On

'Get out of the car,' breathed Edwards. She didn't need telling twice. He grabbed her arm and pulled her into the woods where she backed up against the trunk of a massive oak tree. She felt the power of him standing in front of her; he was big, even for a cop. Her unconscious mind was telling him: I'm vulnerable, I've surrendered, I'm waiting.

She didn't want finesse and she didn't get it. Within seconds his hands were all over her.

Other books by the same author

FIRE AND ICE

On the Edge

LAURA HAMILTON

Black Lace novels contain sexual fantasies.
In real life, make sure you practise safe sex.

First published in 2000 by
Black Lace
Thames Wharf Studios,
Rainville Road, London W6 9HA

Typeset by SetSystems Ltd, Saffron Walden, Essex
Printed and bound by Mackays of Chatham PLC

ISBN 0 352 33534 3

Prologue

e-mail from Mark Williams to Julie Gibson, 27 March

Two vacancies coming up on this paper! You've got to come. Wintersea is a crazy town gone to seed, people a mix of DSS b&b, foreign language students, hippies, oldies and the odd refugee. Think of sitting on the beach in summer! Riding the Big Wheel! You've got to get out of that backwater kid and get your arse down south again. The editor's OK, but news ed's a shit – still, can't have everything! Ad in Press Gazette next week, apply! Must go, have got exclamation markitis!

Extract from Julie Gibson's diary, 3 May

Cannot believe trip down here. On train opposite nice Irishman, got those smily green Irish eyes, dark hair, accent to die for. Chat a bit, tell him about interview etc., wanting more excitement than on offer in N Yorks. He says he's going to London for couple days for exactly that, needs more excitement than his girlfriend can give him! Now looking at me meaningfully with green eyes. V turned on. Legs brush under table, etc. No-one sitting next to us. He asks about boyfriends, told him truth, like zilch on scene at moment. He's looking at me saying can't understand why not – glad I had hair cut – gets drinks. Nice body as well, V-neck jumper, black Levis. Hands touch as I take my can. I am getting *hot*! I get my round in, he's looking me up and down like you won't believe. Glad wearing all black, feel amazingly sexy, thank God put underwired bra on. He says he bets Mark can't wait to see me again, well couldn't deny it, bound to be true. Two cans of lager and I need to pee, open toilet door afterwards and there he is, pushes me back in and locks door, hands and mouth everywhere. Thank God floor wasn't soaking wet, my trousers round ankles, knickers round knees, his hands between my legs, was I wet or what. His cock rock solid. He lifted me on to basin and put it in then lifted me and slammed me down with his hands on my hips. Train decides to pick this moment to lurch all over the place, really weird but exciting. All the time those eyes smiling, no talking. He comes really fast then brings me off with his hands. Rubber wouldn't flush down, God knows if anyone noticed we were both missing at same time, well who cares. What a trip. Not exactly the mile high club but probably something like the zipless fuck Erica Jong was looking for in *Fear of Flying*. He goes out before me, try to calm flushed face with cold water. Arrived in London ten minutes later, said goodbye, just like that. Fantastic. Took as long to get to Wintersea as it did to London, and quarter distance! Meant I could com pose myself. Mark met me at station, said I looked vibrant. Wonder why? He wanted to fuck but two in one day seemed too much. He was pissed off – tough. Had nice evening, couple of different bars, both amazing, nothing like Yorkshire, then Italian. Town seems really cool in a seedy way. Have high hopes for this interview. Think the train shag good omen.

Notes of interview of Julie Gibson by David Hammett, editor, Evening Light, *4 May*

Former colleague Mark Williams from *North Yorkshire Express*. Single, 29, tidy, confident, smiling. Originally from London. Senior 14 mths. Wants work on evening, move to livelier town. Given two small jobs, fine, cuttings good. Likes crime but note limited exp on NYE. Bob OK with her but wld prefer two men (tough). Take up refs, if good offer £18K start, review 6 mths.

Extract from Julie Gibson's diary, 4 May

Sure I've got it. Got on fine with ed, news ed real arse, but hey. Loads reporters, bit different to NYE. Seem OK. Really nice photographer, all in black, bet he never wears anything else, called Stevenson. Cool. Don't know if they'll let me do crime reporting to start with but if they make offer I'll go and worm my way in. Can't wait to get inside new police station with loads of horny cops.

Chapter One

Evening Light, Friday 14 June

BIKE THUGS KILL PET DOG

by Julie Gibson

A DISTRAUGHT dog owner was in tears last night after heartless motorbike scramblers ran over her pet Yorkshire terrier on the grassland behind the sand dunes at Wintersea Point.

Sheila Haylock, 41, broke down as she described how the thugs appeared 'as if from nowhere'. Rusty, her ten-year-old terrier, was running across the grass towards her and one of the bikers swerved as if to avoid him but caught him with his wheel and sent him flying.

The bikers did not stop. Despite the efforts of local vet Rodney Forbes, Rusty had to be put down.

'Good job, Julie. Not bad getting the splash in your first week.' David Hammett smiled paternally, his eyes twinkling through his thick glasses. 'Hope you've enjoyed week one.'

5

'Thanks, David. It's fun so far.'

Fun nothing. It's been one high after another.

Just walking into the newsroom with its dozen reporters, phones ringing non-stop, noise and buzz and everything newspaper life had lacked in North Yorkshire was a thrill. Four banks of three desks each manned by a reporter, half of them on the phone, and in the middle the editorial assistant explaining something earnestly to the grumpy face of Bob Underwood, the news editor.

Julie's desk: next to the crime reporter and a chubby redhead.

New computer modems and sleek grey desks. A radio with local news at one end of the room and one with national news at the other. A copytaker complete with headset in a corner. Ranks of filing cabinets.

She compared it to what she was used to: a tiny office comprising three reporters sitting at old wooden desks with probably the first computers ever invented glowing a ghostly green and nothing else but a tea tray. The editor, in an adjoining cubbyhole dominated by a cocktail cabinet, spent more time entertaining than editing.

Next door three photographers, one the cool man in black, in an office with a computerised scanner plus a darkroom and studio. High tech for someone who was used to reporters doubling as photographers, supplemented by the occasional grudging employment of a freelance.

Upstairs advertising and telesales, a fleet of girls with headsets, eyes down, motivating slogans pasted around the room, constantly being heckled by the sales supervisor, a blonde Scandinavian Amazon.

What a contrast.

Even better: before she had even got to her desk on day one, David had told her she was provisionally assigned to crime. Just what she wanted.

Assistant crime reporter meant doing the donkey work, the editor had explained. It wouldn't be a full-time

6

job, either, as he wanted her to cover all different sorts of stories to find out where her strengths lay.

What he called the donkey work on crime meant visiting the police station every morning to get the low-down on what had been happening in Wintersea during the previous 24 hours.

She tried not to let her smile get too wide as he told her. He wasn't to know that if there had been one place Julie would have chosen to visit every day it was the police station.

John Swarbrick, the chief crime reporter, had taken her along on that first day to meet the local law.

Just walking into the building gave Julie a frisson of excitement.

She had never understood herself why she was so turned on by policemen. It wasn't even the uniform. Detectives were just as exciting.

If she had to guess, it was nothing more than the overpowering maleness. Despite equal opportunities, policewomen had been thin on the ground in the Yorkshire stations she had visited during her last job. And on first sight this one appeared to be exactly the same.

Or perhaps it was more the *type* of male who took up police work.

The confident type. Assertive. Used to bonding with other men, but also experienced in dealing with women.

Whatever. Julie felt her temperature notch up steadily as they walked through the corridor to the superintendent's office, passing uniformed men in spanking clean white shirts who nodded familiarly to John and smiled at her, maybe with a raised eyebrow and an appraising look. She was hooked on the place even before she reached the main man's office.

'Julie Gibson, Tony. Julie, this is Superintendent Tony Greene.'

'With an E,' said the super, standing and holding his hand out and shaking Julie's for slightly longer than is

7

customary. 'Please call me Tony. It's nice to meet you, Julie.'

'You too,' she replied, taking in all six feet of him, his thick grey hair and hazel eyes. Nice face, nice handshake. Not that she would ever expect to get off with a super, but a little flirtation always helped a relationship along.

'Of course, you won't always see me in the morning. I'll introduce you to Adam Arnside, the chief inspector. It'll usually be one of us, but if we're both tied up you'll see one of the inspectors – I'll take you through in a minute.'

'Great. I've been working up in the country in Yorkshire and this is a bit bigger than the stations I was used to up there.'

He chuckled and Julie noticed how his tanned face crinkled around the eyes as he smiled. 'I would think so. You might find it a bit busier as well. We don't have much in the way of stolen tractors or rustled sheep, but there's a fair bit of crime in the town itself, though once you get on the fringes it's pretty quiet.'

'What have you got for us today, Tony?' asked John, businesslike.

'Right.' He moved his gaze from Julie's face on to the computer printout on his desk. 'You want the lot? OK. Robbery at Milo's Mart on Dover Street at ten o'clock last night, just before closing, but he'd already gone round to the night safe at the bank so the robber only got away with sixty quid. He said he had a gun and held up something inside a plastic bag but Milo doesn't think it was real. Obviously he wasn't taking any chances though. He also took about a hundred pounds' worth of booze, all he could get in a couple of carrier bags – obviously he'd relied on getting the day's takings. Description: male, white, mid-thirties, five eight to nine, woolly hat, sallow skin, stubble, fleece jacket and jeans. In other words, about a fifth of the male population.'

He continued going down the list of crimes. Julie's shorthand pen flew over the pages, concentrating 100 per cent, not wanting to mess up on day one. She had to interrupt to get unfamiliar street names repeated but otherwise contented herself with asking the minimum of questions. John was also taking notes, she noticed, and she wondered if he was testing her or if he just planned to split the stories. She was amazed that there was so much to report, but of course it was Monday and the last meeting with the station had been 48 hours ago. On Saturday night alone there were a couple of drunk and disorderly cases and a fight in a town centre pub.

After the seemingly interminable list, Tony Greene took Julie in to the next-door office and introduced her to the chief inspector. He was a harassed-looking man of about 40 with receding hair and a thin face that lost its worried look in an amiable smile. Julie smiled back and knew he too would be a good contact.

The DCI was next – too shark-like, Julie thought, not someone she would trust – then two DIs, both youngish, niceish, and ripe with potential. The uniformed inspectors were both middle-aged, one jovial and one miserable.

That was only Monday. Things had just gone from good to better.

By the end of the week Julie and Tony Greene had struck up quite a rapport. He had a good sense of humour and liked a joke. By Wednesday he was ribbing Julie on her lack of hard crime experience but in a nice way – she knew he didn't think she was incompetent. He was also giving her advice on different areas of town she was looking at flats in.

Staying at Mark's was a godsend at first but it was irredeemably a bachelor pad and definitely out long term. And by long term Julie meant like two weeks. Monday lunchtime had seen her visiting the local letting agents and for three evenings she saw all there was to rent in Wintersea.

There wasn't much choice. Only one flat met all the criteria she had laid down.

First, it was secure. Second, it had a balcony – she wanted either a patio garden or a balcony for sunbathing. Third, it was clean. Fourth, it was in her price range. Fifth, it had a power shower.

And she could move in on Saturday.

'I like having you here,' said Mark when she broke the news to him on Wednesday night. 'Stay a bit longer.' He unplugged the iron and put it carefully on the shelf.

'You only want me here in case you fancy a shag.'

He shrugged. 'Is that or is that not a good reason? Admit it, Gibbo, you're bloody horny yourself. I know how much cops turn you on.'

Julie fluttered her eyelashes and smiled. 'Yeah, you've got me bang to rights, guv. I'm a cop groupie and I can't help it.'

Mark's fingertips grazed her breasts, her nipples immediately starting to tingle. 'OK, Gibson. Keep talking. How many policemen have you screwed?'

Her eyes closed as his fingers found her hardness. She'd changed after work and flat hunting and had taken off her bra, wearing nothing but a cotton vest under a loose linen jumper. He opened his hands and moulded them around each breast.

'Only two,' she murmured, her breath short. 'Didn't you guess?'

'No. Tell me,' said Mark, pushing his crotch at hers. She felt his stiffening cock through the fly of his jeans.

'Terry Wilkinson at Low Road. And Brian Henman at North Yorks Central.'

'Jesus! You bagged a chief inspector!'

'Yeah, and wasn't I discreet?'

'So what was it like?'

'I'm not telling.'

'Come on, Gibbo. You know it'll turn you on.'

'It was like sex. You want me to tell people what sex with you is like?'

'Sure. I've got nothing to be ashamed of.'

He moved his hands down to her arse and pulled her

towards him, rubbing his erection more firmly against her. She was wet and ready but didn't just want a quick release.

'Your arse is such a beautiful handful,' said Mark. 'And you look so sexy with your hair short. Come on, tell me about those big bluff Yorkshiremen.' His lips sucked gently at the skin of her neck, giving her goosebumps.

'No.'

'OK, so tell me who you're planning to screw in Wintersea.'

'No way.'

He sighed, lifted her long sweater and undid the side zip of her stretch pants. He slid his hand in and pushed it sideways into her high-leg briefs.

'You're wearing white vest and knickers again. Are you trying to make me think of schoolgirl fantasies?'

'No, perv. I just think they're sexy.'

'Yeaaah –' his hand had found her slick wetness. 'You are, actually, probably the sexiest woman I know.'

She whimpered as he rubbed her wetness over her clitoris.

'I know what I will tell you,' she said.

'Yes?'

'My favourite cop fantasy.'

Mark drew his breath in sharply and stroked down from her clitoris, his fingers just pushing inside her and then back again. Julie could feel her face falling into its dreamy, heavy, sexy poutiness.

'Go on, then.'

He pulled her knickers and trousers down and Julie automatically kicked them off her ankles, her mind already in its fantasy world. She leant her shoulders back against the kitchen wall and thrust her pudenda forward. Mark resumed his stroking.

'Mmm. I go in one morning and there's no-one there but one of the inspectors, a really nice, horny one. He tells me there's been a serious haul of porn, that's why

11

the super and chief are out – he can't tell me much at the moment. I call back later and they're still out, but the inspector says I can go round and have a look at the stuff if I want.

'So I go round and he shows me a few magazines. It's quite exciting, nothing horrible, and I'm like, well, this is no big deal, then he says the main thing is the movies. They're just going to have a look – do I want to go? So I say sure, and go into one of the interview rooms. There's about ten cops in there. I sit down in the front row with the nice horny inspector on one side and a sexy DI on the other. They turn out the lights and put this video on. It's quite a big screen, and it's amazing quality, hand-held sort of stuff, but well done, and it is so exciting. There's a woman getting ready for a hot date, putting suspenders and all that stuff on, then the doorbell rings and it's another woman and they have this incredible scene. I am getting so hot watching this. Then a man comes in through the patio windows and shouts at them. It's the woman's husband. She's obviously petrified but the other woman points out that he should be grateful his wife is fucking another woman rather than a man, and if he wants to join in she won't mind. So there's a three-way going on and just as he's sticking his cock in the other woman and licking out his wife, I feel this hand push up my thigh under my skirt.

'It's the nice horny inspector and before I can say piss off, his fingers are under my knickers and I'm obviously soaking wet and I'm a: not wanting him to say, "Jesus, you should see how wet she is," and b: fancying him anyway and c: let's face it, *grateful* for this bit of manual action in view of how excited I am. So I go with the flow and next thing he picks up my hand and puts it on his cock, and I don't mean his fly. He's got his prick hanging out already, so I start pumping.

'Next thing the sexy guy on the other side puts one hand on my tit and the other up my leg and I'm thinking, Well, he's just going to find another hand there, but it's like he's expecting it, and one of them takes my slit and the other my clit and my left tit's getting a working over. So I think, Fair's fair, and move my other hand over to the other guy's lap and get his cock out and I'm pumping them both. In the meantime, of course, the husband's shooting all over the girlfriend's tits and the wife's licking it off, and in no time, like synchronised swimmers, both my little inspectors are shooting all over my hands, not to mention their trousers, and I'm not far behind. In fact, I'm almost there now, Mark. Jesus, if you want to fuck, fuck now . . .'

Julie opened her eyes. She always liked to come with her eyes open. Mark carried on stroking her.

'Come on then, Gibbo, come for me now. I'll fuck you in a minute. Your eyes are gone. You're coming, aren't you? Great story. What happens next? I suppose one by one all the cops fuck you one way or another.'

'Yeah.' Julie stared emptily at Mark as her sensations deserted the usual five senses and concentrated themselves in her sex as it pulsed again and again like a sub machine gun. It was long and hard and as it faded she smiled lazily.

'Nice one, Williams. Your turn?'

'Oh, yes. Bend over the sink for me, Jules, baby. Put your arms in it. Oh, brilliant. Your arse is beautiful.'

Julie bent her elbows so she could lift her rump as high in the air as possible for Mark. I do love this guy, she thought, as he rubbered up and entered her, whispering words she couldn't hear. In my fashion.

She looked out of the window as Mark rode her with swift strokes. If anyone glanced up, could they guess? She was wearing her sweater, and could easily be staring out of the window, lost in thought. Would a casual observer see Mark pumping away behind her?

Never mind a casual observer. Say one of the cops from Wintersea was passing by, maybe that blond DI whose name she hadn't got yet. Say he was just passing by and looking up at windows because a suspect might be hiding out in one of the flats? Say he saw her and started to wave then saw Mark behind her, and realised what was happening? Say he told the other guys down at the station that the new reporter was hot for it?

Her hips had started moving in response to Mark's thrusts. He was still whispering and she pushed back as he hammered forward, feeling his cock connect with her G-spot.

Hang on, I can go again.

She concentrated on what he was saying.

'Gibbo, you are one sexy bitch. You sexy bitch. I love it. I love you. Fuck me, Gibbo. Jesus Christ, I'm going to download any moment. Come with me, Jules. Fucking come with me. Never mind your cops, come with me.'

She came, but she was thinking about the blond DI.

And that was only Wednesday. Thursday, after a not very exciting week crimewise, the dog bought it.

Julie was on the mobile at the police station. 'John, dog run over by bikers, had to be put down. Not much else exciting. The woman lives at Wintersea Point. Do you want me to go over now to see her? Sure, I'll try to get a pic. See you later.'

She was a good reporter, she knew. OK, there were weaknesses, like council tax calculations or financial reports. But one thing she could do to perfection. She could drip sympathy.

The dead dog's mother was in her 40s. She'd obviously been crying all night and was still wearing her dressing gown and fluffy mules. Julie empathised so well she almost found herself near tears as the woman talked about her precious Rusty.

'He was ten years old. He didn't have much longer. If only God had let him live out his last days in peace –' She burst into a fresh storm of sobs. Julie scribbled.

'Sheila, do you have a photo of Rusty?'

This was a redundant question. There were photos of Rusty all over the walls. He wasn't Julie's type – she

14

couldn't stand little yappy dogs. Border collies, labradors, retrievers, they were real dogs with personalities. Little ones – well, they yapped.

What she meant was, have you got one not in a frame I can put in the paper?

Julie sat patiently while they went through Rusty's photograph albums. She selected one, then had a better idea.

'Sheila, would you mind if we took your photo for the paper?'

'Oh, I couldn't, Julie. I mean, I've been crying all night. Won't it be better to have Rusty's picture?'

'Probably, but I'm just thinking, it might not come out very well. Can I just call one of our photographers over here, just to see?'

Stevenson arrived ten minutes later. Julie answered the door.

'Got a good pic of the dog you can put through the scanner, but thought it might be good to have one of tearful owner looking through scrapbook, pics on walls, if you like?'

God, he was handsome. He smiled, his thin face taking on a strange beauty.

'I think you have a nose for news, Julie.'

'Sure. Let's go for it.'

And so Friday's paper was a triumph. Front-page splash, dead dog pic, interview, then on page two poor tear-stained Sheila slamming heartless yobs. Comments from police, two whole pages, all bylined Julie Gibson.

She'd arrived.

'You have to come to the pub. It's Friday night.'

'For God's sake, I'm working at the police station tomorrow morning and moving in the afternoon.'

'I know that tone of voice. She just wants to be persuaded.'

'Sod off, Mark.'

'I'm working early shift tomorrow,' said Derek West,

one of the older reporters. 'So's Wendy. We're still having a drink.'

Julie laughed. 'It's all right for you, Derek. You've been in journalism through the good old days when you weren't a proper reporter unless you could down six pints at lunchtime. I haven't built up your immunity. Anyway, OK.'

Mark was snorting something about never knowing anyone else who could drink as much vodka in an after-work session and then go off for dinner and throw a load of wine down them and then go clubbing and drinking God knows what but no-one was really listening as they left the office and headed for the Vaults.

'I can't believe this town has got such cool places in it,' Julie said as they went down the steps and entered what used to be the crypt of an old church transformed into a bar. Wooden pews were used for seats and incense sticks burning at every table recalled the building's past. 'I mean, you look at the b&bs full of no-hopers and it seems like this is Lostville.'

'It's an incredible town,' said Wendy, the other young female reporter. 'Just look through the listings pages in the paper. Loads of students live here who can't afford most of the other chichi places along the coast and they put on all sorts of alternative stuff – theatre and so on.'

One thing Julie had missed while in rural Yorkshire was access to the arts, especially fringe-type stuff, so she was pleased to hear it. She was even more pleased to find out that one of her new colleagues was also up for that kind of stuff, and she looked at Wendy with renewed interest. Like her body, her face was podgy, her only make-up a flash of bright red lipstick. Her hair was cut in a hennaed bob; her clothes were cool, layered in a way that did nothing for her figure, but interesting all the same – quite a contrast to Julie's pared-down minimalist style.

She surveyed the other reporters.

Derek, late 50s, probably coming up for retirement

16

fairly soon. He was blond and tanned with premature age spots on his face, and bright blue eyes and broken veins that warned he might be too fond of the bottle. He wore good clothes on his spare frame and, from what little she had read, his writing was as elegant as his dress.

John Swarbrick, her mentor in crime reporting, dark and quiet, a pipe smoker once out of the no-smoking office. He seemed to get along well with everyone but went off alone to the pub for lunch. She had heard him talk of a daughter who'd just gone to university and suspected his home life took precedence over his work.

Claire Johnson, 50-ish, angular face with jutting cheekbones and hollow eyes, expensive blonde-streaked hair, very thin – close to anorexic, maybe. She had been on the *Evening Light* since she was sixteen, Mark had told Julie in mock horror. Every assignment was greeted with a theatrical sigh but at least she knew practically everybody in town and, were it not for the drifting student and bed and breakfast population, would be related to at least a quarter of them.

Alan Surman, her fellow new recruit who had started a week ahead of her. Public school trumpet of a voice, red haired and freckled, jolly. Nice but dim, she decided.

Her glance fell on Mark, with affection and regret – regret because she had decided it would be best to give up their occasional screws. For one thing, it had been every night this week and he was getting used to it. And she didn't want him to get in the way of her new sex life in Wintersea. He was sweet and smart and career hungry, but his tastes were for sport and lager and too much TV. No way was Julie starting off with the tag of Mark's girlfriend.

The other reporters had made their excuses more successfully than Julie and gone home, but she suspected that the Friday night drinkers would be the ones she would get on with best. She would make friends with Wendy, who was about her age, and she guessed she would hit it off with Derek as well.

As John went up to the bar for the next round, Stevenson walked in.

I think he'll be my first conquest, Julie decided.

Meeting him at the interview, she had guessed he always wore black and after a week he was still monochrome. Although he was slim, his black T-shirts revealed defined arm muscles and Julie suspected he worked out, unlike reporters who in her experience usually did nothing at all unless they went in for team sports. If they were into keeping fit, they would jog rather than go to the gym.

His thick brown hair was shoulder length and pulled back into a ponytail, framing his thin face. Heavy eyebrows and an aquiline nose gave him a commanding appearance, which together with his tan reminded Julie of sexy tour guides on Spanish holidays. His eyes were pale blue like a wintry sky – not exactly cold, but not warm. They were compelling to look at and Julie thought they were the sort of eyes that could make you do things you didn't necessarily want to do.

Which could be interesting.

Wendy uncurled herself from her slouch as he appeared in the doorway and Julie noticed a slight flush on her cheeks.

Sorry, Wendy. I think I'll take this one.

He paused at the bar to help John back with the drinks. Unlike the rest of them Stevenson had a glass of wine.

He slid on to the pew in the space John had vacated, almost opposite Julie, who was on the end of the facing bench. She was fascinated to see with what incredible physicality he relaxed his body as he lifted the wine glass. His shoulders lowered and his whole torso loosened as he breathed out and closed his eyes. He held the wine to his nose and inhaled deeply, then sipped sensuously, still with closed eyes.

Opening them, he smiled at Julie. 'Welcome. I hope you're getting good vibes from the paper and the town.'

'Oh, yes. I am getting very encouraging vibes.'

18

Without breaking eye contact, she lifted her beer glass and silently toasted him, a smile playing around her lips. His smile broadened.

'I would have taken you for a wine drinker.'

'You name it, she drinks it,' Mark interjected teasingly. Julie ignored him.

'And I would have taken you for a – mmm, let's think about this –'

For a quickie in the toilet, a long night of sensuous pleasure, a grope in the developing room – you name it.

'– for a vodka drinker. Wyborowa, the Polish one that tastes like something, straight out of the freezer, no ice, straight down.'

Stevenson raised one of his thick eyebrows. 'Good guess! It's been known. I just will not drink this brew. It's appalling.' He was pointing at Julie's beer glass. 'I bet you only had it because it's local and you were too polite to say how horrible it was.'

He was right. Julie was very unimpressed with the Wintersea brewery's Whinger bitter, even less by the whimsical name, but indeed had kept her reservations to herself as all the others apart from lager lout Mark and g&t Claire were drinking it.

'Oi! It's a decent pint!' protested John.

Stevenson laughed derisively.

'It's dishwater. Derek, don't tell me you like that beer.'

'Christ, no. It wets the whistle after work and the body doesn't recognise it as alcohol so it puts off the moment when I really start drinking.' So she was right about him and booze.

'What's wrong with it?' asked Wendy, round eyed.

Stevenson sighed. 'Insipid is almost too extravagant a description. The flavour falls somewhere between sour and bitter, the aftertaste is like vomit and as far as body is concerned it makes Claire seem voluptuous.'

Julie snorted with laughter and he turned back to her.

'Confess. You don't like it.'

'Well – to be honest – you know, Yorkshire's famous

for its beer, so I expect I've been a bit spoilt over the last few years,' she prevaricated diplomatically.

'Indeed. Now I'm going to get a round in, so come up to the bar with me and you'll see that this place actually has a decent choice of drinks. I suppose everyone else wants the same again?'

They did, although Julie read in Wendy's eyes not only uncertainty about what she wanted to drink but also unhappiness at the attention Stevenson was paying her.

'Draught beer is a definite no-no here,' he was saying as they reached the bar. 'But they do a great selection of bottles – not just bitters but wheat beer, Czech lager, Belgian beers and so on.' He waved his hand towards the refrigerated display. 'And good wine by the glass. Taste this.'

He offered her his glass, which was still half full. He watched her as she lifted it to her lips. Again she locked her eyes on his, while her lips closed around the glass his had only just moved from. He had given it to her deliberately, and it wasn't lost on her.

The wine was good, butter soft with a tang of sweet English apples. Julie wondered if his lips would taste of it.

'Semillon Chardonnay. It's the best of the whites, but all the reds are good.' He took his glass from her, his fingers closing briefly around hers before moving to the stem and raising it to his mouth. As he sipped, Julie snaked her tongue around her own lips. They were dry. Unlike the place between her legs, which was most definitely damp.

She picked up the wine list and decided on an Argentinian red, a Malbec.

'I am so glad you said that about the beer. I didn't want to seem rude.'

'It's shit, isn't it? Actually there are a couple of really good breweries not far away and even a microbrewery in the town which does great beer, but only sells it at its own pub, down at the Old Harbour. That's one of *the* places to go in town, but it's a bit far from work.'

'Right, that's the Far Pavilion?'

'Yes, that's it.'

'Mark took me there when I came down for the interview, but I didn't realise about the brewery – I guess I was a bit nervous.'

Stevenson laughed softly. 'I don't believe you do nervous, Julie.'

'Hey, unfair!' She smiled complicity with him. 'OK, not often. How about you? What do you do?'

'Mainly pleasure.' He handed her two of the drinks. 'Take those over. Oh, and it is a real pleasure to have you working here.'

Julie floated over to the table and handed John and Wendy their pints and went back to help him again, taking her wine and Mark's lager. She resumed her seat and was pleased to see John move along the pew so Stevenson was right opposite her.

He lifted his glass. 'Welcome to Wintersea, Julie.'

'Cheers.'

The others chorused their welcomes and she looked happily around the table as they drank together, but again her eyes were drawn back to the man opposite.

She was immediately warmed by the rich wine. The beer had had no effect on her at all – Derek was right about the alcohol content – but the wine was already working its way through her, relaxing every muscle in her body apart from those that Stevenson had already put on red alert.

'Your eyes change colour. Sometimes they're as grey as a sullen sky, and then they can look almost mauve.'

She nodded. 'Yeah. I used to say I had violet eyes, but I was just kidding myself. The nearest they get is sort of lilac, like a fading bruise.'

'I see what you mean. And you have got superb skin.'

Julie couldn't deny it. Her pale, porcelain-transparent skin was one of her greatest assets. Along with her eyes.

And her dark hair, especially now it was short and spiky. The rest of her regular features were rather boring, she felt, but she did have a great smile which threw the rest of her face into relief.

'Thank you.'

'I'd like to photograph you.'

'Well, that's a dead cert,' interrupted Wendy. 'We all have to have our pics taken to go along with the byline for features.'

'Wow, a picture byline! That's a bit more sophisticated than the *North Yorkshire Express*,' laughed Julie. 'Tell you what, do it on Monday. I'll make sure my hair's perfect and wear my best earrings.'

Stevenson smiled. She guessed he wanted to talk more about photographing her but not in the present company, and the talk became general.

John and Claire left after they'd finished their drink, and Mark said he for one fancied something to eat. Derek wanted counting out, which left Mark, Julie, Stevenson, Wendy and Alan. Julie said she didn't mind where she went and the others debated noisily where to go.

The unanimous compromise was, predictably, an Indian restaurant.

'Take any five people,' said Alan loudly, 'any five anywhere in the country, and get them to decide where to eat and I bet you the only place they'd agree on would be an Indian.'

The One Nation Curry House wasn't a boring compromise, though. It boasted dishes from all over the Indian sub-continent. No flock wallpaper or sitar music; the decor was cool blue colourwashed walls, plain pine tables and chairs and modern art prints. The others greeted the owner by name. Laitan was 30-ish and handsome, with cropped hair and a thin trace of moustache and beard. Unlike the waiters in white shalwar and kameez, he wore a pale green shirt with grey linen trousers.

'Julie, welcome to Wintersea. I hope we shall see a lot

of you here.' He kissed her hand gravely. Not bad, she thought. Definitely one to put in the pending file.

Did she choose tandoori chicken so that Stevenson could see her raise the meat to her lips and nibble the red flesh from the bone? And to let him know that she enjoyed the sensuality of picking up her food? Whatever, she enjoyed it. He chose a vegetarian thali. If she'd been sitting opposite him she would have asked permission to take a taste of each dish. Maybe he would have speared a morsel of each on his fork and held it over the table for her to take in her mouth. But Julie was against the wall on one side of the table with Mark next to her, and he was on the opposite side on the gangway.

It's not going to work tonight, she realised. She was too far away to make a discreet play for him and, anyway, Mark would know. From tomorrow she would have her own flat, be able to invite anyone she wanted to come round, or to spend the night at someone else's place. There was absolutely no point in annoying Mark and antagonising Wendy by going for it now.

Oh, but she was so turned on already. What the hell, there would have to be a farewell fuck for Mark. Maybe a bit unfair on him, but tough. He wasn't exactly sentimental about their relationship. She knew he'd rather screw her than not, even if she had been revved up by someone else. He certainly wouldn't complain that her engine was ready to go without any help from him.

Stevenson was going to have to wait. Anyway, deferred pleasure always had its own rewards.

Mark was all for going for another drink after the curry. Stevenson had gone home after reminding Julie he would see her on Sunday when they were both covering the Spiritual Age Festival, a New Age event taking place at the old Winter Gardens. The others were keen for another pint but Julie was adamant this time.

She knew Mark was vacillating between making the most of Friday night, as he wasn't working over the weekend, and the fear that she might be in bed and refuse to be disturbed when he got in. And she was moving the next day.

He went home with her.

'We can have another one at home. There's some beer in the fridge.'

'OK. Just while we watch *Frasier*. But I'm going to bed after that.'

Turning a corner they were separated by a multinational gang of about twenty language students on the way to the pub, no doubt merely to practise their English.

Mark skipped back to Julie after the kids passed. 'Does that mean you want to fuck in bed, or while you watch *Frasier*?'

She laughed. 'Decisions, decisions. You're presuming a lot.'

'Jules, you're moving tomorrow. I won't have you on tap any more.'

You won't have me at all, she thought.

'You know, it is quite a turn-on, watching TV and pretending not to be interested while someone gives you the full treatment –'

'Full treatment costs extra, lady.'

'Hey, something's just come into my mind – me in my vest with a can of beer in my hand slumped on the sofa watching TV like an archetypal male slob, and you on your knees with your face in my pussy. How's that sound?'

He pushed his face into her neck and nuzzled her.

'Perverse. But that's what I expect from you. Haven't you got any lacy G-strings for a change? Call me old-fashioned, but I quite like to see tits falling out of a push-up bra rather than roaming around inside a vest.'

'Get your face back in my neck – you know it gives me goosepimples – and I'll see what I can do.'

Despite her predilection for comfortable white cotton, Julie had a large sex underwear wardrobe. She guessed that after all the white, black would please Mark the most and went for an all-lace see-through underwired bra with a matching thong, and in a moment of amazing generosity decided to treat him to stockings and a suspender belt as well.

She started to make her way out of the bedroom then stopped and put her work clothes on again over the outfit. In the sitting room, Mark was stretched on the sofa, his tie off and his shirtsleeves rolled up to the elbow, sipping from a can of Budweiser.

'Shit, Gibbo, thought you were dressing up for me.'

Julie stood, hands on hips, blocking his view of the TV.

'I didn't want to make it too easy for you. You've got to do some work first.'

He stood and put the can down.

'OK, I don't mind stripping you.'

He ran his hands over her breasts, which stood proud under the grey high-necked lycra top she'd been wearing all day.

'That top's probably a bit damp under the arms from all the excitement today. I thought maybe that'd be a turn-on.'

'Jesus, Jules.'

He burrowed his nose under her armpit. 'You don't smell. But you are sweating a bit. Perhaps just because you're getting excited.'

'Yeah, I expect.'

I was definitely excited in the pub, anyway, she thought.

She closed her eyes as his grip on her breasts firmed and felt her nipples jolt into erection. He pulled her top over her head, sighing as the bra was revealed.

'Oh, just what I ordered. Christ.'

He buried his head between her lacy tits, his hands running down her short jersey skirt.

'Gibbo, what am I feeling?'

'Horny, I suppose.'

25

'No, I mean, I think what I'm feeling is an arse with no knickers on and a suspender belt. Tell me it's true.'

'One way to find out.'

He unzipped her skirt and she wriggled out of it. He stood back and sighed again.

'It must be my birthday.'

'It's more like, make the most of it because I'm moving.'

She moved away from him and draped herself on the sofa, turned on herself by the effect she was having on him, obvious not just by his face but by the erection straining against his trousers.

'Actually, Williams, I don't want to rush things. If you don't mind.'

'Hell, no. You call the shots, Jules.'

'Yeah? Well, to be honest, I don't feel that sexy at the moment, because I've got all this tandoori chicken spice on my fingers. Look.'

She thrust a hand out for his inspection. The red spice mix was all around and under her short nails.

'I thought you might just do me a favour and get that off. I reckon your teeth and your tongue could do the job.'

'Oh, Gibbo. You – Jesus, you horny cow.'

'Take your clothes off first, though. I want to watch your cock get harder.'

Mark pulled his shirt and trousers off. 'In my experience it doesn't get much harder.'

She nodded. 'OK. You just kneel down here and give my hands a proper going over, then I'll tell you what you can go over next.'

Julie propped herself at an angle in the corner of the couch, her right arm along the back and her left hand extended for Mark's attention. She bent her right leg and rested it on the settee. Mark had to kneel close to the sofa to reach her left hand, his cock on a level with her pussy, but because of the angle she was sitting at he had to turn

26

so that his erection brushed against the inside of her left thigh. Her pussy tingled with anticipation.

As Mark took her hand in his she closed her eyes and concentrated. He started by sucking her thumb and then scoured around the cuticles of her nail with his teeth. His tongue rimmed the top of her nail and he ran his teeth under it. The intimacy and singularity of the contact sent Julie's sex muscles leaping into overdrive.

'It's pretty good for me, how is it for you?' she enquired as Mark finished with her third finger.

'Finger lickin' good,' he joked. 'Though to be honest, my tongue prefers other bits of you.'

She smiled knowingly. 'Right. It can move on to its favourite bits if it likes.'

Assuming he was talking about the bits of her that were slickly wet, contracting jerkily and with a small but yearning hard-on, that is.

Still kneeling in front of her as if in supplication, Mark hooked his thumbs in either side of her thong and slid it down her legs. Julie kicked it off and tilted her pussy forward, keeping one leg on the settee for maximum exposure. Her vagina gave a massive contraction, almost orgasmic, as it felt his warm breath on her.

'Hey Williams, let me tell you a secret for your future reference: that is one major turn-on,' she breathed, as his tongue settled softly and teasingly on her clitoris. 'Don't stop. When you go down on a woman, just prolong for a couple of seconds the time between being close enough so that she can feel your breath hot on her, and your face just brushing against her pubes. That is one – oh, nice – really cunt-jerking moment.'

She closed her eyes as he changed rhythm, from dancing on her clitoris with the tip of his tongue to brushing up and down from her clit to her vulva with broad strokes of his now-flat tongue. Just as she was getting used to it he changed back to teasing her clit.

'If you were as good at journalism as you are at this,

you'd be on the *Guardian* by now,' she purred. Mark raised his head indignantly.

'*The Times*, if you don't mind.'

Julie groaned as he resumed his task by pulling the lips of her pussy apart and lapping gently around the wet orifice for a minute or two, then she felt his tongue harden and push in and out of her.

'You need more than a tongue up there,' he said as he raised himself to face her.

'Yeah, go on, stick it in,' murmured Julie breathlessly, on the verge of orgasm.

'Not yet, I've got a better idea.'

He disappeared into the kitchen, leaving her tempted to put her hand down to her clit and bring herself off, but he wasn't gone long. The first thing she saw reappear in the sitting room was his erection, the second a towel.

'If you're planning to make a mess, it had better have nothing to do with pain on my part,' said Julie acerbically, afraid he might have assigned himself a starring role in *Last Tango in Paris*.

'Don't be suspicious. Lift your arse and lie back on this.' He arranged the towel over the sofa. 'Haven't you heard of the sixties?'

He flourished a Mars Bar.

Julie felt relief that he was obviously more in a Mick Jagger than a Marlon Brando frame of mind.

'Oh, yeah, but that was supposed not to be true, wasn't it?'

Mark shrugged and removed the wrapper. 'Who cares? Just lie back and think of Mick and I'll pretend you're Marianne Faithfull.'

She giggled. 'OK, I'll be your honky tonk woman. Oh, shit! Has that been in the bloody fridge?'

The chocolate bar was freezing.

'Yeah, sorry. I put it in the microwave for a couple of seconds but I was afraid any more would melt it. Let's face it, the heat of you will make this into chocolate sauce in no time anyway.'

No doubt. She luxuriated in the bliss of having something inside her. The smooth chocolate slid like a silk-clad penis up and down her. Shame it's not longer, she thought. But it was a nice prelude to Mark's cock.

With his other hand he was stroking her clitoris, gently, then harder. Her breath shortened. She almost didn't want to come yet – wasn't he supposed to eat the chocolate out of her? – but she couldn't help it.

'Come on, Julie. Is that right? Yeah, you've opened your eyes. God, I can feel you coming just by holding this. Come on, Lady Jane.'

Despite being absorbed in the spasms shaking her leaping sex, Julie registered a reference to an old Rolling Stones song – or was it Lady Chatterley?

'Oh, wow, a cross-cultural deconstructed orgasm,' she breathed, as she wrung the last contractions from her cunt. 'Oh, holy fucking hell, what the fuck is happening?'

Someone had removed the Mars Bar and jammed a load of ice cubes up inside her.

'This is *torture*! I mean, this is really what they do to torture women! Get those fucking ice cubes out of me!'

'Relax, Gibbo, enjoy the sensation!'

'It is not sodding enjoyable. Get them out of me.'

She pulled away from his hand, only to find him holding a tiny remnant of a Mars Bar – the ice-cream variety.

'Shit. Very funny. Most amusing. No wonder it felt cold when it first went in.'

Mark was looking crestfallen.

'Sorry, Jules. I really thought it would be exciting. I wanted the chocolate outside to melt off just as you came, but it was a bit late. Don't you think it would have been the most wonderful orgasm if it had happened then?'

'Yeah, if you like your orgasms to feel like electric shocks. Jesus Christ, it's still cold. I'm going to stick the shower head up it.'

'Oh God, I'm really sorry. It wasn't supposed to be like torture, honest. It was supposed to be a treat.'

Julie saw the funny side. And had to admit although it had been a heart-stopping shock, it had got her adrenalin flowing.

'OK. You meant well. But try that again and I'll be on to Amnesty International. Now just get down there and eat as much ice cream as you can suck out of me and I'll let you come in the shower with me.'

Having got over the shock, she felt amazingly stimulated. Anyway, she owed him an orgasm. And it was going to be the last one.

As a special treat, she got in the shower as she was – bra, stockings and suspender belt – and let Mark hold the shower head to her still-chocolatey insides. He had ice cream around his mouth and she licked it off. His cock seemed even bigger than ever, and was reddening nicely from the warm water.

'I'm getting desperate for you, Jules,' said Mark thickly. 'That bra on your wet tits, those bloody stockings. Let me fuck you.'

'No, I insist, let me fuck you,' said Julie. 'Get down on that bathmat.'

Still wet, he lay down and she poised herself above him for a second before taking his cock in her hand and guiding it inside her. The water had washed away not only the ice cream but also her slick juices, and it was a rough penetration. Sometimes that was how she liked it, and she thrust up and down on his cock with mounting excitement. Water dripped off her on to his torso.

'I'm not going to last long. You'd better get a johnny.'

'Can you last one more stroke?' hissed Julie quickly as she pulled away and then slammed back against him, her pubic mound clashing deliciously with the root of his cock.

'Yes.'

'One more?'

'Yes – no –'

She pulled off and put her mouth around him and took him down as deep as she dared, sucking as hard as

30

she could, and within seconds he came with what seemed like a pint of semen in her mouth.

Spit or swallow?

She spat.

Julie's diary, 14 June

One of the better days of my life. So far. Got the splash plus page 2. David pleased. Drink after, me and Stevenson are meant for great things, physically that is. Got horny, had to have Mark, he made me come then tortured me with ice cream. Jesus, not 100 per cent successful but A for effort and inventiveness. What a sweetie. Was going to be last time but – no need to say anything now anyway. Showered together then fucked him on bathroom floor, sucked him off at end. What am I like.

Chapter Two

Evening Light, Saturday 15 June, late edition

MAN DEAD, TWO SERIOUSLY INJURED IN CRASH

A YOUNG man died after the car he was driving was in collision with another car on the bypass in the early hours of the morning.

His passenger, Kelly Holdsworth, 15, of Granary Lane, is in intensive care at Wintersea Infirmary. The driver of the other car, William Robinson, 58, of Youdale Road, was in the operating theatre as we went to press.

The dead man has not been identified as police have yet to trace his relatives. Friends of Miss Holdsworth claim that he stole the car after leaving a party with her at around midnight, having consumed quantities of alcohol. Police cannot corroborate the accusation.

Moving was delayed thanks to an accident on the Wintersea bypass in the early hours of the morning.

Julie got the information on the phone from the police voice bank at seven o'clock, holding the receiver on her shoulder while trying to pack last night's damp undies.

There was nothing to do until she got to the station, which Chief Inspector Arnside had warned her not to do until 9.30 on a Saturday. Never mind her deadline, he told her – if she turned up earlier they'd just make her wait till ten. She believed him.

She tried the hospital just for form's sake but knew they wouldn't release any details.

As she had expected, Adam Arnside was in a sombre mood when she arrived in his office. Julie had never met a policeman of any rank who wasn't brought down by death, however many times they encountered it.

The dead man was one of the drivers, eighteen years old, and his girlfriend was in intensive care. The driver of the second car was in the operating theatre.

'I can't give you any further details. We haven't been able to trace the dead man's relatives.'

Why not? Maybe a transient? If so – maybe reckless driving, maybe a stolen car?

'Was it his car?'

Adam sighed. 'As I said, I can't tell you any more. Not until we've contacted relatives.'

'Sure. But couldn't you just confirm it was his car?'

'No. I can't confirm it.'

'So how about the other driver? Can I have his name? Have you got hold of his next of kin?'

His brow furrowed. 'His wife's at the hospital. Julie, I don't know how they do things in Yorkshire, but I don't want reporters badgering wives at bedsides here.'

Reporters do what they have to do, Adam, she thought.

'Look, I won't cause any trouble, I promise. If you could just let me have his name and address?'

I know you won't, but I have to ask. I'll just do this my way.

She didn't even have to try. The minute she walked

33

into the hospital waiting room with her notebook out, a girl with an angry, tear-stained face grabbed her coat.

'Are you a reporter? Get this, then. My dad's in there fighting for his life thanks to some drunken yob who can't even drive, pinching a car to get home after a party. Get that in your paper!'

Of course she couldn't. But she could get a few details of poor Mr Robinson and in a quick prowl around likely smoking areas outside found a trio of sobbing pierced underage girls whose friend had gone home from a party with a lad they didn't know. And now she was in intensive care.

'He didn't have a car. We left at the same time as them. He must have pinched it.'

'He shouldn't have been driving – he was drinking Special Brew all night.'

Jesus!

'Kelly's only fifteen. It's her birthday on Friday . . .'

Altogether enough for her story. Mobile out. Hold the front page! Well, not really. But she was in time for the last edition.

She was pleased with herself.

Eventually she got moved. As she'd hardly unpacked the previous Sunday, it didn't take long to get ready to go again. Most of her stuff was still in boxes piled up in the sitting room. Mark was out – by the time she'd returned to the office, written up the story and got back to the flat, he was in the pub for the pre-match warm-up.

The old Clio groaned – again – under the weight of the books, stereo, PC, clothes and photos. At least it didn't have far to go to its new parking space.

The new flat was on the edge of the Old Harbour area, as near as Julie could afford. It was the top floor of a thirties house in a reasonably quiet street where half the houses had been split into flats, the remainder lived in by old ladies with hats and men with sticks.

Her flat had been occupied by the owner until recently

34

but he had been transferred to Paris, the agent had told her, and had left the flat as it was. Not exactly *Elle Decoration*, but comfortable enough, with reasonable furniture and carpets, basic kitchen – which was all Julie would need – and it was clean.

And at the back a balcony with a view – just – over the sea. Today it sparkled moody blue with white ruffles of waves under the early summer sun. A sun lounger was folded down ready by the door.

Clothes in wardrobe and drawers. Duvet on bed. Bright red poppy rug on floor. Books on shelves. Moment of panic when she couldn't find the diagram showing how to reconnect the computer bits, but it was there. Mini hi-fi connected, tapes and CDs stacked, bathroom stuff arranged. Condoms in bedside drawer. Pictures on the walls – her two beloved Jack Vettriano prints in the sitting room, two sultry black and white erotic photos in the bedroom.

The rest of Saturday to settle in, relax, explore, walk on the prom, organise some food. After a week with Mark drinking out of cans and eating toast in front of the TV, she was looking forward to cooking something simple but proper – maybe pasta with a bag salad – and opening a bottle of wine. Alone.

She started exploring the identical streets to her own. It was like a small estate with all the streets named after lakes. Her new address was Grasmere Avenue, and she noted Windermere Close, Derwentwater Villas, Haweswater Terrace and Bassenthwaite Gardens. Not a street or a road in sight.

Seagulls cawed overhead and she caught or maybe imagined a whiff of ozone in the air. Julie couldn't wait to lie on the beach and swim in the sea once summer got going properly.

Tony Greene had told her that the Old Harbour had once been a no-go area, its narrow cobbled streets lined with ramshackle houses which were former fishermen's cottages, a couple of pubs, shops and ship chandlers. Her street had been on the front line of the respectable neighbourhood behind the harbour.

As in so many towns, though, the old and quaint had been reclaimed by the modern and forward-looking business crowd and the Old Harbour was now the only place to be seen in town. As demand for housing increased, the houses on Julie's estate had been converted into flats and definitely gone down in the world.

But not as much as many of the hotels in town.

Rounding the corner of Windermere Close, Julie came across what was becoming a common sight. A large old hotel gone completely to seed, the decline in seaside holidays written all over its cracked paintwork and grubby windows. A knot of men wearing baseball caps and puffa jackets stood outside smoking and arguing in a language she couldn't remotely identify, but presumed came from somewhere in the Balkans. Whey-faced children with dried snot above their lips crouched over a toy while older ones were kicking a ball around. A woman who couldn't have been more than eighteen lifted a pushchair with a squalling baby in it down the hotel steps while two toddlers moaned behind her. None of the men stepped forward to help. Julie reckoned she would have rejected them anyway.

Welcome to the new millennium.

Turning her back on the live fifties tableau, Julie zipped up her hooded sweatshirt against the sea breeze and entered the cool modern world of the Old Harbour.

Straight away she recognised the Italian restaurant she'd been to with Mark on the eve of her interview – bright blue metal tables and chairs on wooden floors with the menu written in black on wooden boards. *Adesso!* was written large in blue italics on the window, its only decoration. A waiter was lugging a board outside to replace the menu she was just about to contemplate.

'Lunch is finished, darling, but we could make an exception for an old customer.'

Julie laughed back at his warm brown eyes.

36

'I'm not an old customer.'

'You came once, about a month ago. With the journalist.'

'Very good! You remember everybody?'

He shrugged. 'It's my business.'

'Mine too.'

He put his head on one side and looked at her doubtfully.

'Don't tell me you're a waitress!'

'No, a journalist too.'

He laughed. *'Fantastico!* You can write a review of my *ristorante*. Then I promise I'll stop putting on the fake Italian accent.'

'Hey! You must be Italian. You certainly look it.'

'Sure, second generation. I was brought up in Muswell Hill and this is my own London accent. But in this game I just can't help mimicking my father, and the punters love it.'

'Keep it up! Look, I'll think about the review, OK? I've just started, so I don't know what the policy is.'

'Bene! I'm Luca. Come soon!'

Yes! This was what she was good at! This was why she was a good reporter! People talked to her – and she liked it. It was almost as good as sex.

Next shop: crystals, semi-precious stones. Followed by an organic baker's. Deli – Julie popped in for pasta and a jar of pesto and inspected the takeaway section, which would be a good alternative to the chore of cooking pasta. Small pub, not very interesting. Bookshop, good. Second-hand designer clothes – definitely worth a look on a rainy day. Antiques, of course. Harbour Lights, an upmarket lamp shop. A fishmonger. Flower shop – all artless bunches of daisies tied with string and anemones bursting out of brown paper bags. Very smart.

On the way back I'll treat myself to a bunch, she decided.

Wholefood shop and organic café. Hey, what about lunch?

Half-portion of Caesar salad with organic croutons. Delish. Back to the counter afterwards for organic coffee. In walked Stevenson.

It's meant.

'Good thing I caught you in time. The coffee's appalling. It might indeed be organic but they haven't got a clue how to make it.'

Julie was amused. 'I may not be quite as fussy as you.'

His blue eyes fixed her. 'Almost certainly not, though I don't think you're completely without discernment. But it's a good excuse to get you back to my place.'

Oh, yes.

His hair was released from its workday band and brushed his shoulders. Still in black jeans, the usual T-shirt replaced by a black shirt with a double row of buttons, done right up to the neck. A black linen jacket. Good stuff.

'Don't forget I want to photograph you.'

'What, now?'

And how? Full face, profile, or strictly X-rated?

'After coffee, perhaps. I want to talk to you.'

That deep, cultured voice could talk to me for ever, she thought.

Like Julie, Stevenson lived on the top floor of a house, although it was an older, Victorian house with steep stairs. The flat door led on to a small lobby with a hatstand and two doors off. Julie followed him to the sitting room and stopped in her tracks.

The small window meant the room was fairly dark but a fire glowed in the hearth. A chaise longue upholstered in rich crimson velvet and draped with silk throws in kingfisher blue and purple faced the fire, while two equally sumptuously dressed chairs sat either side. Embroidered and mirrored cushions were heaped on the floor by the window, tangled up with the taffeta curtains gloriously striped with rich red, yellow, blue and purple.

And everywhere there were candles. No visible electric

light at all. Candles in wrought iron holders, lined up on the mantelpiece, in sconces on the walls. All white and all the same size apart from the large ones above the fire, the only ones which were as yet lit, which Julie suspected were responsible for the sensual perfume pervading the room.

'Oh, my God. This is fantastic.'

His lips curved into their beautiful smile which almost lit up his eyes. In this setting Julie could visualise him as Mr Darcy in *Pride and Prejudice*. He had that aristocratic air.

'I'll light the candles and put the coffee on. You can pick out some music.'

He indicated a stereo in the corner of the room.

'Oh, you don't live completely in the nineteenth century, then?'

He laughed as he lit a taper with a match then slowly made his way along the candles. 'God, no. When we're lit up you'll see there actually are some electric lamps for when I just can't be bothered with these, though that's not often.'

She surfed through the CDs. 'I don't know what music will go with this room. And quite honestly I haven't heard of most of these people.'

'OK, you go through the door at the end and put the kettle on. There's a cafetière on the worktop and the coffee's in the cupboard just above it.'

Julie wandered into the kitchen. It was no more luxurious than her own, but there was an array of gadgets on the worktop she would have put in a chef's kitchen rather than a photographer's. A wine rack held half a dozen bottles and she inspected the freezer. A half-bottle of Polish vodka – 'ha!' – some ice cubes and not a trace of an ice-cream chocolate bar.

The coffee was in bean form, but she found the grinder. Aware that her efforts at making coffee would be no better than the café's she made do with putting the kettle on and leaving the beans next to the grinder.

A plaintive saxophone accompanied by what sounded like a medieval male-voice choir penetrated the kitchen as Stevenson opened the door.

'Thank God you didn't start without me.'

To fill the grinder with beans he moved sideways past Julie. Their bodies were close. Very close. Her body blushed.

He fixed her with his blue eyes over the noise of the grinder. When it finished he warmed the cafetière and made the coffee, then turned to face her. They were maybe six inches apart and she was melting as though someone had poured boiling water over her as well.

Raising his hand to her face, he traced a line down her cheekbone with his finger and then cupped his hand under her chin, turning her face to inspect her profile. His touch felt like an electric shock.

'Isn't sex wonderful, Julie? We've barely even talked to each other and my hand on your face is our only physical contact, and that was purely professional.'

He moved his hand away and turned to pull cups and saucers out of the cupboard. 'And yet,' he continued, 'we're both excited. The erotic tension is building. Like any other sort of tension it will build up and up until it explodes – if we let it.

'Milk? Sugar? The firework is lit and soars up to the sky. Anticipation fills everybody's soul. Then it goes off – wow! ooh! ah! – then what?'

You're trying to say something I think I don't want to hear.

She took her coffee and followed him back to the sitting room. The candles provided more light than she had expected. He had drawn the curtains and the vibrant colour in the room glowed richly in the soft but clear light. The fire was still burning low.

He sat by the fire and indicated the chaise longue to Julie. She perched uncomfortably on the edge.

'You really do need to recline on it,' he said. 'Although if you don't mind me being blunt you're not dressed for

40

it. Neither are you dressed for a photo. What do you think, Julie? Shall we raise the tension a bit higher? Will you undress for me?'

Those blue eyes were telling her she would, whether she wanted to or not.

And she did want to. What she wanted to do was take her clothes off and have him fall helplessly on her and take her with a rough passion.

Then the anticipation would be over.

But well, hell. She wouldn't make much of a picture plonked on the chaise longue wearing a hooded sweatshirt.

'I seem to be doing all the talking,' he observed. 'But as I said when serendipity brought us together today, I want to talk to you. About our relationship.'

'We have a relationship?'

He frowned. 'Of course. As I just pointed out, we have a sexual relationship, one which I want to continue. But I have to tell you my terms, and you have to understand why they are what they are.'

She smiled and shook her head. 'You're not making sense yet, though I expect all will become clear in a minute. But as long as we're having a relationship, I may as well get undressed. Though I'll be honest, I don't know if I'm stripping for a lover or just taking my clothes off for a photographer.'

'Oh, surely it's worth investing a little effort in it in any case!' he said impatiently. 'That's the problem with all of us. Everything is done without thought. I believe in concentrating on what you're doing. A good job doesn't take much more trouble than a bad one.'

Good point, Stevenson. Strip, girl. It might just drive him over the edge. She stood and unzipped her sweat-shirt slowly. Not an erotic garment but she heard and felt the clasp of the metal zip running over each of the teeth.

Under there my tits are nice and snug in their white vest. My nipples are hard.

So's my breathing.

As she reached the bottom of the zip she could feel the heat of her sex directly below it. She disengaged the zip and the two sides fell apart, and she shrugged the garment from her shoulders. Although she was still wearing cords and a T-shirt, she felt almost naked.

Stevenson sipped his coffee and then leaned back in his chair, watching her with a smile on his lips.

'After university I decided to travel and went off to India. It was amazing. An incredible culture shock – the heat and colours and vegetation of southern India really blew my mind. I moved about a lot, spent time on the beach in Goa, did the usual tourist stuff, and met loads of other backpackers. I teamed up with one Australian guy for a while.

'He was a pretty laidback bloke. He'd got into Buddhism and out of curiosity I went with him to a Buddhist monastery for a retreat. We had instruction in meditation and lived just like monks in cells for a week. It was free which was great because of course we were trying to make our money last. But after we left I felt really blissed out and I decided I'd stick to this meditation stuff.

'I left India and went to Thailand. After a bit of beach bumming I met up with another guy who'd been on a retreat in a forest monastery there. I was still meditating and feeling pretty good about it and decided I'd try it again, so I set off for the forest.

'They weren't running any retreats but said I could stay and help out. Unlike the place in India there were European and American monks which didn't make it seem so alien. After a while I got really into it and decided to become a probationer monk.'

Fascinated by what he was saying, Julie had taken off her T-shirt and shoes. She was pleased to see his eyes on her breasts, soft and round under the cotton vest. As she slowly brought her hands to the zip of her trousers, he continued.

'The serenity of the existence was indescribable. There

42

were frustrations, of course – we all had our jobs to do and some of the monks didn't get along. And the privations – you ate what you were given, which was usually pretty dire. No furniture, just a cell with a sleeping platform. No amusement, unless you were working with a monk you got on with – preferably one you could communicate with! But I was hooked. I didn't think I would ever want to do anything else. After my probation I took vows and became a novice.

'One of the tasks was to go on *pindapati*, which was the daily begging round. The meal had to be eaten by midday, so we would set off in pairs early. We just walked into the village and people would put food in our bowls. Often it was disgusting, rotten fish, stews made from tatty vegetables, all mixed up. You weren't supposed to raise your eyes to the donors, though sometimes you were aware it was a young girl, and God knows those Thai girls were beautiful, but you had to let the thought go.

'There was one big house on the edge of the village and sometimes a servant would come out and put stuff in our bowls. Then one day the servant asked me to go in. The monk I was with went off to the other side of the village. We weren't supposed to separate, but we hoped maybe it would be rich pickings from the big house. Maybe some decent meat!'

Julie pushed her cords down over her hips, moving them slightly from side to side, nothing too obvious, and sat on the chaise longue and pulled them off her feet.

Shall I go further? Don't I look pretty good like this? Maybe not naked on the first date.

The tight white vest moulded round her breasts, its racing back style showing off her shoulders. White briefs today rather than high-legs, which left satisfying nakedness around the belly. Unshaven bikini line meant black pubic curls escaping from the knickers.

Never mind him, I'm turning myself on.

She lay back properly on the chaise longue, her head

resting on the tasselled velvet cushion and one arm caressing the silk throw over the back. It felt good. She propped one leg up and smiled – partly with self-satisfaction – as he went on with his story.

'My eyes were on the floor as I was led through a courtyard to stand outside the house. I heard the door open and someone stood in front of me. Amazingly, she spoke to me in English.

' "Hello, American monk. I got something for you."

' "English, not American," I said spontaneously, but still looking at the floor. She laughed. It was a musical voice. Sometimes Thai-accented English sounds fierce, but she sounded adorable.

' "Why you not look at me?"

' "Lady, you must know that monks should not look at women."

'Again that musical laugh. "No-one here to see us, English monk. You come to beg, I give you something. You sit here!"

'She pushed my shoulders down on to a bench in the garden. She smelt wonderful. I hadn't been so close to a woman, let alone touched by one, for over a year. She sat next to me. I was already breaking the rules by sitting alone with her, so I decided I might as well look.

'She was beautiful. All the Thai girls had perfect figures, small and lissome, but she had a really lovely face, tiny nose, heart-shaped lips, almond eyes. A lot of the women would curl their hair and cut it, but hers fell straight like a length of black silk. Her eyes were sparkling with intelligence – and sexuality.

'Despite my vows I thought straight away of putting my arms round her and feeling that body against mine. She sensed it, and she laughed again.

' "You a good monk, Englishman," she declared. "You no want to fuck me. But I want to fuck English monk."

' "Please," I started, then her lips were on mine.

'I knew the rules. As long as I didn't respond, I was safe. OK, I shouldn't have let myself get in this position,

44

but provided I made no move of acceptance, I wasn't breaking my vows.

'I sat like a statue while she kissed me and ran her hands all over my face. Of course I got an erection. God knows that was rock hard and more like a statue than the rest of me! She was laughing, amusing herself, then her breasts were in my face. She pushed my robe aside and uncovered my erection.

'"Hey, you do like me, English monk," she teased, running her hand up and down it. I knew that if I came that would be it – the rules count that as a response. So just like when I was young and having sex for the first time I thought of other things to take my mind off it – football league tables, times tables.

'She stopped touching me and I thought, thank God, but she had only stopped so she could take her clothes off. You can't believe what it was like. I was a monk, for God's sake. The Thai people generally have immense respect for monks, so it was hard to believe this was really happening. I don't know, she was rich, intelligent, and maybe she just didn't give a damn.

'I knew what was coming next. She straddled me on the bench, her face touching mine and her breasts grazing the front of my robe as she lowered herself on to me. "OK, English monk, you do nothing. I do all the work, then you not in trouble."

'You can't imagine what it felt like, that wet, tight hole pushing down on to my cock that hadn't so much as had a hand round it for almost two years, not even my own. But I wasn't going to come. I was determined. As long as she rode me, I kept thinking of something else, and after a while I knew I'd conquered it.

'She got off and stood in front of me and brought herself off with her fingers. That was nearly as bad as her fucking me, maybe because I thought I'd beaten her then almost lost it again. Then after she came she got dressed and went inside the house. She came out with a big steaming saucepan of a rich, fragrant stew and filled my bowl. It was the best thing I'd smelt for months. Apart from the smell of her.

'"You are a good monk," she told me. "You come back and I give you food any time. You are good monk with big cock." Then she opened the garden door and I went. The other monk was waiting for me, annoyed that I'd been so long. I told him the lady of the house made me wait, and when he smelt the stew he shut up because it was worth waiting for.

'Then I spoilt it all. The next day I went back.'

Julie drew in a deep breath. She'd been so caught up in the story that she'd unconsciously been stroking her thigh. She could feel the heat of her sex on her hand. Bringing her bent leg down to cross over the other brought a welcome throb from her sex.

'The other monk said we'd better go back for some of that meat stew. You know, I hadn't even had any. It felt wrong, as though I'd prostituted myself for it. But I didn't dare explain to him why we couldn't go back. I thought of asking him to go instead, but what if she did the same to him? He would know it had happened to me too.

'So I went in. She was delighted that I'd come back for more. This time she made me go inside the house and pushed me down on to the bed. It smelt of perfume and stale night sweat. She uncovered my cock again and sat on it. Again I didn't allow myself to come. But then she put her mouth around it and started sucking and I knew there was no way I could resist, and quite frankly I didn't want to. She was well practised and I just lay there and let it happen. I came for what seemed like minutes, pouring out gallons of the stuff.

'To give her credit, she swallowed it all – no tell-tale stains on my robe. But I knew then it was all over. I took the stew and went back to the monastery and told the abbot.

'If only I had told him the day before and not gone

46

back, I could have stayed a monk. But I knew that. Maybe I really wasn't suited for the monastic life.

'I got a lift to Bangkok and went back to being a backpacker, albeit one with a shaved head. I threw myself into having sex. I met a South African guy who was in Thailand taking girlie photos and he taught me how to use a camera in exchange for help in finding girls, especially ones who would pose with another girl, and even got me in some of the action shots. That lasted about a month. It was crazy – I must have had fifty girls. Not all Thai ones, sometimes other backpackers. I'd meet them and take them back for Barney to photograph. They thought it was way out, and sometimes they'd fuck me for the camera, sometimes that'd just be later and private.

'There were times when it ended up with Barney joining in as well, and other times he didn't even have any film in his camera, and we'd get a couple of girls and he'd pretend to take pictures of the three of us, then he'd get turned on and I'd pretend to do the photos.'

He paused. Julie was silent, absorbed in the sensations her muscles were creating. They were contracting hugely like the aftershock of a climax. Her clitoris felt as though it was as hard as Stevenson's cock had been for the Thai woman and her nipples pressed furiously against the soft cotton of her vest.

She nodded as he looked at her appraisingly. 'I'm beginning to see what you mean by building tension.'

'Yes, but not just over a few minutes. Imagine it over a day, a week, a month, maybe longer.'

Are you serious? Doing this sort of thing for a month without screwing? Me?

'I couldn't stand it.' Honesty's the best policy.

'You could! I knew as soon as I met you at your interview. You're not just sexy, you're sensual – even if you don't know it yourself. Don't tell me you don't love that velvet and silk on your bare skin. The warmth of the fire and the candlelight. The bitterness of the coffee.'

'You can't turn me into you.'

47

'No way do I want to. Think about it, Julie. You love flirting, that's obvious. Think about the longest flirtation you ever had, unconsummated. A bit of eye contact for a while. Then maybe your hands meeting accidentally across a desk. Passing close in front of or behind each other without actually touching. Building the tension. And then compare that unconsummated flirtation with one you gave in to, for a quick screw you would probably regret.'

She sighed. 'Yeah, I know what you're saying. But though you managed to live as a monk there's no way I can sublimate my urges like that.'

Stevenson's thin face broadened with his smile. 'I don't mean you have to be a nun, Julie Gibson. But as far as the two of us are concerned I want us to build up this eroticised state for as long as possible.'

Thank God there's always Mark and DIY, she thought. She looked into his clear blue eyes.

'OK, that sounds good. Like a game. But when you say as long as possible, do you mean we get to fuck in the end?'

He raised his eyebrows. 'I don't know. It's a game without any rules. But to go back to my story, after my orgy in Bangkok, I vowed not to have any casual sexual relationships. As time went by I upped the stakes and the ground rules gradually changed.'

He got up and knelt in front of Julie. 'Pleasure, Julie. I told you that was my thing. And there's nothing better than deferred pleasure.'

She had to laugh. 'Do you know, that's what I was thinking last night when you went home. I didn't think it was going to be quite as deferred as you're planning, though.'

'Enjoy every sensation. Feel that velvet on your thighs. I'm enjoying the sight of it. Turn on to your front and feel your sex pressing on the chaise longue.'

Turning, her mons connected with the hard surface

48

under the velvet. She rocked gently from side to side. 'Oh, yes, that's good.'

'It's great for me, too. I can see the profile of your right breast where your vest has fallen forward. Your nipple is hard and rosy.'

'Are you allowed to touch it?'

'OK, let's make a rule – yes. But not every time we meet. Today I can touch it.'

Julie closed her eyes as his fingers lightly circled her nipple.

He's right about this. I have never ever felt so sensitive. This could lead to something amazing.

'Can you touch anything else? Are you going to take your clothes off? Can I touch you? Can we kiss? Are we allowed to masturbate each other?'

'We play it by ear. Today, I'll take my shirt off. But that's enough contact for now. I still want to photograph you.'

Moving to the far end of the room, he picked up his camera and took it back to the chair. Watching Julie all the time, he unbuttoned his shirt and removed it with care.

His muscled arms were matched by his torso. With his long hair he looked like a candidate for the role of Tarzan.

'Why do you work out?'

He raised an eyebrow. 'I like to have pleasure in my body as well as in things around me.'

Raising the camera, he squatted on the floor. 'I spent eighteen months with no hair, no exercise except for work, nothing to wear except a robe, no drink except water and a largely rotten diet. After I came back home and started to get my head together, I realised that I wasn't meant for such ascetic practices. But I didn't want to just fall into an ordinary, accepting life. So I promised myself that I would make the most of everything that I could now have, and as far as possible have the best I could afford.'

His camera was on her face. 'We've rather lost our drift here, though, Julie. I want you to look as though you're in a state of excitement in this photo. Are you still feeling turned on?'

'Are you kidding?'

He put the camera down and slowly and tantalisingly ran a finger down her back.

'Turn over.'

She turned to lie on her back once more, feeling vulnerable as his body loomed over her. Her face looked up at him and she wanted to reach her arms up to his, but stayed still. He was looking down her body consideringly, and with a faint pang of disappointment she realised he was just looking for the best shot.

'Put one arm up under your breasts, and the other down between your legs.'

She felt self-conscious as she followed his instructions. He went back to regarding her through the camera lens.

'So what turns you on, Julie? What do you dream about?'

Easy.

'Believe it or not, policemen. Constables, sergeants, inspectors – I'm not fussy. Uniform or plain clothes, it's all the same. As long as they're nice-looking.'

'And do you fuck policemen or just fantasise about them?'

'God, yes. When I get the chance. I haven't had one here yet.'

His voice was amused. 'What, in six whole days? Of course, you've had Mark.'

'How do you know?'

The camera whirred.

'That was a nice secretive smile on your face. Because you obviously have a sexual relationship with him, though I bet it's casual.'

'You better believe it.'

'Have you ever made love to a woman?'

'No way! I am strictly heterosexual.'

50

He smiled. 'Let's put it another way. Have you ever fantasised about making love to a woman?'

Well, that's different. But fantasies are one thing, and it's not the sort of thing you tell people. You don't want your friends getting nervous.

She nodded.

'Good. I'm just thinking how nice it would be to watch your nipples being sucked by a nice round lipsticked mouth, and thinking how it would turn you on. What do you think?'

Can you not see the sudden contraction you caused?

'Especially with you wearing that outfit. How nice to have a contrasting girlie girl, wearing lacy bra and undies, giving you some attention.'

'Is this for real? Is that part of the game?'

'Just thought your tension level had dropped a bit. So are you visualising it? I think you are. Girlie girl pushing your vest up and caressing your breasts, how about that? Then maybe pushing those briefs down, maybe a nail-varnished finger sliding over your clitoris. Maybe even pushing inside you and coming out sticky wet. It would be wet, wouldn't it, Julie?'

He took a shot of her and she knew that she would look as though she was almost in the throes of coming because she was now in mega turned-on mode.

But he hadn't finished.

'She'd play with you until you felt like you were on the verge of orgasm, but then of course I'd make her stop because I didn't want you to come.'

Oh my God. How about a spontaneous, no-hands-on orgasm?

'Then when you'd calmed down a bit you could play with her as much as you liked. As a parting shot, I'd let her give you a gentle licking, a flicker of tongue over clitoris, just for long enough to bring you back to the brink but not let you go over the edge.'

She was molten like lava; one touch and she would

51

blow. But he wasn't going to let her. He just took one more shot and was silent.

Julie opened her eyes. 'This game – I'm not complaining, but I feel like you're the rich Thai woman and I'm the monk.'

He laughed. 'Maybe. But don't forget I'm not taking my own pleasure either. Now you know the game, you can play too. Next time you can turn me on.

'Not,' he added, glancing at the thick ridge of his cock in his black jeans, 'that I'm not in a state of some arousal already.'

Julie sat up and looked closely at him. 'How many women have you played this game with?'

His smile broadened as he sat on the pile of cushions under the window.

'Redundant question.'

'OK, this is relevant. How many women at work have you played it with?'

His forehead creased into a frown. 'Why is it relevant?'

'Because if there's a long list then everyone'll know and I'm not into that.'

'I can't believe you would think I would have wanted a relationship with a long list of women in the office.'

She giggled. 'No. I don't. But I'd still rather know.'

'One. And it didn't last that long. She couldn't handle it. She was too controlling. I just chose the wrong woman.'

'Who was it?'

'Well, you can guess who it wasn't.'

Obviously none of the reporters. None of them would be attractive enough for his fastidious taste. And someone controlling?

Of course. Amazon woman.

'Monika. The Danish pastry.'

He laughed. 'There's nothing remotely pastry-like about her, I can tell you.'

'You don't have to. She's pretty stunning.'

'It was her I was imagining making love to you. Her

52

blonde hair compared to yours, her tanned skin, her dark vampish lipstick. What do you think?'

Julie stretched luxuriously on the chaise longue. 'Actually quite nice – in fantasy, of course. And it's nice to know that she was the one you played the game with. I don't mind the thought of her.'

'Well, that's a relief! Anyway, game's over. I've got things to do, people to see, and it's almost five o'clock.'

She jumped up. 'I hope people to see doesn't mean the girl you're really shagging, and our game is just something you're playing so you can turn her on by telling her about it.'

'A terrific imagination. You're going to be good at this.'

Julie dressed. 'Well, I'm off to celebrate my first night in my new flat. It'll be great to be alone instead of having Mark around all the time. Where did I put my dinner?'

At the door she looked at him, puzzled. They didn't kiss – how bizarre! How could they say goodbye? He solved it by hugging her to him briefly and then kissing his finger to his own lips and transferring it to hers.

'See you tomorrow at the festival. Go well, Julie.'

The florist was just about to close as she passed it but as she peered through the door she was beckoned in enthusiastically.

'Always happy to serve one more customer,' said the cheerful girl who was in the process of cleaning her work table. 'What would you like?'

Julie gazed around the brilliant, scented bunches on display. It was going to be something special. She finally chose a bunch of magenta-coloured anemones plus a spray of acid-yellow, exquisitely perfumed mimosa. The florist approved of her choice.

Sensual. Vibrant. Colour. Brilliance. This really is going to be a new life.

Julie's diary, 15th June

Now I'm playing a game with Stevenson called How Long Can I Last. Not without coming, but without fucking at all. Terrific verbal sex, I squelched all the way home. His flat is amazing. I'm going to change my life. Started by buying some fantastic flowers. He used to be a Buddhist monk! Told me how he lost his monkhood and then became a serial screwer of Thai prostitutes. The thought of him sandwiched between two Thai girls and a photographer getting his rocks off watching really got me hot. Put the flowers in water when got back then straight in the bathroom. Thank God I insisted on power shower. Unhooked it and turned the nozzle round to no holds barred and pressure up to maximum. I came in no time, what a knee trembler, in fact bit too powerful, next time won't put it up so high. After all I'm into deferred pleasure now, ho ho. So then tried out lying on new bed with Anaïs Nin and vibrator – calmer than shower, great, intense. Proper dinner for first time for ages, watching *Blind Date*. Fell asleep in front of TV. Blame Stevenson.

No way would I be here if it wasn't work, thought Julie.

'We're living, in a-a spiritual world, and I am a-a spiritual girl' kept going round and round in her mind.

Spiritual girl – not. Just because she was playing an erotic game with a former monk didn't mean she was getting into spirituality.

And this New Age stuff was just mind numbing. Crystals – so what? Alternative therapies – just pass the paracetamol. Aromatherapy, that was the only thing of any interest. What's the sexiest massage oil? She smelt her way through a few before she identified the sensual scent of Stevenson's candles. Ylang ylang. Great name.

Tarot cards, T'ai Chi, Indian head massage and Chinese herbal medicine. The Celestine Prophecy workshops. Spiritual healing.

'You're a philistine,' said Stevenson, grinning as they

walked round looking for a story. Normally Julie could find something newsworthy in even a school sports day but this was impossible. Esoteric or earnest, none of the exhibitors had anything exciting going for them.

'I'm not, you know. I love theatre, books, films and art, and though I wouldn't call myself a believer I get all emotional listening to choral music. But excuse me, Bach is a million times more spiritual than this.' She nodded her head in the direction of a music stand which had the sounds of the Amazon rainforest blaring out.

'Yes, I'll drink to that. Let's do lunch. I noticed a really appealing veggie burger stand near the door.'

She stuck her tongue out. 'You are vegetarian, though, aren't you?'

'Only by discipline, not inclination. Sometimes I just abandon myself to tearing a juicy steak apart and feeling that warm blood run down my throat.'

'Great, that makes you sound like a vampire. What have I let myself in for?'

'Look, there's a macrobiotic food stand. Do you know what the perfect macrobiotic food is?'

Of course not.

'Brown rice. What do you think about that?'

Julie sniffed. 'I'll tell you exactly what I think. I'm out of here to get a proper sandwich or a pizza and I'll see you later – or are you done?'

'I am, just about. There wasn't much point me coming, really. I don't expect we'll bother with any pics of this. After all, it's not as though many of the exhibitors are local.'

'And you've got one of drippy June the organiser.'

He laughed. 'You are very down to earth, Julie. I like that. Tell you what, let's go and have a sandwich and a pint in the Far Pavilion then I can go back to get this stuff sorted and think about verbal sex with you and you can come back here and wait for something to happen.'

'I can tell you I'm going to be thinking about verbal

sex with you if I have to stay here any longer. It's the only way it won't do my head in.'

The Far Pavilion's beer was light years away from the Wintersea Whinger she'd had to put up with two days before. Golden and aromatic with the scent of apricots, fruity in the mouth with a bitter finish.

Stevenson was impressed with her verdict.

'You could become the paper's food and drink critic – we haven't had one of those for a while.'

'Seriously? That guy Luca at the Italian was just asking me yesterday to do a review. I can't believe no-one wants to do that job.'

'Well, who? Claire?' They dissolved into giggles.

'No, that's not fair. What about Wendy? She looks like she likes her food.'

'Now who's being unfair? Poor thing, I don't think she'd have anyone to go with. And I doubt she'd be that discerning.'

Julie raised her eyebrows. 'Oh, I don't know. She fancies you, so she's got some taste.'

He winced. 'So it's not just obvious to me! She's a nice girl, you know. But not my type.'

'I thought maybe we could be friends.'

'As long as she doesn't know we're having sex,' he observed.

'But we're not, my dear.'

It was back. The tension was rising again. Hands accidentally touching reaching for sandwiches.

But first, work. Back to the Winter Gardens for another hour – nothing going on. In office by four; no-one else there. What to say about the festival?

You can't get the splash every day. On auto. Get it done and get home.

RECORD NUMBERS visiting the Spiritual Age Festival at the Winter Gardens on Sunday led local New Age sages to predict that Wintersea would become a major centre for New Age and spiritual culture.

56

The festival attracted over 3,000 visitors, more than any other such festival ever held in Britain according to organiser June Moonchild. They were treated to lectures on shamanism and soul retrieval, given the chance to try therapies such as Indian head massage and reiki, and sampled macrobiotic vegetarian food accompanied by mood music.

Chapter Three

Evening Light, Monday 17 June

ATTEMPTED SECURITY VAN ROBBERY

ARMED ROBBERS were foiled in an attempt to rob a security van of almost a quarter of a million pounds near the Ringway Industrial Estate this morning.

Six hooded men forced the van to stop by barricading the road with two cars just after 10 a.m. but two Houlder Brothers lorries arrived on the scene unexpectedly and the gang fled.

The van driver, Paul Whittle, 30, said that he and his companion, Eric Johnson, 44, had feared for their lives.

The security company, Securajob, would not confirm how much was in the van but it was en route with the weekend takings from the three branches of Biggabuys in town, whose manager George Stephenson told the *Evening Light* would be in the region of a cool £200,000.

Julie suspected Adam Arnside would be annoyed with her for going behind his back on the crash story but he was cool. Even impressed.

'You're not a pushover, are you, Julie?' he asked her in his office on Monday morning.

Oh yes, I am, Adam. Just don't push me right now before I've got the weekend crime back to the office.

'Excuse me?'

He laughed. 'I wondered if you'd just go away and report the bare bones of the accident but you did a bit of ferreting.'

'I really didn't harass anyone. I honestly would not have even spoken to Mrs Robinson but her daughter came to me.'

'OK, I'm not complaining! I like it. You're good at your job. And if you had upset anybody, I'd have known. This might seem a big place to you after your Yorkshire villages but it's my town and I know what goes down.'

Did she detect an admiring look on his face as he shuffled the morning's crime report?

'Anyway, back to business. I can give you the dead man's name now – Wayne Hodgson, eighteen, of Silverlea Hotel, The Promenade. Also I can confirm the car was stolen from Inkerman Terrace some time after eight o'clock Friday night. Mr Robinson and Miss Holdsworth – I don't need to give you their details as you've found out for yourself – are in a stable condition, as I expect you've also got from the hospital.'

Check.

Down the list of Saturday night and Sunday crimes. Nothing much had happened while Julie was engaged in erotic mindgames with Stevenson or while she was at the Spiritual Age Festival.

The phone rang.

'Yup. Yup. Who's there? No-one hurt? OK. Sure. Cheers.'

He put the phone down and raised an eyebrow at Julie.

'So, here's your chance to be practically on the spot.

59

Attempted security van heist near the Ringway – that's an abandoned industrial estate on the edge of town. Go on, get yourself down there, and don't say I don't do you any favours.'

She could have kissed him but there was no time.

'Adam. Thank you so much.' She was already backing out of his office, getting her mobile out to get a photographer on the scene. 'I'm rushing. See you tomorrow.'

'Sure, sure.' He was smiling.

By the time she called in and got her map out to find the scene of the crime, Mike Phillips, one of Stevenson's colleagues, had beaten her to it, and told her that the security guards had already been taken to the police station to make their statements. After a few shots of the van he went to the station to wait for the men with strict instructions from Julie not to let them get away before she could speak to them.

There was really nothing to see apart from an abandoned security van, still with its booty, guarded by cops. Except for the DI.

She had noticed him fleetingly in the station, but just a casual look had been enough to register those eyes, deep Bournville-chocolate dark, with what you might call a spark but was more like a flame. A slow-burning flame that properly fed could be kindled into a raging fire.

His hair was dark, too – short, number two, perhaps, slightly receding but not worryingly so. High cheekbones, a straight, full-lipped mouth and a big nose, slightly hooked.

Not tall – compact. Heavily built but not fat. Strong, like his face.

'Hi. I'm Julie Gibson.'

He nodded. 'I know. I'm Bryn Edwards.' His voice was as deep and dark as his eyes, which were fixed on her face.

'Is that DI Edwards?'

'Sure is. You've missed all the excitement.'

60

I don't think so, DI Edwards. Not with the intense way you're looking at me. 'So, what can you tell me?'

He gave her as many details as he could, in the middle of which another security van arrived to offload the money. The policemen guarding it drove off, just leaving the scene of crime officers looking at tyre marks and searching the ground for other evidence.

'I'd better get down to the station to talk to the security guards.'

That's what duty tells me. My body's telling me to stay here. That direct gaze is making me melt like hot chocolate. I know it's a warm day, but this is ridiculous.

'Yeah, I think maybe I ought to get going, too. Except I came down with the uniformed guys – any chance of a lift?'

'Sure.' Her voice was faint.

He went to speak to the other officers. Julie was having serious control problems. She felt as horny as hell and she could not believe that DI Edwards felt any different. After all, he could have left with the other cops if he'd wanted. Shit, she had to drive in this state.

She had the map out as he got in the passenger seat.

'Don't you trust me to direct you?' he asked, amused.

'Oh, I'm sure you'll give me very exact directions.' She spoke deliberately, looking into his eyes. He looked back and they locked and they both knew they were heading towards the inevitable.

'First off, drive straight up here and turn right – you can't go any other way.' They passed empty industrial units and the road trailed off into a track.

'Just follow this track down to the end by the edge of the woods and pull in on the right.'

On the right, just under a tree. Thank you, God, for putting us on the same wavelength.

As she upped the handbrake and switched off there was a moment of pure silence, full of expectation. Then they turned towards each other and their lips locked just as their eyes had done a minute before.

'Get out the car,' he breathed, undoing his seatbelt. She didn't need telling twice. He grabbed her arm and pulled her into the woods where she backed up to the trunk of a massive oak tree. She felt the power of him standing in front of her as she felt the power of the tree trunk behind her and without even really thinking about it stretched her arms behind her, as though trying to encircle the trunk. Her unconscious mind was telling him: I'm vulnerable, I've surrendered, I'm waiting.

She didn't want finesse and she didn't get it. His hands ran over her breasts urgently, not quite roughly but powerfully. He undid the two top buttons of her white shirt and pushed his hand inside to knead her breasts. Their mouths clashed again as their tongues sought each other. Julie thrust herself forwards towards him and was rewarded by feeling his cock grinding against her bone. His hands were raking all over her torso, rubbing her hard, fierce nipples and now down past her waist, down her thighs, to lift her short skirt.

The collar of his button-down was open and she undid two more buttons and felt the hair on his chest.

Whimpering, she rubbed harder against him as he pulled her tights and knickers down efficiently and pushed one hand along the length of her sex. She heard a guttural noise come from his throat as he found her wetness and, now cheated of his cock pressed against her, she pushed herself against his hand and brought her own hands round to unzip the fly of his beige Levis. His belly was warm and she could feel soft hair like fur on it.

His uncaged erection felt unnaturally thick, as round as her wrist. A drop of pre-come lubricated her fingers as she stroked, his fingers now inside her, scooping out moisture to soften the roughness of his broad thumb which was circling her clitoris. She knew neither of them could wait and she knew that neither of them wanted bringing off manually. Someone had to move and she slid down the tree trunk and manoeuvred sideways until she was lying on the patchy grass.

He didn't need an invitation. Taking a condom from his pocket he rubbered up quickly, still fixing her with his deep dark eyes, while she took her tights and knickers off and pulled her skirt up. She wasn't stripping sexily for him like she had done for Stevenson. She knew he wasn't interested in that. Like her, he wanted to get to home base as soon as possible.

His legs were covered with the same dense soft fur as his belly, animal-like. It seemed appropriate.

Lowering himself on to powerful arms and still with those intense eyes on her he nudged against her swollen opening. She lifted herself up for him and guided him inside.

It *was* as thick as her wrist. She gasped as he drove it in, distending her as nothing had ever done before. Unbelievable, almost painful, but in a deeply pleasurable way. The slight pain level seemed so right, after the desire she'd had to surrender to him.

Still they hadn't said a word but the tension between them was palpable. She wrapped her legs around him and arched her back up towards him as she got used to his thickness.

She felt full up. Filled. Fulfilled. Whatever. His thrusting, rhythmic cock and his magnetic eyes were doing a good job. She pumped her hips up towards him, taking up his rhythm, slamming her bone against him. He moved his hands to her shoulders, making her take some of his weight, which increased her discomfort and also her passion. She wanted his weight on her, his powerful body riding her roughly; she wanted him to clutch her and bruise her and fuck her and use her oh my God oh my God oh my God.

Julie realised she'd been talking out loud. Hopefully not for long. Anyway, would he have noticed as he too came with a deep and heartfelt groan, also calling for someone other-worldly in his dark voice?

Just quickly the thought arose that she had Stevenson

to thank for her state of eroticised excitement. Then she made like a Buddhist and let it go.

He withdrew and they stood simultaneously, the DI knotting the condom and raising his pants, Julie trying to stand on one leg to put her knickers and tights on.

They smiled at each other. Not embarrassedly, but conspiratorially.

'Great shag, DI Edwards.'

He nodded courteously. 'You're a great lay, Miss Julie. Next time we'll probably take it a bit more slowly.'

'I don't know about that. I loved it quick and rough – didn't you?'

Say you did. I really mean it. Sod these tights. I'll have to get my legs brown.

'Oh yes. But it would have been nice not to have to rush straight to the station. The thought that you might miss your deadline did make me force the pace a bit more than I might have liked.'

'That's very kind of you, DI Edwards. Talking of which, let's get on. At least we've only lost five minutes. Hey, just get this grass off my back, will you?'

He brushed efficiently with his big hands and Julie almost felt like she'd like a bit more hands-on already. But there was work to do.

'OK, more directions. By the way, you have the thickest cock I have ever come across, as it were, in my life.'

'Thank you. Left here. Shame we can't put a siren on. You are living, breathing sex. Just like the real Miss Julie.'

'Are you kidding me? I don't believe it – a DI who knows about Strindberg!'

'Truth? A few years ago Amanda Donohoe was in a production of it and I've fancied her ever since I saw her in *Castaway*. Theatre's not usually my thing but I made an exception for her.'

She laughed. 'Well, you've got one up on me. All I know is that it's a play by Strindberg. Obviously she was a bit of a goer.'

'And some. Although her clothes were a bit more

cumbersome than yours. Pity I couldn't get them all off. Still, next time. And I can savour you in your underwear first.'

'That's twice you've mentioned next time.'

'Too forward? You don't think there'll be a next time?' His voice was amused and teasing – and amazingly confident.

'It seems sort of inevitable.'

'Exactly. That's why I wasn't going to mess about playing hard to get. Turn right here. All the guys have got the hots for you. I can't believe my luck in getting in first.'

'Who says you have?'

He burst out laughing, a throaty, almost dirty laugh. 'Ha! You are kidding, aren't you?'

'Yeah. But what I don't like the sound of is that you seem to think you'd know if anyone else had beaten you to it. I'm not keen on men gossiping in the toilet stuff.'

'That's not my style. Do you know where you are now?'

Julie turned to him briefly. 'Yeah. And so do you. But I'm not going to promise to be exclusive.'

He sighed. 'All in good time.'

'You don't sound too put out – hey, you're not married, are you?'

Those eyes were looking at her. 'Divorced, Miss Julie. Completely at your disposal.'

'Right, then lead me to the security men – if they're still here.'

They had pulled into the police station car park.

'And if you don't mind, make sure I don't get a rocket for parking here. I know I'm not supposed to but seeing as I gave you a lift –'

He reached over and silenced her with a finger on her lips. 'Don't worry. You're safe with me. Come on, I'll find your men for you, then clear your car with admin.'

* * *

She was just back in time to bang the story out for the 11 a.m. deadline.

I'll have a heart attack if I carry on at this rate.

The phone rang at 11.05.

'Newsdesk!'

'I wondered if your tension level needed a little fillip.'

She laughed softly into the receiver. 'I'm afraid you're a little too late, sir.'

'Julie, you have my unreserved admiration if you've already scored by five minutes after the deadline. Unless you took someone home with you last night.'

Aware of John and Wendy close by, she chose her words carefully.

'No, I just happened to be in the chief inspector's office when he heard about the crime this morning, so I managed to actually get out to the scene. But thank you for your call.'

'Oh, you've had a cop. Uniform or CID?'

'Yes, DI Edwards is in charge of the case. Maybe you know him?'

'Ye-es – nice guy. Intense. Is he Welsh?'

'Not noticeably.'

Can you tell? I know he's not Jewish, but . . .

'Well done, Julie Gibson. And you still made it back in time for the deadline. I hope your new chum won't interfere with our game.'

'Oh no, there's nothing exclusive about it.'

'Splendid. I'll be seeing you.'

Well played, Julie. She put the phone down, smiling, and turned to Wendy. John was on the phone.

'Why is it you always get these hot tips after you've got the story? It might have been more useful if that guy had phoned at nine instead of eleven.'

Wendy clucked sympathetically. 'I *know*! And they always go on so much, don't they?'

If only you knew.

She beamed at Wendy impulsively. 'Hey, do you fancy

66

lunch? I didn't get any breakfast and I feel like more than a sandwich.'

'Brill. Twelve?'

We're going to be mates. I might even tell you about DI Edwards once we've got going properly. But not about Stevenson.

Located in the town centre, the office should have been perfectly situated. Except now the paved precincts were half empty with a quarter of the shops boarded up. All the usual suspects were there – the cheap fashion chains, cheap toiletries, cheap jeans and the video rental shop, with just a couple of old family businesses still in place like the jeweller and the men's outfitters. All the decent shops were in the Old Harbour area, and the supermarkets were out of town. The precinct shoppers were the type who couldn't get out of town and couldn't afford the Old Harbour prices.

So not much choice for lunch, apart from pubs – and Julie had been to the only decent one – a couple of scruffy cafes and a wine bar.

They settled themselves in the only remaining table in Bubbles and Wendy went up to the bar for two glasses of Chardonnay while Julie perused the menu. She settled on a lasagne and Wendy a smoked salmon sandwich.

'I think I might try to get into wine,' ventured Wendy as she sipped the chilled Chardonnay.

Surely nothing to do with Stevenson's verdict on the local beer?

'Yeah, I like it. Look, Wendy, I need you to tell me how a girl lives in this town. Hairdresser, step class, clothes shops, lady doctor and stuff.'

Wendy half smiled. 'Hair, clothes and doctor, yes. Step class, you must be joking.'

'Hey, haven't you tried it?'

Julie told herself she wasn't being naive. On the contrary, it would be fattist to assume that Wendy didn't exercise just because she was a bit chunky.

'Do I look as though I do exercise? It'd just be totally embarrassing. Anyway, I pride myself on being the arty type, not a ladette.'

'OK, let me find out about the step classes, and then I'll talk you into coming with me. My bum's big enough when I do exercise – it'll be spreading like a cowpat if I have another week without it. You'll have to come with me – I haven't got any girlfriends!'

Wendy laughed. 'Do you really need them? You're a man's woman.'

'Sure, but I still need some girlie chats. I'm not abnormal. So what about men in your life?'

'Nothing, *nada*, *niente*. Anyway, after working all day and sometimes a couple of nights, then I'm in this experimental theatre group that meets once a week, then going to other plays, meeting my mates, there's not a lot of time.' She took a sip of wine. 'I hope you don't think it's out of order me asking, but are you and Mark an item?'

Julie put on the most incredulous face she had in her repertoire.

'You are kidding! Aren't you? No way! We're just mates, that's all. On the paper we were on there were only three reporters, so for about a year there was me, Mark and the chief reporter, this really old guy who literally knew everyone in the circulation area so he got all the stories without even trying. We had to bond.'

Wendy shook her head. 'That must be really weird. My last paper was quite big – just a weekly but there were six of us. I can't imagine working in a tiny office.'

'Don't do it.'

The food arrived. Julie was starving. Sex always gave her an appetite. She'd already had an iced bun and a coffee in the paper's tiny canteen but it hadn't been anything like enough to fill the hole DI Edwards had left in her.

Unfortunately, she couldn't keep her mouth shut.

'Hey, Wendy, I've pulled a cop.'

With her eyes rounded in surprise over her red lipstick, Wendy did a good impersonation of Bette Davis.

'No! But you've only been here a week.'

Julie giggled and simultaneously kicked herself. Why can I never keep quiet?

'I know. Isn't it great? The dark, intense one – DI Edwards.'

Wendy screwed up her face, obviously not able to picture him.

'I don't really know a lot of the policemen. I've only been to the station a couple of times when someone else was on holiday, and apart from Adam Arnside and Tony Greene and a couple of the uniformed inspectors I don't know anyone else – except the ones who do schools and inquests and so on. Well, well done! I suppose. I'm not keen on cops myself.'

'Oh, why not?' said another voice.

They looked up. It was Monika the advertising Amazon.

'Julie's pulled a DI. They're all just pigs to me,' Wendy blurted out.

Cheers, Wendy. Obviously not used to keeping confidences.

Monika laughed. 'Quick work! Welcome to Wintersea. We'll have to have a night out some time. Must go, I'm with Derek. See you later.'

With Derek? Interesting. Yes, there he was at the bar, now leaning elegantly towards Monika. Surely she's not shagging him? With their blond hair, blue eyes, tans and height they could almost pass for father and daughter, thought Julie amusedly. As Monika spoke to him he looked over and smiled and waved.

'Only blondes go that gorgeous golden tan,' she said enviously.

Wendy sniffed. 'Only blondes have difficulty connecting words like "hole", "ozone layer", "sunbathing" and "skin cancer".'

'Ouch! So what gives with Monika and Derek? Give

me the goss on all the office romances, Wendy. If you won't come to step, you owe me one. Especially as you just told her about me and my cop.'

Wendy was blushing. 'God, I can't believe I did that! I don't know, there's something about Monika that makes me nervous. I really didn't mean to say that. I'm sorry.'

'No problem. Just spill the beans.'

The truth: she didn't know. They were good friends and went to lunch quite often, but Monika was at most in her early 30s and Derek at least 55. But they knew each other intimately, if not sexually.

The rest of the reporters: not much. Wendy confessed she'd had a bit of a thing with Mike Phillips but had decided against it. Cheryl from advertising had made a big play for Mark when he first came and had made a bit of a fool of herself but it was all finished now.

Julie knew that from Mark. Cheryl was married and he'd screwed her once after the Christmas party. Unfortunately she'd proved more difficult to detach than she had to attract and he had to play it carefully so as not to end up with a live-in girlfriend and two kids.

Some girls, really.

'Oh, and of course there's Bob.'

Julie swivelled her head like a possessed woman.

'Ho ho. Is it April Fool's Day? Who on earth would go for Bob?'

Wendy smiled smugly. 'Hilary Dutton on reception. They had an absolutely major thing going for about a year. Then his wife found out. What's worse, she was pregnant at the time, and she came up and shouted at Hilary right out at the desk. Then she broke down crying and it all ended. Hilary and Bob, I mean.'

Julie was still gobsmacked. 'But Hilary's quite nice, and Bob is such a – such an arse. I mean, look at that fat grumpy face of his; I've not seen it smile yet.'

'Right, but that's now. He used to be thinner and better-looking and happier. It's only after the Hilary thing ended he's got like this. Claire reckons that if his wife hadn't got pregnant he and Hilary were going to leave home and set up together.'

Well well. All good grist to the mill.

'Hey, that's incredible. Listen, can I come with you next time you go to the theatre?'

Wendy beamed. 'Sure. Next Saturday there's a two-hander of *Women in Love*, you know? Just Ursula and Gudrun, monologue and dialogue.'

Julie raised her eyebrows. 'What, kind of, *Birkin and Gerald are Redundant*? Sounds interesting. I'm in.'

Sounds dire, but I need a social life. Apart from screwing.

It was time to go. Julie's eyes were drawn to Monika and Derek who were still at the bar. They both smoked with attitude and from a distance looked sensationally attractive. So what was a 25-year age difference? But Monika liked to be in control, and Derek was obviously nobody's pushover. Could be it wasn't sexual at all. Unless they too were playing some sort of erotic mind-fuck game.

The whole world could be playing something similar. The thought heightened the haze of eroticism Julie seemed to be moving in these days.

She thought of Stevenson's Monika fantasy and tightened her muscles. Maybe, just maybe.

Julie's diary, 17 June

How come the girl who always says she doesn't like it in the morning fucks a cop at 0955? Actually I don't know what time it was but hey, what a turn up. Bryn Edwards. Suppose he must be Welsh with a name like that. Never occurred to me till Stevenson mentioned it – well, that's a first. He's so hairy but not like the usual coarse and rough male hairs, he's soft, like an animal. In fact we were almost like animals, sort of primeval, just instinctively knew we had to screw. It was a quickie but not, I mean not like a quickie with Mark which is always so sort

71

of stylised, though I suppose that's my doing. Guess I need some sort of roleplay with Mark. Not much like the heightening tension with Stevenson, goes without saying. Perhaps only because of him I was on heat.

I can't believe the change in me since I've got here. Up in NY I was just grateful for what I could get whenever, now here it's following me around. I mean: Mark on Friday, Stevenson – in a way – on Saturday, now Bryn – must start thinking of him as that rather than DI Edwards – on Monday. Really will have to kick Mark into touch now, temporarily at least, go back to the casual thing we used to have.

This diary was supposed to be the basis for my novel but it's just turning into a catalogue of sex. Move over Bridget Jones – I've turned into Mary Millington.

Chapter Four

Evening Light, Thursday 20 June

LANGUAGE STUDENTS ATTACKED BY VICIOUS MOB

A GROUP of overseas students from the Stoneborough Grange School were punched and kicked by a mob of youths in the town centre last night.

Hurling racist insults, some twelve youths set about the multinational group who had just emerged from The Ship pub at around 10 p.m.

Police say they have no idea who or what was behind the attack. 'No-one seems to have seen the gang arrive and witnesses say they seemed to melt away into the streets surrounding the precinct,' said Chief Inspector Adam Arnside.

'What's going down with this attack, Julie?' Bob Underwood was scowling at the computer screen where he was obviously reading Julie's story. 'Surely the police have got some idea who it could be.'

She shook her head. 'No, they haven't. They're completely mystified. They say there's never been any indication of racism before – I suppose that's right?'

He nodded grudgingly. 'Well, I suppose that's true in the sense that there's never been any violence but there's been a bit of tension since the refugees started piling in. The students have been here for ever, though. I don't understand why they've been attacked. If it was a group of refugees it'd make more sense.'

'Well, I've got all I can find out down there.'

She'd interviewed the students, the teachers, the head, the police, the eyewitnesses – in fact, everyone but the elusive gang. What more could he want?

Bob sighed. 'I suppose that'll have to do then. You've marked it with pics – what have they got?'

'A black eye, a cut face and a few bruises.'

What do you expect?

He sighed again. Less than two weeks and he was already getting on her nerves.

'OK. But keep pressing the police on their enquiry.'

Julie's phone rang.

'Newsdesk!'

'Do you like dancing?'

It was DI Edwards – no, Bryn.

'Yes. Well, within reason. As long as it's not line, square or circle. Nothing geometric. And nothing that involves sequins.'

'Tonight's the night to go to Hell and Back.'

'Hey, I've just done that. Talking to the news ed.'

His laugh was deep and excitingly coarse. 'Best club in town, especially on a Thursday. Next to the Breaker Bar on the seafront, just down from the Old Harbour. I want to dance with you for hours so we're dripping with sweat and then make love to you for more hours.'

'I hope you're not in that communal office.'

'No way. I'm in the town centre.'

Her journalistic nose twitched. 'Looking for racist thugs?'

'No, just hanging out in the mall like an American teenager.'

She giggled. 'OK, going back to what you said – you mean on the beach?'

He snorted. 'What, under the pier with the druggies shooting up around us? Great as long as we don't lie on any needles.'

'God's sake. What's happened to romance?'

He laughed again. 'Yeah, well, when we've finished cleaning up the streets we'll start on the beach. So, are you up for it? Shall I pick you up at your place?'

Oh, no, not yet.

'No need, I'll meet you there. Where?'

'Meet me in the Breaker Bar. I'll be there from nine. OK?'

'Check.'

'And if you won't let me come and get you, take a taxi. Just until we have cleaned up the streets.'

What shall I wear? He said he wanted to savour my underwear next time. Or shall I not wear any?

She was glad she'd spent what she could of the last three evenings sunbathing on the balcony. She wasn't tanned but she'd lost the whiter shade of pale the York-shire winter had left her with. And thank God she'd faked her legs brown.

I love dancing. Especially with someone I want to fuck.

Imagine dancing with Stevenson. That would be amaz-ing. Talking of whom – let's have a bit of tension raising.

First – I've got mail.

JULIE I MISS YOU COME ROUND SOON I PROMISE NO ICE CREAM.

She looked over at Mark and blew him a kiss. He'd just have to wait.

Julie told herself she wanted to have lunch with Steven-son in Bubbles because she liked the lasagne. It certainly didn't have anything to do with the fact that Derek and Monika might be there again.

Whatever – they weren't.

The photographer had been off for two days and as he walked into the wine bar Julie's muscles skipped a beat. He was so cool.

Apart from their oblique phone conversation, Julie hadn't told him about Bryn, and wasn't sure whether the rules of the game meant that she should or whether extra-curricular sex was outside the parameters of their relationship. He soon put her straight.

'OK, tell me everything about the scene you had with your DI on Monday.'

She lowered her voice so no-one else could hear, although the decibel level in the wine bar was high. It meant she had to put her elbows on the table and lean towards him. Their faces were so close together they could barely lift their glasses to their lips. She fixed her eyes on his.

Julie murmured her story. The pitch of her voice sounded sexy to her, and she hoped to Stevenson. His pale blue eyes gleamed with interest and encouraged her to keep talking. Afterwards she told him about her date that night and the promise of their wet and sweating bodies writhing together.

'Very good, Julie Gibson. You're making me quite excited. Don't stop now.'

So what else can I tell you? I could say how exciting it is to tell you this, to talk to you about fucking someone else while our heads are together so intimately in such a public place.

She told him about what she was or wasn't going to wear that night, wondering how much Bryn would be turned on when he realised that she'd been so available to his touch all the time they were dancing. Then she described her major masturbation session that resulted from his turning her on last time.

'More, Julie.'

'I hope this is working for you. I'm turning myself on, anyway.'

76

'It's working all right. In fact, you're going to have to get the next glass in. My erection would be extremely obvious.'

'I'll do that now.'

She came back and told him about her last session with Mark. He was amused.

'And seeing as I've told you about him, I think you should give me the lowdown on Monika and Derek. What are they up to?'

'Oh, do you?' He was looking up from his vantage position facing the door. 'Well, here comes Monika. Maybe she'll tell you herself.'

Oh, shit. Please do not land me in it.

Monika was alone this time.

'Julie, you've only been here five minutes and you seem to have established your usual table in the wine bar. And you don't have to spring apart just because I'm here. I was watching you leaning towards each other so intently.'

And I bet Stevenson was watching her watching us.

'Do join us, Monika. We're talking about sex.'

She pouted her deep plummy lips at him. 'Surprise, surprise. I'll get a drink and a chair. But you've got to put up with me smoking.'

She was back in minutes.

'So fill me in on this erotic conversation.' She lit up a Marlboro Light.

At least she's not mentioned the fact that she knows I'm shagging a cop. That's good. For all she knows I'm after Stevenson – maybe that's why she looks so amused.

'Julie was telling me about her conquest of one of the DIs the other day.'

'Oh, yeah, I know about that.'

He was surprised until Julie explained about Wendy's big mouth.

'So, you're talking about sex. Does that mean you're playing his game, Julie?'

Julie felt out of her depth with Monika. She looked helplessly at Stevenson, who came to her rescue.

'Before she answers that, she has her own question that she's too embarrassed to put to you. Are you playing a game with Derek?'

He was smiling his thin-lipped smile and Monika was laughing. Julie shook her head.

'Oh, wow, this is too much for me.'

'No it's not,' said Monika. 'This is what happened, Julie. I tried to play Stevenson's game but he kept moving the goalposts. It was like playing that stupid Mornington Crescent thing on the radio. I suppose you have to be English to understand it, but I can't hack it. I like rules. So I decided to make up my own game, with my rules. I have to admit I've stolen a couple of this guy's ideas. Anyway, I chose Derek to play with me. It's cool.'

Julie's embarrassment was turning back to excitement.

'So, Julie, you're screwing a cop and playing Stevenson's game. What about Mark?'

'Jesus, does everyone have to know everything about everyone around here?'

The other two laughed.

'We're just raising our tension levels.' Stevenson smiled at her. 'I'll tell you later, Mon. Mark is a man with more imagination than I gave him credit for.'

Well, he said he didn't care who knew about his sexploits.

'I told Julie that I fantasised about the two of you making love,' he went on, turning to Monika. 'She was wearing a white vest and knickers, and I thought of you in black lace and high heels pleasuring her. It was a real turn-on. Not just for me.'

'So what were we doing in this fantasy?'

'You were having little nibbles with your lipsticked mouth on Julie's pale skin. It glows translucent, Mon. You'd love it. Then your painted nails were disappearing inside her.'

This is surreal.

Monika looked at Julie, a suppressed smile on her face.

'Well, interesting. I'd like to see that masculine underwear of yours.'

'He took enough pictures. With film. I think.'

They laughed conspiratorially together.

'Don't you need to go to the loo, Julie?'

Double take – oh, no. I don't want a quick grope in the ladies, Monika. If I'm going to have sex for the first time with a woman, I want to take my time about it.

'No, I only go to the loo with men. Anyway, I'd better get back. I haven't even had anything to eat.'

Monika was still smiling. 'Derek will enjoy hearing about you. But don't worry. That's as far as it goes. We're tight together, Julie. Is that OK?'

'This is all fine – I think. I'm just so pleased I'm seeing my DI tonight.'

Stevenson smiled with a touch of malice. 'Well, if you weren't there's always the power shower and the vibrator and your collection of erotic literature.'

Jesus, I'm blushing. I'm out of here.

John had left a Post-it on her screen – two refugees had been stoned by a gang of youths outside the Ravenscroft Hotel. He had gone out to talk to them and would she get something from the police?

That was just typical. This morning Bob had tried to make something more out of last night's assault than had seemed to meet the eye and now this happened as if to prove that his suspicions were correct.

And typical that it should happen on only the second day she'd ventured outside the office at lunchtime. Good thing John had been in.

She got hold of Tony Greene.

'I can't add anything to what Adam told you this morning about the first assault,' he said.

'But this has got to be the same mob, Tony, hasn't it?'

'You're not putting words into my mouth, Julie. We're still looking into both incidents. I can't tell you any more.'

She had that familiar desperate feeling, the one where you understand exactly what someone's saying but you know the boss won't let you get away with accepting it. Bob was listening, she was sure, willing her to press harder. She realised she was in the catch-22 where she was going to have to alienate her contact in order to please her boss.

Sod it. She wasn't going to upset Tony Greene, not at this early stage of their relationship. She thanked him and put down the phone.

'So what do the police say now?' Bob was straight on to her.

She shook her head and tried to let her voice remain neutral. 'Nothing new. They're still looking into both incidents.'

Bob sighed.

Oh, please. Just shut up and give me a chance to do the job.

'Surely you could have got something more out of him. You weren't on the phone for long. He must have some idea whether they're connected. At least he can tell you where they're concentrating their enquiries.'

'He said not.'

'Look, we need something. If nothing else a statement about how seriously they're taking the incidents, something about racist violence, whatever. Try again.'

Julie was seething as she dialled again.

She lowered her voice. Maybe he would realise she was acting under duress.

'Tony, Julie again, I'm sorry about this. Can you just give me some form of words about despicable racist violence or something? I know this is a pain.'

Short silence.

'Who's standing over you? Not David Hammett?'

'No, no.'

'It's bloody Underwood, isn't it?'

Thank God.

He sighed. Everybody was sighing. Even Julie sighed.

80

'All right, kid, it's not your fault. I'll sort him. Tell the little sod I'm not giving any statements until after my men get back from investigating the latest incident, and you can tell him as well that I'm going to phone you with my statement and seeing as it's Thursday you can have it exclusive so the weekly don't get it out before you in the morning.'

'Tony, you're a star.'

'And if he tries to get you to phone me before I'm ready I'll give it straight to the *South Coast Courier*, and I mean it.'

'I believe you.'

Of course, it wasn't good enough for Bob. He wanted something right now, right there, and she couldn't deliver. He snapped open the diary and sorted out everyone who wasn't busy.

'Claire, get on the phone to anyone you might think of who'd know these yobs. Mark, get down to the Hornbeam Estate. They're bound to come from there.'

Mark raised his eyes to heaven as he stood and put his jacket on. He passed Julie's desk and squeezed her shoulder. Wendy too was looking sympathetically at her.

The phone rang. David wanted her.

'Only week two and you're turning into a superstar.'

That wasn't what she was expecting.

'I've just had Tony Greene on singing your praises. Unfortunately he's not so keen on some of my other staff.'

His eyes were twinkling at her. It was like working for her father.

'I don't want you telling any tales, Julie. But when I get a complaint from a police superintendent I have to look into it. Did Bob tell you to phone Tony Greene back after you'd already spoken to him?'

'Yes. He thought I hadn't pressed him hard enough.'

'And was he right?'

Julie chose her words carefully. 'I haven't been here

81

very long, but from what I know of Tony Greene I guessed it would be unwise to press him any further. Bob disagreed.'

'And so you phoned him back on Bob's instructions and you still didn't get any more.'

'To be fair, David, I did get a promise that he would give me a statement this afternoon, and that it would be exclusive to us.'

'Good. Do you think that's because Bob pushed you to phone him back?'

Bugger Bob, I'm going to look out for number one.

'No, I think we would have got it anyway.'

'So do I. That's fine, Julie. We'll wait for John to come back and we'll wait to see what Tony comes up with.'

'Yeah, except Bob's just sent Mark off to the Hornbeam Estate to see what he can come up with, and he's got Claire phoning various contacts.'

David sighed. It was catching.

'Go back to your desk, Julie. This conversation didn't happen.'

Five minutes later he wandered into the office to find out what was happening with the stoning story. Bob told him.

'So, Julie, Tony Greene is going to phone you this afternoon with an exclusive statement?'

She nodded.

'And John's out on the case?'

Bob nodded.

'So I'm not exactly sure what Mark's doing. He might put his foot in it poking round Hornbeam. You know how touchy the folk there can be. And who are you phoning, Claire?'

She shrugged. 'Everyone I know who knows a yob, but nothing so far.'

'Yes, so stop it. Julie, get Mark on his mobile and tell him to get back here. Bob, we need to talk.'

* * *

They talked for over an hour. In the meantime Tony Greene phoned Julie with a full statement. Detailed descriptions of the yobs. Same for both incidents, strongly believed to be connected. Police abhorring racist violence and emphasising very small minority of population. No need for public to worry. Appeals for eyewitnesses to come forward. John came back soon after and they worked the story together. They were both pleased with it.

Julie was called in to the editor's office again. She wondered what on earth the others thought. For the second time in just over an hour she had a phone call which made her leave her desk without a word.

David was scanning his screen.

'I see you and John have just finished the violence story. Very good job, good teamwork. And you're going great guns with the police.'

'Thanks, David.'

'We've decided –' he looked briefly at Bob, whose face was set grimly and looking at his hands '– that as well as helping John with crime you should have a crack at getting some inroads into the council estates, especially Hornbeam. It's a bit rough but most of the people there are pretty decent. We've tried from time to time to get to grips with it but it's hard to get the confidence of the folk down there. I think you can do it – how about it?'

'I'll give it a go.'

'Bob's just noticed in the diary that there's a murder trial coming up in a couple of weeks which happened at Hornbeam, so you can start by ferreting around to see what background you can come up with.'

Excuse me? Murder?

Bob pushed a couple of old cuttings towards her.

'It's coming up at the Crown Court on the fourth of next month. John'll be covering the court but when we get the verdict and can print the gory details we'll need some background. All you need to do is get down there and talk to anyone who knew the victim and the murderer.'

'Alleged murderer,' corrected David. Julie hid a smile as Bob glowered.

'It's all there. Ask at the police station if they can tell you anything. It's likely they'll have known him – the alleged murderer, that is. He might even have had a record. If Greene can't come up with anything knock on doors. There was a woman living with the murdered man. I don't know if she's still around.'

Julie leafed through the cuttings. Girlfriend had let alleged murderer in about ten o'clock one night. He might have been a bit drunk, but they were friends. She went up to bed, thought they were settling down with a drink but half an hour later they started arguing, then she heard her boyfriend cry out and the door slammed. When she got to the sitting room she found him semiconscious, knife sticking out of his ribs, blood everywhere. Dead on arrival at hospital.

The alleged murderer – surely there wasn't much doubt about it? – had fled and his picture was on the cutting. He looked more than a bit rough, with his close-cropped hair and small cruel mouth, vacant eyes beneath one ringed eyebrow. Police had appealed for information as to his whereabouts and eventually he was found in Brighton and brought back to stand trial. The committal was four months ago and now he was due up before the jury.

Heavy stuff.

'Great,' she said briskly. 'I'm off till Monday but I'll see what the police can come up with then, and diary permitting I'll start knocking on doors as soon as I can.'

David was still twinkling and Bob was still glowering. Julie went back to the newsroom smiling. Mark looked at her enquiringly as she went in. She gave him a wink, smiling mightily. He winked back.

Reporters 1, news ed 0.

Julie's diary, 20 June

What a day. Bob Underwood made a complete prat of himself. I won. David loves me and so does Tony Greene. I love everybody. (Except Bob.) Stevenson and Monika and Derek are all in this game business, and me I suppose. I bet Monika's a dominatrix. God knows she looks like one. Did she really want to touch me up in the ladies? It must have been a joke. Just keeping the erotic tension high, and getting S going. I was so embarrassed when he went on in front of her about me wanking – he enjoyed it. Warmed me up nicely though. Won't be able to do this later as hopefully will be having my brains fucked out by DI Edwards, no, Bryn. Can't believe everything can carry on going so well. He'll probably stand me up (not really). Amazing he should ask me out tonight when I'm off tomorrow in lieu of last Sun. Can't write any more, too restless with all the excitement.

It was easy enough to narrow the possibilities down to three outfits but the combinations of different underwear, or none at all, came to about 23. Or so it seemed.

She so wanted to do the no underwear thing but it would have meant wearing the red dress because it was long and she really wanted something short to dance in. And no way did she want the whole club to find out she was knickerless if she turned too quickly. And if she had to wear knickers, she'd have to go the whole hog with a matching bra.

It really only left the black cap-sleeved button-through which moulded itself to her body. The shocking-pink balcony-style push-up bra and matching briefs looked good under the unbuttoned dress – she was pretty sure Bryn would approve. Though when she did the dress up, it needed something else – brilliant, the Christmas present arm bracelet, a fragile tangle of twisted metal like barbed wire that wound around her upper arm.

Pink lips to match her underwear and a stain of

blusher along her cheekbones. A smudge of pink and lilac around her eyes and a touch of kohl underneath.

Julie got a taxi and arrived at the Breaker Bar at 9.30 to find Bryn standing up at the bar holding a long colourless drink. In his black T-shirt and jeans he looked like he was trying to impersonate Stevenson.

Of course, he didn't know she was – or not – having a sexual relationship with the photographer. Odd coincidence, though. But what a contrast they would have made stood next to each other! In black Bryn looked almost menacing. His darkness gave him a saturnine air and the muscles rippling from the sleeves of his T-shirt looked power-packed, rather than Stevenson's gym-refined, sculpted body. Bryn's sleek black head was covered closely with fur like an animal – a mole, perhaps – and his slightly Arab-looking nose commanded attention.

He turned and slowly his smile spread over his face – a smile that expressed absolute delight at seeing her.

'Miss Julie. You look great.'

She smiled back. 'So you're going to the *Reservoir Dogs* audition as well! I think you better be Mr Brown, and I'll be Miss Pink.'

'Have a drink, Miss Pink.'

He pulled out a bar stool.

'Once we get dancing I won't want to stop, except for one thing –' his eyes were caressing her face '– so get a large one down you now.'

I'll be getting a large one down me later, Mr Brown.

She picked up the cocktail list to hide her smile. 'Anything with vodka.'

'Only one thing for Miss Pink – Raspberry Ripple,' the barman put in.

Oh please do join us.

Vanilla vodka, *framboise*, raspberry juice and cream.

'Cream? I'll be sick.'

'There's only a dash of cream,' the barman reassured

her. 'And loads of ice. And with a double vodka and the raspberry liqueur it'll get straight to the point.'

It was delicious, and almost the same colour as her underwear.

Shall I tell him that? No, he can find out later.

She took the straw out. Much as she wanted to pout her shocking pink lips around it for Bryn's benefit, she knew it got you drunk quicker.

He wasn't paying much attention to his vodka, or whatever it was. He was drinking her in, his eyes not moving from her face except to run quickly over her body. She felt as though he was an undercurrent sucking her in, his deep brown eyes pulling her towards him. She had to consciously move back against the bar stool to stop overbalancing.

'Have you had a good few days?'

Julie nodded. 'Not bad. Thanks partly to your super. Hey, anything new on the mob you're looking for?'

He laughed. 'Rule one, Miss Julie, we should not talk about work. Especially mine. I don't know what they'll think anyway about me taking you out, but I will definitely not be very popular if I start giving you little titbits over a Raspberry Ripple.'

Rule one? Is this a game, too? OK, I can play as well.

'Rule two, DI Edwards, is that we should actually start calling each other Bryn and Julie.'

He nodded. 'Sure thing. My turn? Rule three, Julie. We have to enjoy every minute of this relationship. Or stop.'

She shrugged. 'I can't top that.' She finished her drink. 'I want to dance.'

'Yeah, me too.' His fathomless dark eyes burned into her face. 'I want to dance very close to you, brushing against you accidentally sometimes, then other times touching you very deliberately. I want your body to drive me crazy with its movements.'

Her eyelashes fluttered involuntarily.

'Yeah. Come on, then, Bryn.'

The club was already packed though it was only just

ten o'clock. Bryn seemed to know loads of people as they threaded their way past the bar, and Julie even thought she recognised one or two of the crowd.

'This is the best club night in town,' he told her. 'Branford plays a mix of world music, Tamla and blues, and seventies through nineties stuff. It's brilliant. Everyone over twenty comes here apart from the hiphop and techno crowd.'

There were little knots of what had to be language students, some hippychic students from the university, the main crowd expensively dressed twenty- and thirty-somethings, two thirds of them in black. Not a striped sweatpant in sight and no-one looked out of their head as far as Julie could tell. Apart from the crowd at the bar everyone was dancing, involved in the music, which was an insistent African beat with a lot of brass on top.

Julie threw herself into the dance. She loved dancing and she loved to dance with her whole body. She could only do it sexily; she didn't know how else to do it – or what the point would be.

She liked to move her hips and her arse and lift her arms to show off her breasts. And what she was really liking was the look of pure enjoyment on Bryn's face.

It turned her on even more than her dancing. His whole face was a mask of sheer delight. She had never seen anyone look so actively happy. It was incredible. She couldn't help but respond to his pleasure with her own.

The music changed to a faster ska-type rhythm and Julie adapted, economising her movements in time to the music. She was already warming up nicely. It wouldn't be too long before he could have his wish of having her body slick with sweat. She leant towards him to tell him, but gave up. It wasn't possible to talk, and anyway, he was absorbed in the music and in contemplating her.

He was a good dancer – not an athletic one but one who moved in his own natural rhythm, happy in the small space available. Obviously enjoying the music, his mouth opened slightly and his nostrils flared as he moved his head from side to side in tandem with the backbeat.

Julie was bound up in his full-on enthusiasm. Neither of them needed to talk, just to lose themselves in the music and the movement of their bodies which they were creating for each other. And the contemplation of the other's body.

They'd covered three decades and five continents before the music slowed, with the velvet voice of Cassandra Wilson singing a Van Morrison song. Bryn put his hands on her arms and they danced together, close but not touching. She could feel the heat coming from his body, imagining the warmth of the flat hairy stomach and remembering the thickness of his cock.

But I want to dance some more. I hope he does.

He did. They went upbeat again with The Divine Comedy and a French avant-garde sound Julie didn't know, then they were back in Africa, followed by some old-time Tamla then into the seventies with Blondie. They had been dancing for well over an hour and Julie was getting distinct dehydration vibes when the DJ slowed it down again and Bryn mimed drinking at her.

She followed him to the bar and they both had a pint – Julie orange squash and Bryn lager.

She watched his body as he poured the beer down his throat, standing with his back to the bar. Every movement was completely unselfconscious but naturally powerful. She had a sudden urge to push herself between his arms and rest her head on his shoulder, submissive and pliant. It was the same impulse that had caused her to wrap her arms behind her around the tree when they were in the woods. He was the strong one, the master, and she was happy to be his slave.

I never imagined I could want to be dominated. But there's a pulse between my legs that's telling me it's so right.

Time to go to the loo.

* * *

89

'Hihi, Julie!'

Monika followed her through the door to the ladies.

Oh-oh.

'I am as horny as hell. Don't worry, I'm not hitting on you.'

Julie shook her head as if to clear it. She couldn't believe her brain was doing a good job in deciphering the words her ears thought they were hearing.

Monika was – inevitably – also in black, a backless collared halter top over a black leather mini and high silver-studded boots. Her skin gleamed golden brown, natural as opposed to Julie's fake-tan legs. Her long blonde bob swung over her shoulders. If she'd been dancing, there was no sign of her hair being dishevelled or sweat on her face. But her eyes were dislocated and Julie wondered if she'd taken something.

There were a couple of girls making up in front of the mirror who greeted Monika.

'Hihi. Scram!' she said briefly.

Julie watched amazed as they giggled and went out. For the first time she registered the girl who had followed Monika into the ladies.

'Hey, Julie, you go in that one and stand on the seat.'

'Excuse me?'

'Go on! You can bolt the door. I'm going in here.'

This is my new life. Go for it.

Julie stood on the seat only to see Monika's head popping up right next to her own.

'I want you to watch. Get your head over here.'

Julie leant over the partition. Monika smiled wickedly at her and Julie realised she was raising her skirt. Beneath it she was naked. Completely.

'Hurry up, Anna. I'm desperate.'

'Just because you like an audience doesn't mean to say that I do.'

'Get on with it, you little tart. Oh, fantastic! Julie, can you see properly?'

How properly did she need to see? What was obvious

90

was that the girl called Anna had her face buried in Monika's crotch. And that she couldn't tell whether Monika was a natural blonde, because her sex was completely hairless. And that she was pushing her pubic mound towards Anna, her skirt pulled around her waist like a black leather belt.

'Anna, you're a virtuoso. Julie, she'll do you next if you want. She loves it, don't you, Anna? Don't bother answering. Let me tell you, Julie, she's got her tongue right up inside me now. God, I'm wet enough already. I was fucking desperate. Now she's right on my clit. That is *so* good, don't stop that, Anna, you beautiful little tart. Oh, shit, I said don't stop that. She's moved back inside me, Julie, but that is good. Hey, she's fingering my clit now, Julie. I'm going to come any minute. Oh, God, Anna, you beauty, I love you, baby, you lovely little slut. Don't stop, oh, God, stop, I can't take any more.'

Julie felt she must be at least as wet as Monika, who had dropped her skirt and was clutching the partition on either side while she convulsed in pleasure. Her eyes were closed and a pulse moved in her cheek, maybe in tune with the contractions she was experiencing down below.

Monika opened her eyes and leant towards Julie. 'I would have liked to kiss you while I was coming. Are you sure you don't want the same treatment? I'll do it for you, beautiful Julie, if you want. Or Anna. Or both of us.'

Julie swallowed. She wasn't sure her voice would come out right.

'No, thanks. Not right now.'

The Amazon smiled her wicked smile. 'I'll interpret that as maybe some other time. That'll do.'

She clattered down from the toilet seat in her high-heeled boots. 'God, I need a cigarette. Anna, have you got any left?'

The other girl pulled a packet from her pocket. 'Mon, what about me?'

Monika stroked Anna's pubis through her skirt. 'You have to wait. I want you totally desperate. Now wash my juice off your mouth or I'm not going back in there with you.'

She lit up and turned to Julie. 'I saw you at the bar with your cop. I know him. He looks like he'd be a great lay – is he?'

Julie laughed. 'I think I'll reserve the right to tell you about that another time, Monika. And I'd better get back to him – he'll wonder what's going on.'

'Tell him there was a queue, of course. We might come and say hello later, eh, Anna? Or even better we'll come round to your place sometime. Julie's got quite a collection of erotic literature, Anna.'

For the first time Julie looked properly at the other girl. She was quite young, early 20s, with short brown hair and a small pixie face dominated by huge brown eyes made up sixties dark. There were the remains of beige lipstick around the mouth that had just been licking Monika. Gay? Bi? She wasn't clued up enough to tell.

'Don't believe everything Stevenson tells you. Anyway, I'm getting in there. I still need to pee.' Julie locked the door behind her, just in case. Before she peed she ran her finger experimentally along her pussy. It was creaming nicely. She gave her clit a tiny massage but forced herself to stop and get on with it.

The other two were quiet. What were they doing? When she came out Monika was still smoking but with one hand stroked Anna's breasts lazily. The young girl had her eyes closed. Two girls walked into the loo but Monika took no notice of them. Julie repaired her lipstick, still watching from the mirror. The two newcomers had disappeared hurriedly into the cubicles.

'Well, I'm shagged out now. Come on, Anna, let's dance a bit more and recharge.'

'If I get any more charged I'll seize up,' said the other girl sulkily.

Monika slapped her behind, quite hard. 'Tough shit. See you later, Julie.'

I bet Bryn will enjoy hearing about this. But not now. Maybe later, when we've already come a couple of times and we need recharging as well.

Bryn was talking to a shaven-headed black guy with wraparound shades. It was Branford, the DJ.

He introduced him to Julie.

'Amazing music. Thanks.'

'Respect, Julie. Must get back to my machines. There you go, man.'

He pulled a key out of his pocket and gave it to Bryn. They embraced. 'Later, man.'

What door does that key unlock? Never mind. I bet I find out, thought Julie.

'We've got to dance some more, Julie, I've almost cooled off.'

Shame you didn't come with me and watch a big beautiful blonde being eaten by another woman.

She just smiled. 'Yeah, let's go for it.'

And when we've danced some more you're going to open a door somewhere not too far from here and we're going to fall on each other like it was the last fuck in the world.

The music was just as good and Julie threw herself into it even more than before. She wanted Bryn to feel the slick sweaty body he'd fantasised about. Her excitement at watching Monika fuelled her energy level and Bryn's intense, glittering gaze sent her body into overdrive.

It seemed like at least an hour before the pace slowed. The throaty sounds of Macy Gray seemed to wrap around them like wreaths of smoke, pushing them towards each other. They locked together at the pelvis, their hands on each other's arms, faces far enough apart to read the signals. Bryn raised one eyebrow almost imperceptibly and she nodded equally minimally. He led the way through the slow-dancing crowd, holding tight on to her hand. At the back of the room was a door set discreetly in the wall. He unlocked it with the key Branford had given him and locked it again from the other side.

Up a staircase, another door, same key. Into a dark room, Bryn ahead, turning, slamming her back against the door, both breathing hard. Her body revelled in the authoritativeness of his touch. They kissed hard and seriously.

'Let's get some light. I want to see you properly.'

He didn't turn on the overhead light but a table lamp which revealed the large ghostly gleaming lump in the middle of the room as a white leather sofa. Desk, computer and filing cabinets against the walls.

As he turned back towards her Julie saw – or was it sensed? – that he was almost trembling in his intensity. She shivered in response.

'Undo your buttons for me, Julie.' His deep voice was cracked. She guessed his excitement was such that he couldn't trust his hands to stay steady enough to undo her dress.

He sat on the sofa and turned a knob at the side. The back lowered to rest side by side with the seats. It was almost as big as a double bed.

It's not the first time he's done that. But then again it's hardly the first time I've done this.

Julie undid her dress, not too slowly but steadily, starting at the bottom. When she pulled the last button she pulled the dress aside with each hand and stood with her elbows bent and her hands on her hipbones, in a stance that said only one thing. Fuck me.

She watched him as he pulled his T-shirt over his head and removed his shoes and socks, then stood to unzip his jeans and pulled them off with his briefs. His strong jaw was set and his mouth a straight line. A classic study of desire.

Shrugging her dress off her shoulders, she waited, taking her time in running her eyes over his naked body for the first time. His pores might have been secreting sweat but it was nothing compared to the carnal virility that emanated from them. The soft hair she'd briefly seen and touched covered his chest and described a line down to his groin, where it was thick once more. His massive thick prick reared up out of the black cloud of hair. She felt almost as though she was waiting to be mounted by an Arab stallion.

The expectation between them was tangible and too excruciatingly delicious for either of them to want to move.

His chest was visibly rising and falling and Julie realised that her breasts were moving too in time with her quickened breathing. Her skin was glowing pink in the lamplight and sheened with sweat from dancing. The tension was almost unbearably exquisite then, a split second after she wondered how long they could stand it, he moved the three paces towards her and pulled her to him by the shoulders, hard. Their mouths met at the same time as she felt his cock grind against her and his chest fur rub her breasts.

His fingers were clamped to the top of her arms and again she wished he would hold her roughly enough to bruise her and mark her. She drank in the musky smell of his sweat as his hands swept round to her back, circling down either side of her spine until he reached her arse.

The pink briefs were cut away at the back exposing her round buttocks. Bryn made a noise in his throat as he felt the bareness, describing circles with his hands on the voluptuous flesh.

'Turn round. I want to see your arse.'

He propelled her around in any case, hands once again on her shoulders. He let go and Julie stood with her back to him through a silence that seemed to last a minute but was probably just a moment. She could feel his rapt concentration on her backside and the throb it was causing between her legs and knew she had to have him inside her. Now.

Without turning she knelt on the floor and raised her arse high in the air and offered herself to him. She moved the pink knickers aside with one hand and bent the other arm in front of her and cradled her head on it.

Take me like an animal. Don't bother with preliminaries and please don't say anything. And hold me hard.

She heard the tearing of foil and a moment later his cock was pushing inside her. Despite its girth it slid easily into her wetness. She felt its warmth against her hand. He guided it in until he was sure it was on course and then grabbed the cheeks of her arse and thrust the whole length inside her.

How did he guess just what she wanted?

She moved her hand: no need to hold her knickers aside now. She lowered both hands to the floor.

Her instincts were to push back against him but she wanted him to do the moving. She was the meek passive female and for probably the first time in her life she wasn't taking charge of her own orgasm. There was no doubt that it was going to happen and her submissiveness was arousing her so much that she almost felt she could come from pure passion.

Bryn clenched and unclenched his hands on her buttocks and slowly slid half out of her and pushed back again. She imagined the red marks his hands would make on her white skin.

She imagined what his thick cock looked like half out of her.

He pushed in again, hard, and again stayed without moving for a moment while he mashed the flesh of her arse again, pulling the plump globes apart. Then he withdrew almost completely, this time pushing in harder. Then again. And again.

She settled into his rhythm, her G-spot responding automatically.

But I don't actually want to come yet. And I certainly don't want you to.

The warmth of his chest hit her as he bent over her back and then his fur was rubbing up and down on her as he moved his hands up the underside of her body to grab urgently at her breasts. They had almost fallen out of her bra and he pulled them out completely, rubbing and rolling her nipples and squeezing each breast in his large hands. His position made him breathe heavily, almost grunting. Again the image came to her of being covered by a big glorious animal.

But he was pulling out.

'Turn round and take it all off.' His voice was deep and guttural. And authoritative.

She swivelled on her knees to face him head on. His breathing was coming even harder and his rubbered cock looked bigger than ever. While he watched she took her bra off but had to sit to pull her knickers over her ankles. She had barely removed them when he pulled her hips forwards and upwards and, still kneeling, entered her again. Despite its size his cock slid in as smoothly as a hand into a silk glove.

Julie wrapped her legs around him. With the lower half of her body angled upwards from the waist, her arms and head trailed unneeded on the floor and she thrilled at the unaccustomed feeling of helplessness as Bryn drove into her, pulling her backwards and forwards with strong hands clamped hard on her hips.

One of his hands moved to her clitoris and started rubbing and she knew he must be near coming. Half of her desperately needed to come but the other half wanted to delay the moment for ever.

'Put your arms above your head, Julie,' Bryn murmured, his voice still thick and cracked. 'I wish I'd brought a pair of handcuffs. Never mind, I'll tie you down another time. I'd like to see your arms struggling for release.'

He knew too that she wanted him to dominate her.

And if he hadn't known before, her involuntary moan at his words, the thought of being tied down, would have left him in no doubt.

She couldn't last much longer.

They both froze as the door opened. Branford.

'Oh shit, man, I'm sorry, I thought you'd be done. Look, I've just got to have a shower. I'm on a seriously massive promise. I'm not looking, man, I'm straight through the door –'

'Shut it, Branford, and get over here a minute.'

No, no, not an audience. Don't do this to me, Bryn.

'Just hold Julie's arms, man. She's looking for restraint.'

Oh, my God. Yes, I am looking for restraint. But like this?

She looked up at Bryn's face. He had a half-smile on his lips.

'If you want, Julie. I know you want to feel his big hands holding you down but I can't disembody him – what do you say?'

I say yes. I have to say that I feel slightly cowed by the thought of this stranger holding me and watching me come. But I have to say too that that is another turn-on.

She nodded.

Branford knelt behind her head and smiled down at her.

'Just think of me as a big warm pair of handcuffs.' His eyes were still hidden by the shades which made his participation seem all the more sinister. And exciting.

'You're beautiful, Julie. I'm going to hold you tight but tell me if it's too much, you hear?'

She nodded and then gasped as first one then the other hand clamped firmly down on her wrists, pinning her to the floor. Although she wanted the restraint she reflexively tried to raise her arms. As Branford's grip tightened, a low moan escaped her.

Now her upper body was confined to the spot, Bryn had to shift forwards and move himself instead of pulling her on to his prick. He began to drive into her faster and

98

his hands moved again to her arse, still raised off the ground, and his nails dug in as he scooped up a handful of flesh with each hand. Julie cried out, half in pain and half in delight, and tensed the muscles of her buttocks against him. It only heightened both their pleasures and as Julie saw a lost look come into Bryn's eyes she struggled with her arms and clenched her arse and hammered her pussy up to meet his cock, mashing her clitoris against his bone. She knew she was bucking like a bitch on heat and she growled as she came. Part of her registered that this was no way to perform in public but a darker side of her took an extra thrill from the humiliation.

His eyes closed as he came, calling her name. Although her eyes were glazed by her own climax she caught fractured glimpses, as though under a strobe light, of his face lost in sensual oblivion.

It was a while before they stopped moving and moaning. Julie suddenly felt her wrists free and remembered Branford. She looked at him upside down and, hoping to forestall embarrassment on either side, winked.

He whistled softly. 'I wish I was staying here with you guys instead of going off to this gig with Monika.'

Monika!

Bryn looked up, interested. 'The big Swede! Sure you can handle her, man?'

'She's a Great Dane, mate. I'm telling you, I'm Mr Voyeur tonight. She tells me she's got to give this big-eyed kid a going-over first but I can watch if I want.'

'Yeah, Anna. I saw her licking Monika out in the ladies.'

Bryn did a double take.

'Wasn't this something you thought you might share with me, Julie?'

'I was going to after the first round. Mind you, I don't know if I can handle another one after that.'

Branford got up. 'Right, so if there's nothing more I

99

can do here, I'm getting that shower and leaving you to it.'

He stopped in his tracks halfway across the room. 'Hey, you don't fancy coming round to Monika's too?'

'Fuck off, man,' laughed Bryn. 'You were strictly hardware just now. I don't do orgies.'

'Yeah, well, two women're probably more than enough for me.'

He went through the door at the end of the room. Julie sat up and leant back against the sofa.

'Wasted your time putting this down.'

Bryn smiled. 'You never know. I wasn't expecting you to drop to your knees and offer yourself like a slave girl.'

Neither was I, DI.

'And believe me, Branford was not supposed to come in. That wasn't a set-up.'

'Never occurred to me.'

Not much.

'Actually, it never occurred to me that I even wanted to act like a slave girl.'

He looked surprised. 'No? The other morning, the way you put your arms behind you and pushed forwards, that was so sort of submissive, I thought it was your thing.'

She shook her head. 'Just instinct. Never has been my thing. Though I think it might be now.'

Bryn put his arm round her. She snuggled into his armpit.

'I never thought it was my thing to want a hairy man to mount me from behind like an animal, either, but that seems to have taken a major place in my repertoire.'

'A hairy man who fucks like an animal. Great description. Thanks a bunch.'

Branford re-emerged looking exactly the same as he went in.

'I'm out of here to grab a bit of action for myself. You behave yourselves now, you hear?'

'You look after yourself, man. I hear that Monika can be wicked.'

100

'I'm hoping.'

The door closed again and Bryn turned to Julie.

'Maybe we ought to get some use out of this couch. I need to get more acquainted with your body, so you just lie down there and tell me about watching Monika and I'll watch you telling me.'

Seconds out, we're heading for round two.

Chapter Five

WOMEN IN LOVE – BUT WHAT ABOUT THE WRESTLING SCENE?

IN A FASCINATING new take on D. H. Lawrence's *Women in Love*, Wintersea's experimental feminist drama group Medusa pushed the envelope of the avant-garde by featuring only the women in love themselves in a two-hander, writes reporter Julie Gibson.

Gudrun and Ursula discuss their relationships over coffee in the local Starbucks like Frasier and Niles Crane comparing neuroses in the Cafe Nervosa, interspersed with soliloquies – Gudrun's whilst masturbating in the bath and Ursula's howled at the moon. An interesting scenario but those who have seen the celebrated film by Ken Russell will feel the loss of the nude wrestling scene between their respective lovers.

'You don't seriously expect me to use this, do you, Julie?'
Bob had one eye on the screen and another on Julie.

She laughed. 'Not in its current form. At the very least
you'd have to knock out the reference to masturbation. I
just got in five minutes early so I thought I'd bang it
out.'

For a moment she thought there could be a smile
twitching at the corners of his mouth, but he wasn't
going to ruin his reputation.

'Sure, well, if you see anything you think might be
worth a review, by all means. But I think this is – I don't
exactly know where this could go.'

'Pseud's Corner, if we had one,' she said slyly. 'Just
don't tell Wendy.'

Unbelievable. He *was* smiling.

'Oh, is she showing you around?'

'Sort of.'

'Did she really masturbate in the bath?'

Julie laughed. 'What, Wendy? Oh, sorry. I doubt it. The
bath was sideways on so all you could see was her head
and arms, though she was moving as though she knew
what her right arm was for, if you know what I mean.
This is amusing you, isn't it?'

He laughed. 'Yes, though not as much as the fact that
a lump of cliff the size of a cross-Channel ferry fell into
the sea last night. Bloody good story.'

Shit. Should've listened to the news on the local
radio.

She usually did, but after a relaxed and mellow long
weekend she just couldn't be bothered. Thanks to a
thunderstorm she hadn't slept too well the previous night
so instead of the usual routine she'd just floated in a bit
early and banged out the review.

'Storm have anything to do with the cliff? Presumably
no-one was hurt.'

'They think it was a lightning strike. Unfortunately no
casualties except a few trees. Bit further to the west and

103

half the White Bay caravan site would be floating by now
– still, can't have everything.'

Ghoul.

The town had been surprisingly quiet over the weekend
apart from a few small drug busts and petty thefts. No
reprise of the violence of the previous week.

'Obviously waiting for you to get back on duty, Julie,'
said Tony Greene. 'Have a good long weekend?'

She looked at him carefully before she answered. Bryn
had sworn he wasn't a gossip but she never quite trusted
men. As much as she liked flirting with Tony she didn't
relish the thought of him knowing that her weekend had
begun with one of his DIs shafting her while another
man held her down.

'Very good, Tony. Were you off?'

'Yes. The weather was so good I spent most of the time
in the garden.'

Julie had also made the most of the sun, apart from
sleeping half of Friday after being up till dawn with
Bryn. Friday night she'd booked a step class; she almost
cancelled it because her muscles were aching from the
various positions Bryn had put her through, and his firm
hands had left marks on her buttocks and shoulders. But
hell, she had to keep fit. She covered up and put up with
the aches.

Bryn had wanted to see her again on Saturday night
but she already had her theatre date with Wendy, so
instead they met for Sunday lunch at a pub outside the
town. His shift started at six so they'd made do with a
car fuck, something Julie hadn't done for a long time.

And never like this.

He had driven to a remote spot where the car was
shaded by trees. She assumed that like the first time they
would leave the car for the seclusion of the woods. But
she had gone out dressed as she had wanted to the
previous Thursday, and when he ran his hands up to the
top of her thighs and found nothing but wetness and

fleece his excitement had intensified even more than usual.

Adjusting the car seat so she was practically horizontal, he had pushed her skirt up around her waist and in a hoarse voice ordered her to hold it there. She wondered if he remembered her telling him about Monika holding her skirt up while Anna had made her come. Was he going to go down on her?

Julie's T-shirt was already off the shoulder and Bryn pulled it down even further and scooped her breasts out of it, so they sat artificially high above the pale green top, now stretched tight across her chest, imprisoning her upper arms. She felt exposed and totally vulnerable. Bryn was silent. Though she wanted to raise her head to look at him, to see his face, she couldn't break the moment.

'Why didn't you tell me you had no panties on?'

She smiled faintly. 'I thought perhaps when you did find out it'd be more exciting than knowing all the time. You could hardly have done anything about it in the pub.'

'No? I could have sat next to you if I'd known and slipped my hand up your skirt while you were eating. Could you have come like that, in the pub, pretending nothing was happening except eating and drinking?'

'Shit, I don't know. But someone would have seen your hand under the table.'

'Yeah. What would they have thought? What a little slut, letting him do that in public. But you are a little slut, aren't you, Julie? Otherwise you'd be properly dressed.'

His words thrilled her. As long as he didn't mean it. She had to assume he was playing the domination game. If not, she should smack his face and tell him to fuck off.

There was another moment of silence. Then his dark voice again.

'Fuck the gearstick.'

Her head snapped round towards him. *What*?

'Don't keep me waiting, Julie. Get your wet pussy

round that gearstick and move. After all, you're obviously dying to get something up there – I don't suppose it matters what it is.'

He moved his seat back to give her more room, or was it to get a better view? After another stunned moment, Julie sat up, still holding her skirt.

There didn't seem to be enough room to face him and sit on the gearstick so with her back to him she planted her feet firmly either side and gingerly lowered herself on to the round knob.

It felt uncomfortable as it disappeared inside her. The thickness probably wasn't much greater than Bryn's cock, but the roundness made it difficult to push down on – and then there was nothing except this big, round knob inside her.

'I want to see it come out of you again before you go back down on it,' the deep dispassionate voice came from behind her. 'I want you to feel it going in and out of you. And don't be too artistic about it, I want it fast. Like you might do it for yourself if I wasn't here.'

Like an unwilling stripper in a nightclub full of jeering men, Julie felt completely humiliated. And, God, was it exciting.

She shunted up and down on the gearstick, lifting herself so that the knob almost slipped completely outside her and then sat back on it. Once she adjusted to the shape of it she thrilled each time it pushed her open and filled her up, but as it travelled further inside her there was nothing behind it for her to mould herself around. As he ordered she moved fast and knew she was near coming. Her eyes stared vacantly through the windscreen and the silence behind her, whether from his enjoyment or not, moved her sex muscles almost as easily as the thick round ball of the gearstick.

'That's enough. Get off and take your clothes off.'

'No way! Someone might drive past! I mean, a quick flash of me bobbing up and down, they could have imagined it, but bobbing up and down with no clothes on –'

'Shut it, Julie. Clothes off, turn round and sit on me.' His trousers were down to his knees and he was busy rolling a condom over his thick stalk.

She took her skirt off but hesitated before exposing her breasts.

Oh, well, I'm not exactly a DD cup. Maybe if anyone goes past they won't even notice.

As if!

She pulled off the T-shirt and turned to Bryn, smiling. Was he still in dominant mode?

No.

'Come and sit on me, sweet Julie,' he murmured.

Forgetting her sense of exposure she happily knelt over him and positioned herself over his big cock. Before she could sink on to it he put his mouth around one of her breasts and sucked greedily on the nipple. She mewed like a contented cat and lowered herself slowly and luxuriously down and around his penis as he replaced his mouth with his fingers and switched his lips to her other breast.

After the empty promise of the gearstick knob his cock filled her fatly, satisfyingly. She lifted and lowered herself slowly but he started to move more urgently and she guessed he didn't want it slow and languorous but wanted to see her move like she had on the gearstick but from the front. He had moved his hands and mouth away from her breasts and as she bucked up and down on top of him they danced to their own rhythm and he was looking at them, eyes half closed.

He was nearly there but she needed a little encouragement. Her fingers moved to her clit and she rocked it steadily as she bounced up and down, feeling herself swell inside, ready to come.

Already she recognised the dreamy look that came into his eyes just before he climaxed and she had time to register a small thrill of triumph to have judged it so well before her muscles exploded with her own orgasm just as he gripped her hips tightly and groaned her name.

And here I am talking to Tony Greene with a little smile on my face and it's so hot in here I'm sweating. Especially between my legs.

'Tony, what can you tell me about the Anderson murder?'

He was half smiling, those lovely crinkles just appearing around his eyes. Had she just changed the subject too abruptly? Must concentrate.

'Not much. You'll have the cuttings, I suppose. Suspect got away, Brighton police finally apprehended him, charged with murder.'

'What's he like? Grimley, I mean. And Greg Anderson?'

'Off the record, both low life. Anderson wasn't too bad but Grimley's a nasty piece of work.'

'Did you come across him much? Did he have a record?'

'I can't tell you that, Julie.'

'Well, if you have time to look through your files, maybe tomorrow?'

Tony Greene was fixing her with his hazel eyes.

'I don't mean I don't know, Julie, I mean I can't look through my files. Haven't you heard of the Data Protection Act? Not even for you.'

'Tony, I would be so grateful. Really.'

She gave him her most encouraging smile. He looked at her for a long moment and then got up from his desk and held the door open.

'Julie, I've been on the force for over thirty years and I've never made that sort of mistake. As much as, right now, I want to. So. See you tomorrow.'

She smiled and took the hint and then, halfway along the corridor, fell in.

He thought she meant that she'd be grateful enough to – surely not.

Yes, she was right.

108

For God's sake, girl, he thinks you've tried to bribe him with a shag.

Which is a bit of a shame, because I'd happily shag him for nothing.

There had been many times when Julie had been depressed by her job. Visiting the recently bereaved. Trying to put council tax computations into journalese. Most especially, trotting round muddy, smelly farm-yards. But nothing had prepared her for the Hornbeam Estate.

She could hack the place itself, despite the boarded-up unlettable houses, the grilles over many of the occupied windows, the rash of baseball-capped sweatpant-wearing poverty-faced yobs on every corner.

But for the second time that day she found herself in one of the grimmest houses she'd ever seen in her life with its equally undesirable occupant.

David Whitworth had been a friend of both the dead man and the alleged murderer, and if they resembled him in the slightest, society was better off without both of them. He was probably in his early 40s, though he might as well have been 60. His hair could more accu-rately be described as grizzled rather than grey. There was no way you could label that stubble designer and no way any designer had any hand in the making of his clothes. His eyes were blue and unnaturally bright, prob-ably enhanced by the pint mug of cider he was drinking from. At least his second. When she'd knocked on the door at around noon he'd been three-quarters of the way through his first.

He was smoking, of course, though it was barely necessary for the whole house stank of cigarette smoke and Julie felt she was taking in as much as he was just by – almost reluctantly – breathing.

Occasionally a dog barked from the room it was shut up in. It was loud and gruff and she would have put money on an Alsatian. The settee she was sitting on the edge of was covered in hairs, grease and dust, with a pile of washing dumped on the other end.

Thank God she didn't have to see the kitchen or use the bathroom.

'Well, we all grew up together, didn't we?' He constantly sought her concurrence with his statements, the most innocuous of which he managed to make sound aggressive. 'Greg, Peter, Gary Altman and Jonny Drew. We was all mates. These houses went up when we was toddlers; we all moved in about the same time. Mind you, it was a bit different then, this estate, when it was new. People had a pride in it. Look at the state of it now.'

Yeah, and how on earth could that have happened, pal? Nothing to do with slobs like you living on it, I suppose.

He had been rambling on for long enough. Either he knew nothing or he wasn't telling. Still, there was another name in there.

'I've seen Mr Altman, David, but who else did you mention? Was it John Drew?'

'Yeah, Elm View Road, right on the corner by the bus shelter, can't remember the number. Well, course it was his wife who old Greg had shacked up with.'

Oh, yes?

'Of course, Mrs Drew – Sandra, wasn't it? I tried her house but I didn't get an answer.'

'She'll be at work. You might get her later.'

The last thing she wanted to do was to come back later for more fruitless door knocking. None of these people seemed to have heard of doorbells. And she had a nasty feeling that at least a couple of the houses she'd tried in vain had people lurking on the inside, just not answering.

Maybe she'd try John Drew and then get back for lunch. She looked at her watch. Quarter to one. She'd been here far too long for nothing.

'Well, thanks very much, Mr Whitworth, I really appreciate your help.'

'Think nothing of it, darling. I just hope old Grimmo

don't go down for too long. He's a diamond. Well, so was old Greg – don't understand it at all.'

She couldn't shut him up. By the time she finally managed to close the door her watch beeped one o'clock. A whole hour wasted.

The house by the bus shelter in Elm View Road actually had a doorbell. It worked. And it was answered by someone she could have done without meeting at that particular point in her life.

He was tall and blond with an indeterminate hairstyle, mid-length and slightly wavy, layered a bit like Mick Jagger's. His face was big and open, his nose large and straight, but not too large for the face. And his eyes were so, so blue.

Forget-me-not blue. The azure of summer skies. The intense blue of waves where they met their white, foamy crest.

Not the cold dawn ice-blue of Stevenson's eyes. A warm blue. And as he smiled enquiringly at her, she saw the sun rise in those blue eyes.

'Yup?'

'Oh, sorry. I was looking for John Drew. I'm Julie Gibson, from the *Evening Light*.'

His smile broadened. He had a large mouth, the sort they call mobile. As if most people's mouths don't move.

'You've found him. Jonny, actually. No "h". Short for Jonathan. What can I do for you?'

By now she'd taken in the fact that he was wearing jeans and a battered black leather jacket. Nothing under the jacket but warm-looking, tanned flesh. A small, fine tangle of golden hairs on his chest. A thin silver chain round his neck with a – crucifix, maybe? – charm of some sort. Not what you could call a medallion.

What can you do for me? You can lift me up high and run my body down over your warm skin until it sits perfectly on your cock, then you can fuck me while you look at me with those incredible eyes.

'I'm talking to people who knew Greg Anderson and

111

Peter Grimley? David Whitworth gave me your name. He said you were all friends. And that Mr Anderson's girlfriend was your ex-wife?'

He nodded slowly. 'Well, that's all true. So is that it?'

'Oh, no, I wanted to ask you about Mr Anderson, and Mr Grimley, if you have a few minutes? Just a bit about them, you know, what they were like? As I expect you know, the trial's coming up at the Crown Court next month.'

'So I hear. I'm sorry, Miss Gibson, but I really don't have the time. I'm just on my way back to work. My shop's usually open again at one-fifteen, and it's nearly that now.'

Although I'm still looking into those eyes, I am not lost, I really am not.

'Oh, right, what sort of shop have you got?'

He was looking amused. 'Motorbikes, spares, repairs and stuff. On Winter Avenue?'

She vaguely remembered it, a row of uninspiring shops leading from the town centre out towards the old industrial estate. Hardware, TV repairs, that sort of thing.

'Sure. Well, maybe I can catch you there a bit later?'

He shook his head. 'No, sorry, I'm going to be working on a bike this afternoon and I've got to concentrate. You can come back here about six if you like.'

Shit. She was not planning on working late. But look at him!

'That's great, I'll do that, if you're sure. OK, I'll see you later. Have a nice afternoon.'

I'm rattling on like an idiot.

I am an idiot.

Julie picked up a prawn mayo sandwich and a low-fat fromage frais on the way back to the office. As she neared the front entrance, Wendy came out and stomped off in the other direction. Julie called her but she didn't hear – or did she? She had an uneasy feeling that she was ignoring her.

112

She soon found out why. The late edition was open on Wendy's desk at page three.

INDECENT THEATRE PRODUCTION CALLED OFF

AN OBSCENE version of D. H. Lawrence's *Women in Love* by a local women's theatre group at the Phoenix Theatre has been called off after protests, writes Bob Underwood.

The two-hander by the experimental group Medusa featured a scene where the character Gudrun, played by Janine Hinchcliffe, is depicted masturbating in a bath.

The mayor, Mrs Linda Edwards, and other councillors joined in decrying the production and local church leaders added their weight to their pleas until an emergency stop notice was put on the public performance licence for the remaining three nights of the play's run.

She slumped into her chair. 'Thanks a lot, Bob.'

You shit. You slimy little turd. You sad, grumpy-faced, fat git.

No wonder he was so amused this morning. That idea had obviously come to him after he'd read her review.

'I thought Wendy deliberately ignored me just now. I can see why.'

Mark was giving her sympathetic glances from the other side of the room. She looked at the screen. Incoming mail – guess who from.

'She'll get over it. You're on an evening now, Julie. We have to fill a paper every night and that means if you get a chance like this you've just got to make it happen. That's good journalism.'

113

She shook her head indignantly. 'No way! That is being deliberately provocative.'

He shrugged. 'What if it happened this way? What if Mrs Edwards' teenage daughter went to see the play and went home and told her mum about it? Same outcome. All I did was spread the word a bit.'

'OK, Bob, if you want to run a newsroom where no-one tells you anything in case you use it the wrong way, that's your business.'

His jowly face was flushed.

'I don't want any advice from you about running this newsroom. When you've been here a bit longer and what's more got a bit more experience both of this town and of the job in general then I might be interested in your opinion, but right at this moment in time I'm not asking for it and don't want it. OK?'

'Check.'

Shitbag.

Derek was standing up and languidly pulling on his cream linen jacket. Are you going to rescue me by taking me to the wine bar, you sweetie?

'Bob, I'm going to the Vaults and I need to talk to you about something – OK?'

Bollocks. Or is he going to give him a talking to?

Stevenson appeared in the doorway of the newsroom.

'Julie. I need you for your mug shot.'

She pushed her chair back quickly.

'Well, you've found a mug all right.'

He smiled. 'Actually, I need a woman for some shots for advertising – are you free for a bit?'

'Tell you what, I haven't even started my lunch hour yet,' she said pointedly. 'Let me pose for you in my own time.'

She picked up her sandwich and followed him out of the room without looking at Bob.

'I suppose you know he stitched me up?'

The photographer nodded. 'Oh, yes, first Wendy came in almost in tears blaming you, then Mark followed her

114

in and told her you'd just written a review and Bob had set the story up.'

'She just ignored me in the street, so she obviously didn't believe him,' lamented Julie.

'Wendy's been here long enough to know what Bob's like. She should have warned you not to mention anything controversial to him. I think she's more mad at herself than you.'

They went through the photographic room past Mike Phillips working on the scanner into the studio, a cream room with two modular sofas facing each other, a small table and lights. It reminded Julie of a padded cell.

Stevenson flashed up the 'Busy Do Not Enter' red light and turned to her.

'Mug shot last, when you're a bit happier. Eat your sandwich and relax all the muscles in your body. Close your eyes and eat.'

She sat down opposite him and unwrapped the sandwich, trying to follow his instructions. God, she was tense. Her shoulders must have been up around her ears.

It was weird eating with her eyes closed, feeling that Stevenson was watching her. She told him.

'Yes, it's making me think of blindfolding you and feeding you, like 9½ Weeks, with some really interesting things. Like oysters. And figs. You know what they say about figs?'

'Hey, who's the English graduate around here? It's talking of Women in Love that has reminded you of figs. But you know, that's not in the book, only in the film. It was in a poem.'

'Really? I'd like to hold an open fig next to your cunt, to contrast them. I don't think it's a good comparison at all. They're too red raw, the seeds make them too rough and grasping. Your cunt will be pink and smooth and caressing.'

'When will you find out?'

He laughed softly. 'Maybe today.'

Julie's breath was shortening. In the next room Mike

115

was working. Although the no entry light was up, if there was an emergency it would be ignored.

She finished her sandwich. 'Now what?'

'Are you relaxed?'

'I was until you started comparing me to a fig. But I suppose I mean yes, in the sense that I'm not worrying any more.'

Suddenly the door opened. Not the one leading from the photographer's office but the one used to bring the public up to the studio.

'Hihi. Got delayed. What's up?'

Monika.

The photographer stood and clicked on the other no entry sign, the one on the door Monika had just entered by.

'I've been thinking about you both in your underwear. Julie needs cheering up and I need a lift and let's face it, Mon, you always need something new – so how about it?'

Julie shivered, but not with cold. 'It's one way to distract me from that little shit Bob.'

'Why, what's he done now?'

'We're not talking about it,' Stevenson interrupted. 'Talk about something else. Tell us about your DI, Julie.'

'Actually I'd quite like to hear about Monika's session with Branford and Anna,' said Julie, hoping it wouldn't reveal that Branford had told her about his role as human handcuffs. 'But – excuse me if I'm being prudish – Mike's right outside the door.'

'If you shout fire, he can hear you. Otherwise this room is pretty soundproof. So tell all, Monika.'

The Danish girl had already pulled her silk knit top over her head to display her breasts, small and tanned, in a satin and lace bra. It was pale grey, embroidered with tiny lilac flowers, and Julie knew it hadn't come from a chain store.

She couldn't deny it was exciting to watch Monika undress, and to look at her cleavage, pushed together by the wired bra. Of course she'd seen the rest from her vantage point in the next-door toilet cubicle, but it was still a thrill when the other girl undid the buttons down the front of her cream linen skirt to show briefs that matched her bra. They were cut high in the leg and the folds of her sex pouted from the crotch.

She stood tall in her high-heeled mules. Julie remembered her orders to Anna and wondered if Monika wanted to make love to her, and if so did she want to dominate her. The new role she was playing with Bryn was exciting, but she wanted to reserve it for him.

'It was a good night – are you getting undressed or not, Julie? First off, Anna had brought me off with her tongue in the toilet, while Julie watched. Then I went home with her and Branford, you know, the DJ?'

Stevenson was looking suitably interested. Julie stood, feeling awkward, then before she could start to undress Monika stood right before her and undid the top button of her shirt.

She was taller than any of the men Julie had been involved with lately, and she felt a thrill of smallness and docility, the same she felt with Bryn. With him it was strength that made her feel that way, but with Monika it was pure length.

'Anna wasn't interested in a three-way but I was. She just wanted me to make her come then crash. Shit, she's so boring. I knew Branford was up for more than just me, so I told her if she wanted me she'd have to play ball or I'd lend her a vibrator and send her home.'

Julie's shirt was on the floor. Monika smiled as she put her hands round Julie's waist to undo the button and then the zip of her skirt. She was very close and Julie caught her breath as she felt Monika's breasts graze her own as she leant forwards.

'She always says she doesn't come with penetration – you know, that pseudo-feminist shit – so I sat her on Branford's cock for a bit and watched them, then I knelt facing her and we took turns going up and down on him. That was really cool – he was trying so hard not to come! Then I sat on his face and fingered Anna while she fucked him, but she is just such a bitch – she said she hadn't come and I knew she had: she just wanted me to go down on her. So I made her wait till I came, then I put my tongue in there and did not stop. I mean, she was coming and coming and you know what it's like when it won't stop, almost painful. Branford was amazingly getting off on this so he came up behind me and fucked me for ever while I tongued her for ever. My jaw ached all day Friday. But shit, it was a good scene. Branford is a very talented man.'

Julie, innocent in white broderie anglais bra and briefs; Monika, totally wicked in opulent satin and lace the colour of smoke and bruises.

'He guessed you had something special in mind,' she told Monika.

'Oh, yeah? How do you know?'

'We were fucking in his room upstairs. He came in to shower for you and Bryn got him to hold me down.'

Monika smiled, her wide lips moving slowly and sensually. 'That sounds very good. I like you, Julie. Seeing as we're standing this close why don't we see what our bodies feel like together?'

Just one small step for woman. Julie moved forwards and put her hands on Monika's back, her fingers on the fine grain of her satiny flesh, feeling her smooth, wide-boned body against hers. The height of the other girl meant that her pubic bone pressed above Julie's and it felt better than good.

Monika's hands ran lightly over Julie's arse then she pressed it firmly forwards so that their sexes ground together harder.

'Do you want to kiss?'

'No. What I really want . . . is what Stevenson fantasised about.'

'Remind me.'

He was watching intently with a ghost of a smile on his face.

'You suck Julie's nipples one by one, then you finger her until she nearly comes.'

'I just lie back and enjoy it.'

The girls looked at each other and Monika smiled knowingly.

'You want to be passive, Julie.'

She nodded and lay on the couch.

Monika knelt in front of Julie and lifted her right breast from her bra with her nail-varnished hands, then ran a fingertip around the nipple until it was bullet-hard. Julie saw her plum-coloured mouth gather into a pout then close over her swollen tit and suck, gently, then harder. Same on other breast. Stevenson turned on the light and took photographs.

Julie was hot. Hot from lights, hot from tingling excitement. Eyes closed, totally passive.

Monika pulled Julie's knickers down and off and pushed her thighs apart. Julie couldn't see but felt her slip two fingers inside her and heard her laugh at her wetness. She pulled her fingers out and stroked Julie's clit.

Julie was on the verge of coming.

'I'm coming,' she murmured. She'd forgotten the plot. Monika stopped.

'Oh, shit.'

'Isn't that right? You said nearly comes?'

'That's it,' said Stevenson. 'Now my turn to choose what happens. Mon, on the floor, head other way round to Julie. Take your knickers off and do the same to yourself.'

'All the way?'

'No. The same. I don't want you to come either. Move along a bit – I want Julie to see you properly. Julie, prop yourself up and watch.'

'Can I touch myself too?'

'No, you'll cheat. Tell Monika something you've done with your cop. Go on, Mon.'

Julie shivered to see Monika's hairless sex again, this time in close-up. It looked so exposed, brazen. She wanted to shave hers too.

The fingers that had just dipped into her own sex dipped again and came out and circled the other clitoris.

She didn't want to talk about Bryn. Instead she told Monika about Mark's ice-cream dream. Stevenson shot.

Monika stopped. 'I'm being honest and stopping, but it's my turn to say what I want and I want to come.'

'You can't. You're in my game and I make the rules.'

'Oh, fuck you. That's exactly why I stopped playing the stupid bloody thing. So what can I do?'

'What you like. As long as you don't come.'

'I want to suck your dick.'

'OK. As long as you don't make me come either.'

'God forbid.'

Stevenson unzipped. My first time as a voyeur, thought Julie. Even his cock was elegant – circumcised, smooth and dusky pink and loftily topped with crimson. Monika knelt before him, and Julie moved to the floor to watch closely. She picked up the camera and looked through the lens. Stevenson's rapt face was registering every touch of tongue.

God, he appreciates every sensation so fully an orgasm would probably be too much for him. That plum-coloured mouth looks so sexy going up and down that shaft.

Suddenly I want that mouth on me. That tongue that's licking upwards lightly, little flicks all over the head, I'm wanting that licking me.

Still, it's not my turn and, anyway, do I really want to get into a thing with Monika?

'Enough.'

Monika lifted her head as Stevenson spoke.

'I don't believe you're near it. You're cheating.'

'Mon, trust me. Anyway, look at the time. We all have

to get back to work. How do you feel, Julie? Cheered up?'

When wasn't I cheerful? Seems like aeons ago.

Clothes back on. Monika left by the back way. Just in time, Stevenson remembered the mug shot, then Julie left by the front. Mike was gone, anyway.

Bob and Derek were still out but Wendy was back at her desk. Julie started to explain.

'It's OK, I know, I shouldn't have ignored you. I was upset with Bob, really, not you.'

John told them he had heard Bob make the phone calls and tried to stop him. Mark and Alan came over and commiserated and they reached a consensus that while not exactly on a work to rule, they wouldn't tell Bob anything for a bit, just do the job but stick to the diary and not volunteer any information.

'Don't you ever read your mail?' said Mark as Alan drifted back to work.

'Sorry, Mark. Bit busy.'

'Have a drink with me tonight at the Far Pavilion. Come back after if you want.' He murmured discreetly, which Julie was pleased about, especially as she'd told Wendy they weren't into sex.

God knows I need a quick fix of something, or should I say someone.

'OK. I've got a golden wedding this afternoon then I'm back at Hornbeam at six, but that won't take long. See you there at eight?'

Should give me time to get the car back here, trot home, shower – certainly need that – and grab something to eat, she thought.

Mark blew a kiss in confirmation.

I really think this should just be a drink. Life's getting complicated.

'I cooked you dinner. You're a bit late.'

Dinner? Are you nuts?

'Well – thanks – I wasn't expecting anything –'

'No. But I was hungry, and it seemed rude to go ahead and eat while you were here. I like cooking – makes a change to have someone to cook for.'

'Right. Sorry I was late. The staff cars were both out, and I didn't have time to go home to get mine, so I had to get the bus.'

Julie was actually hot and cross. The golden wedding couple turned out to be an excruciating combination of stone deaf and garrulous and the job had taken far too long. She had sped back to work and written up the story, such as it was, then she and John had had a discussion about the crime situation generally and her morning on the estate. By the time they wrapped up she found both the pool cars were out.

Now it was after 6.30 and she had to get home on the bus, change and get down to the Far Pavilion by eight. She really didn't have time for dinner.

But when Jonny Drew smiled his careless, friendly smile, she forgot all that.

I have to watch out here. I'm having a full-on relationship with one man, playing a sex game with another, possibly on the verge of my first girl-on-girl encounter, meeting an old friend and occasional fuck for a drink after this, and this morning apparently offered sex for information to a police officer. Whatever I said to this guy earlier on, he seems to think we're on more than professional terms.

'So, what's for dinner? Smells good.'

He pulled the two plates that were warming from the grill pan. '*Spaghetti alla puttanesca*. Translates as tart's pasta.'

'I don't think I'll take that personally.'

Did you just read my mind?

He laughed, a warm, genuine sound. 'You weren't meant to. I often make it because it's quick and I like it. Just tomato, garlic, anchovy and olive sauce. Here, put the salad on the table.'

Watercress and corn salad, with proper dressing. He piled the pasta on the plates.

'Whoa, not so much for me. I haven't been doing physical work all day long.'

Apart from a quick stint during my late lunchbreak.

'I bet you've got a good appetite. I like a girl who eats, rather than just picks at food.'

It was delicious. Julie wasn't a great cook but he was right, she loved to eat.

'This is so nice. And – unexpected.'

'You think I'm a nut, don't you?'

She laughed. 'No! But I've never had this happen before.'

'I miss cooking for someone else.'

'Since your wife left?'

'Yeah, it's nearly two years ago. Serves me right, though.'

'Why?'

'Oh, stuff. Do you want some wine?'

'Just a glass – if you're having one.'

He poured two glasses of Chilean cabernet sauvignon. 'Sorry it's not Italian. Cheers.'

'Cheers.'

She felt oddly comfortable sitting across the table from this obviously rather eccentric man. He was still wearing jeans but had a clean white T-shirt on instead of the biker jacket. She wondered how old he was. The other guys he'd grown up with were in their early 40s.

'You know I told you I went to see David Whitworth and Gary Altman this morning?'

'Mmm-hmm . . .'

'Well, you're not much like them, are you? I mean, they went on about you and them and the other two guys being lifelong mates and so on, but you're – well, you know what I mean. The state of their houses, drinking mugs of cider all day, and here you are in this nice little house cooking Italian food and drinking wine. I just don't get it.'

Jonny twirled spaghetti round his fork. 'Well, I just had a bit more of an education, that's all. These guys lived with their parents for years, never got married. David's parents died, and Gary's divorced and then his mum remarried and moved out. They're a couple of sad old men – not that they're even old. Neither of them has ever had much in the way of work either.'

'What about Greg Anderson and Peter Grimley?'

He laughed shortly. 'Greg wasn't too bad, but Peter – well, grim by name and grim by nature. If he goes down for a long stretch he won't be missed round here.'

'I thought he was supposed to be your friend?'

'We grew up together. In recent years we played cards once a week, but that was about it.'

'David Whitworth said he was a diamond.'

'Fucking rough diamond, more like.'

She nodded. 'I tried to call on your wife, I mean ex-wife, earlier, but she wasn't in. How's she coping with it all?'

He took a large swallow of his wine. 'I can't speak for her. Mind you, I bet she won't speak to you either. But that's her business.'

'Sure. So you had this education and then came back and stayed on the estate?'

He shrugged, concentrating on his food. 'Sandra got pregnant.'

'Oh, shit. So you've got kids.'

Looking up, his eyes struck her again. 'No. We did have . . . a little boy. He died when he was a year old.'

'Oh, Jonny. I am so sorry. How awful for you, and for Sandra.'

'It was rough at the time. We were a bit young and stupid. Not that I'm much better now.'

He smiled, the warmth in his eyes dazzling her. 'Anyway, that's enough of my sob story. I'm not complaining, you know. I like my life. I actually prefer living on my own, to tell the truth, apart from having no-one to cook for. I love my bike, I enjoy my work, and I like this town.'

Julie cocked her head to one side. 'Yeah, I like this town too. But you don't seem to me the type to go to trendy bars and restaurants or the theatre, so I don't think you like it for the same reasons that I do. What's in it for you? Familiarity?'

'Familiarity breeds contempt, doesn't it?'

He leant over the table towards her, his face animated and absorbed. 'I'll tell you. This town is disintegrating, Julie. The old buildings are crumbling and no-one's trying to stop them. Any industry we once had is dying. The social fabric is tearing, we can't cope with the immigrants and the unemployed, and families are falling apart. There's a massive hole in our policing structure: there just aren't the numbers to keep up with the petty crime. The council has more or less given up on the place and they're only in it to line their own pockets. And I see from your paper tonight that the town is literally falling into the sea. The ground's giving way underneath us.'

His words excited her. She felt like she was living in a *Blade Runner*-type future rather than a crumbling seaside town.

'This town's on the edge, Julie. It's on the edge of lawlessness and social destruction and physical collapse as well as on the edge of the sea. And that's what I like about it. That's what gives it a buzz, not your fancy restaurants or experimental theatre.'

His words sent volts through Julie's body. The adrenalin surge shortened her breath and twitched her muscles into action. They called it the fight or flight response but as usual fuck was the word that came to mind.

I know what you're going to say, Julie, and it's crazy. Really crazy. Don't do it. Please don't look at him so intensely.

'I think I'm feeling that buzz right now.'

You silly cow.

The warm eyes blazed a look that scorched her.

125

'Mutual, Miss Gibson.'

She laughed, breaking the tension.

'Why can nobody just call me Julie? I'm either Miss Julie, Miss Gibson or Julie Gibson. What's wrong with just Julie?'

He caught her wrist with his hand. 'How about a fuck, Julie? I'll call you what you like.'

She closed her eyes as his words sent sweet shivers through her.

'I'm going to have to say no. But I'll tell you why. First, I'm meeting someone else at eight o'clock.'

'Your boyfriend?'

'No, just a friend. But a friend I sometimes have sex with.'

'Well, I appreciate you not using me to warm you up for your friend.'

He was so warm, so at ease with himself, so unfazed by her rejection.

'And, I do have a boyfriend. Although he's new and we're not committed to exclusivity. And while I'm being honest with you I have a sort of sexual relationship with someone else. But that's sort of – it's not exactly fucking.'

He sat back and laughed his careless laugh.

'You're a bit twenty-first century for me, Julie. I got my first girlfriend pregnant before I left university and had to get married. Apart from joining in the sexual revolution at college, I've led a sheltered life.'

'You mean you were faithful to your wife?'

'Not that sheltered.'

'Anyway. I'm sorry, I really have to go now. I'm without wheels, I live on Grasmere Avenue and I really need to shower and change before I go out.'

'I'll give you a lift.'

'Oh, that's really nice of you. But I don't want to put you out.'

His eyes looked innocent and amused. 'I didn't have any plans for tonight, Julie. Unless you'd stayed, that is. I'm really sorry you can't.'

126

He stood and pulled on his leather jacket. 'Been on a bike before?'

What have I always said? Four wheels good, two wheels bad.

'Er . . . no. Well, once, in Corfu. I fell off. Said I'd never get on one again.'

Hiding a smile, he handed her a crash helmet.

'Well, it's that or take two buses and get to your friend late. All you have to do is hold on and lean the same way I do. Come on, Julie, it's a thrill. You'll love it.'

I'm sure it's all very exciting but I usually get my thrills with most of my clothes off. Still, what can I say to this guy who likes life on the edge? No, I'm a scaredy-cat?

On the edge, Julie. Go join him, girl.

Julie's diary, 24 June

What am I doing now? I really need to sort myself out. I'm desperately madly deeply in lust with an *older man*! And, one who lives on a rough council estate and gets his hands dirty during the day. But with the most beautiful blue eyes! This morning he was wearing a biker jacket and jeans and was about the sexiest thing I have ever seen since I first set eyes on David Ginola. He's not stupid either. He cooked me dinner when I was only going round to ask him about his old mates, for God's sake. Not that I got much out of him, I was more interested in looking at him. And even more major, he gave me a lift on his bike. I'm like, oh what if I fall off, I was weeing myself but it was so great. I want to get one, I felt so sexy! He wanted to fuck but I put him straight. Wish he'd not had his T-shirt on tonight. Anyway going off to meet Mark, am not going to write this later in case we fuck. I just don't want to look back on this period in my life and think, what a little slut.

Chapter Six

Evening Light, Friday 28 June

BIKE PROJECT HELPS
LOCAL KIDS

The Julie Gibson Weekend Feature

WINTERSEA'S YOUTHS are unanimous in their approval of a motorbike club that meets on Thursdays near the old industrial estate.

And police are equally pleased that the youngsters are learning how to ride and maintain bikes legally.

The project is run by local bike shop proprietor Jonny Drew, with the co-operation of Wintersea District Council and financial assistance from various local charitable organisations.

'Hey, what's the Julie Gibson Weekend Feature?' asked Mark, as the customary silence descended on the newsroom as the reporters pored over the first edition of the paper. 'I gave you that story, Jules, and now you seem to have got yourself a regular slot.'

Julie shrugged. 'Nothing to do with me. You said you weren't interested in writing it, so I did, and then David called me in yesterday and said he wanted me to try a weekly piece. Don't get jealous; it's all supposed to be about Hornbeam and the other estates. Part of the ongoing project to boost sales among the lower orders, as Claire calls them.'

Mark was tutting, but amused. 'I bet you didn't tell David you only did the story because you fancy Jonny Drew.'

Julie stuck her tongue out.

'Well, I can't say I blame you, Julie,' observed Claire. 'He's got great eyes.'

'Yes, not bad for someone your age,' teased Mark. 'Bit old for Julie.'

'Age is irrelevant, dear boy,' said Derek. 'Anyway, he only looks about forty – oh, I see forty-two. A youngster. So did you pull him, Julie?'

'Derek! I'm surprised at you!'

Like hell I am. Bet you'd like the juicy details to tell Monika. Bet Monday lunchtime has featured in your game during the last week.

It was true that Mark had put her on to Jonny's bike club. After the thrilling lift home on the bike on Monday she had managed to shower, change and even write her diary before arriving at the Far Pavilion a cool five minutes late. But Mark knew something had happened.

'You've got that look about you again. Sort of vibrant. Have you been screwing?'

'No, I have not. It's this sexy dress.'

Her halterneck vest dress, tie-dyed in turquoise, lime and fuchsia, looked like it had drunk in the heat and excitement of the summer and was reflecting it right back.

'Bullshit. We're too close to hide these things, Julie. Come on, give.'

'OK. I could have been screwing but I turned it down because I was meeting you. And that's the truth.'

129

'Right. So who wanted to shag you?'

Mark knew of Jonny and gave Julie the lowdown on his bike club. Not only was she even more impressed with him, she was mentally punching the air because she had a good excuse to get in touch with him again.

Julie was on a high thanks to Jonny and Mark was pleased to be out with her again at last, so they had a good time. She had told him, with some economy, about Bryn, although nothing about Stevenson and Monika, and he started dropping broad hints about being the first to see her new flat. It was time it was christened, he declared, and who better to do the job than her good old friend?

She was in such a good mood that she acquiesced and they made their way back to her place. After the grand tour Mark insisted on going down to the off licence for a bottle of celebratory champagne.

'Right, let's get this christening underway,' he said as he got back and started undoing the wire cage. 'Glasses, right. Shall we start in here?'

They were in the sitting room.

'Sure. Er . . . start what?'

The cork popped and they both cheered. He poured two glasses.

'The christening, dickhead. We have to fuck in every room and drink a glass of champagne. You can't miss out on your own flat's christening.'

What a sweetie. What an idiot. What a blatant bloody opportunist. But really what a laugh.

Mark bet he could down his champagne first, and he did. Julie bet she could get undressed faster than him and with only a dress and briefs to remove won easily. He opened the betting on how quickly he could make Julie come with his hands: he said two minutes, she reckoned five. To her amazement it was two and a half. The day's excitement and the raw unsentimental physicality of their relationship had her more than ready, especially when he had her lie down on the table with

130

her knees apart and feet together like a frog, her upper body hanging upside down staring at the curtains. She called up Jonny Drew's face while half listening to Mark telling her graphically how he'd masturbated every night thinking about her while he fingered her to orgasm. After she'd come he pulled her to the edge of the table and entered her still-pulsating pussy, while she played with her breasts for him.

'This is going to have to go quicker than I planned or I'm going to shoot my load before we get to the last room,' he lamented, pouring the second glass of champagne as they moved to the kitchen. 'Jesus, Jules, do you remember fucking over the sink in my flat?'

Yes, it was good. I bent over the sink just like this. This time they sipped at the wine while he pushed into her long and slow, pausing between each thrust. Julie remembered fantasising about a DI when they fucked like that before. Now she had her very own DI on tap.

The bathroom next. 'I've got to wee first,' said Julie, closing the door on Mark. He pushed it open.

'You can do it in front of me.'

She shrugged. She'd practically done everything else in front of him anyway.

'Jules, don't. I've got a better idea. Are you desperate?'

'Nearly. Why?'

He poured the next glass of champagne. 'Drink this fast.'

'Then I will be desperate.'

She drank anyway.

'Haven't you heard of golden showers?'

No way. That is gross.

'You want me to wee all over you?'

'Not all over me. While we fuck.'

'Bloody hell.'

He sat on the toilet, cock up in the air. Apart from squatting down in the bath, she didn't have a lot of choice.

'Mark, it's going to go on the floor.'

'I'll wash it off. Come on, Julie, it'll be a real turn-on.'

Facing him, she sat down on his cock.

'Don't move too fast, I don't want to come till the last room.'

Straddling him she moved up and down his shaft. She really did need to go. Her belly felt big and bloated. Experimentally, she tried relaxing her muscles. It wouldn't come. She tried harder. Still it wasn't working.

'I can't go while you're inside me. Get off and let me pee. I really need to now.'

'Look, try to forget peeing and just concentrate on fucking. Feel your clit rubbing against me. Oh, Julie, you are fantastic. Come on, baby, just like that. Now think waterfalls, rivers, lots of lovely water. Can you hear that water running, rushing? Julie, that river is a lovely golden river of piss. You're coming, aren't you? Let go, Julie, you won't come unless you let go. Yes, brilliant, hello eyes. Oh my God, that is weird. Your piss is so hot.'

Not half as weird as it is for me, Williams. I cannot believe I'm doing this. It's like coming twice in one go, and even more exciting because part of me feels ashamed, as though it wasn't deliberate and I was just a dirty cow.

'When you said christening, I didn't think you meant the bathroom floor.'

Quick wash all round before moving on to the bedroom.

'I'm actually feeling quite pissed,' she observed lazily, flinging herself on to the bed.

'*Quelle* coincidence. I'm feeling quite pissed on.'

'Ha-ha. Let's finish that champagne and have that last fuck.'

He poured a small amount in each glass.

'Hey, what about the rest of it?'

'I'm conducting this christening. How about you just lie on the bed and we'll play husbands and wives?'

'What have we been doing already?'

'I mean for a change let's do the missionary position.'

'Oh, how sweet.'

Julie wound her legs round him and ran her hands down his back, murmuring dirtily. She was feeling languid after the wine and her two orgasms but wanted Mark to have an orgasm to remember.

But he soon withdrew.

'OK, now for the finale.'

She peered up at him in astonishment. 'Mark, there aren't any more rooms. Unless you want to do it in the hall, but it'd be a bit uncomfortable.'

'The balcony, Jules. We have to christen the balcony.'

'You are joking! There are people walking up and down the road past the garden all the time! And it's hardly even dark yet!'

He tutted. 'I'm in charge. We'll just have to be quiet. Come on.'

She opened the balcony door gingerly. There didn't seem to be anyone about and she quickly dived for the sun lounger.

'Coward. Sit up and finish this champagne.'

'Look, if someone comes along the road –'

'Yeah, they'll see there's someone up here but they won't be able to see what we're wearing. Or not. Or what we're doing.' He sat down next to her and poured the dregs of the bottle. 'Cheers, Jules. I get a funny feeling we're not going to do this for a long time after tonight, so let's go out with a bang. As it were.'

'Oh, Mark, that sounds so sad.'

'Bollocks. But you're already going around with a cop and I know you, you can't resist this Jonny Drew. You can't fit us all in, but don't worry, I'll be there when something gives.'

She stroked his cock. 'I do adore you, Mark, in a sort of amused way. Why don't you hit on Monika? She's really interested in you since I told her about the ice-cream Mars Bar.'

Mark did a double take. 'I thought you girls didn't talk about the details.'

'Not usually, but you said you didn't mind me telling

133

about you, so I did. She's amazingly horny. I can guar-
antee you won't be disappointed.'

'You mean she's hotter than you?'

'I reckon.'

'Jesus. Jules, just for me, get your back to that balcony,
put your arms along it, and open your legs. That is
beautiful.'

She tossed her head back and lifted herself so he could
enter her with ease. Despite his arguments to the contrary
she was sure that anyone walking along the road would
see them, but what the hell. It was unlikely to be anyone
she knew.

'No-one's hotter than you, Julie baby, and that's the
truth.' He mashed her breasts, circling the nipples with
his thumbs as he thrust hard inside her. After the strange
satisfaction of her first experience of watersports she
wasn't expecting to come again but her own dirty talk to
Mark in the bedroom, the warm night air on her body
and the blatancy of their public fuck sent her muscles
leaping again.

It wasn't lost on Mark. 'You're the best, Gibbo. Jesus,
your muscles are squeezing me. I'm coming any minute,
Jules. Can you come with me again, baby?'

He leant forwards as he pushed hard and fast inside
her and nuzzled into her neck, sending crazy tingles
round her nerve endings.

Yum. If you insist, Williams. Three in a row. The
second first of the evening.

Julie was starting to feel slightly desperate. She just had
too much on her plate to fit into a week containing a
mere seven days.

She wanted to see Bryn. But equally she wanted to see
Jonny Drew to get the motorbike club story done ready
for Friday, features day. But that meant Bob would need
the story written by Thursday morning so he could
approve it and organise the pics at the club on Thursday
night.

Of course, she could have interviewed Jonny during the day – but that would scupper her hidden agenda.

But if she saw Jonny Drew on Wednesday night, when could she see Bryn? She was down for Wintersea parish council on Thursday night. Tonight – no way. Mark's imprint was all over her body. Friday she could do at a pinch, but she'd missed the Friday night out last week because she was off, and wanted to consolidate her friendships with the other reporters – especially Wendy. There was step to fit in as well but that wasn't till seven so she had the choice of staying in the pub or going to the class, though she had a feeling she knew which would win, fat bum notwithstanding. Then Saturday she was working early shift from seven till two.

As it happened, Jonny Drew couldn't see her on Wednesday.

'Sorry, Julie. I'm tied up for the next two nights, and work's desperate at the moment. I haven't really got time to see you. Can't you leave your story till next week? Or come down with the photographer on Thursday?'

'No, it's too late. They need the Friday features written and ready to go by Thursday morning. I suppose we'll have to leave it till next week.'

Shit. She really wanted to show that she'd come up with something for the time she'd spent at Hornbeam.

'Well, I can tell you everything on the phone, if you like.'

You're missing half the point, Jonny.

'And then maybe you could come down over the weekend and have another go on the bike.'

Perfect. She arranged to phone him back at home at lunchtime to get the story of the bike club. A done deal.

So Wednesday night was free for Bryn. She'd seen him that morning in the police station, though he'd just walked past her saying hi. Should she call him, or he her?

She was the one dictating when she'd be available.

She called him.

* * *

135

By the following night she felt like celebrating. She had turned in the feature on the motorbike club, after getting suitable quotes from the police and councillors as well as Jonny. She half-heartedly felt she ought to speak to some of the kids but that was going too far. She didn't do yobs.

David had been pleased and told her that if she could come up with a feature every week, preferably highlighting the positive side of the town's indigenous community, she could have a regular Friday slot.

Done!

And Bryn was also off on Wednesday night and here they were at Tiny's, a bar overlooking the Old Harbour, which had hardly any space inside but loads of tables on the dock edge. Seagulls wheeled round them as they sank their second bottle of Beck's.

'I love hearing the gulls when I'm inside, but close up they give me the creeps. I keep thinking of *The Birds* and waiting for them to divebomb me.'

Bryn laughed. 'I supposed I'm just used to them. Or perhaps I don't have your active imagination.'

She looked sideways at him. 'I don't know about that, Bryn. I was just wondering how you're planning to use your imagination tonight.'

He groaned and stretched, yawning. 'Don't ask too much of me, Julie. I'm absolutely knackered. How about we just go and eat at Luca's place and then go back to yours early for a nice cosy uncomplicated fuck?'

Bryn hadn't bothered to lower his voice and Julie was amused to see the man at the table next to theirs turn his head briefly towards them. He was sitting with his girlfriend but they hadn't done much talking. She guessed they were in either the first or final stages of their relationship.

He was quite nice. So was the girl. Julie decided to raise their tension level a bit. With his back to them, Bryn hadn't realised they'd overheard him. She raised the volume of her voice by an infinitesimal amount while lowering the pitch.

'I don't know, we haven't done uncomplicated yet – I'm not sure we're ready for it,' she purred. 'But I don't feel quite as submissive as usual tonight. Probably after the way you forced me on to that gearstick last Sunday.'

Bryn laughed his dirty laugh. 'You weren't complaining then, so don't pretend you didn't enjoy it. But if you want to be on top tonight, in a manner of speaking, I'll give it a go.'

The man at the next table had shifted his chair slightly so he could see them both. Julie looked up from under lowered eyelids, caught his eyes, and held them.

'If you really fancied something different, I know Mark's going out with Monika tonight. Maybe we ought to make it a foursome – if you know what I mean.'

That guy is really turning on. Though Bryn's not sure.

'That Monika. I wonder what Branford got up to with her last week.'

Julie filled him in. From time to time she looked towards the man at the next table. He was still listening. She saw him murmur something to his girlfriend and wondered if he was telling her about their conversation. Just in case, she raised her voice a fraction more.

'When she was telling me I was wondering how I'd feel if I was in Anna's position and you were in Branford's.'

Bryn's torpor was evaporating. Fast.

'You ever had a woman, Julie?'

'Not yet.'

They laughed. 'You ever had a man, Bryn?'

'You're joking, I hope?'

She shrugged. 'Just a thought – I'd quite like to watch two men at it. Maybe not actual penetration – perhaps a blow job. What if you were on the receiving end?'

He screwed up his face and shook his head. 'Don't think so. Well, I don't know. If we were in a scene like you said and the girls weren't putting out, I expect I could manage to be sucked off by a bloke if I was watching you and another woman together. Jesus, we can't start talking like this now; we've got to sit through dinner first.'

Julie put all she had into her smile. 'We don't have to sit through anything first. We could see if Mark and Mon are up for it if they're still in and get a takeaway after.'

Briefly she remembered Stevenson's idea of the blind-fold taste test. But maybe not with a Chinese.

Although she knew Bryn wasn't interested in a group scene, his face was telling her he was fast getting into the idea of fucking her. Soon.

'Or, we could run back to my place and fuck then go to dinner. Or we could go along the beach round by the cliff there. Bet there's no-one about round there.'

The headland marked the end of the beach and the start of the rocks. Great for kids looking in rock pools but they would all be in bed by now. They would be out of sight of the early evening harbour promenaders. Unless the couple at the next table decided to take a walk.

Bryn moved his head closer to hers across the table, obliterating her view of the other couple. His face was that mask of sensuality she was starting to get addicted to.

'What do you really want? I can't make you out tonight.'

'I want to perform,' she whispered back. 'Let's go round that headland and if no-one's there already, I want to fuck fast and hard.'

'Who are you performing for?'

'Trust me. Are you ready for me?'

'What do you think? How about you?'

'I'm as juicy as a ripe mango. Come on.'

They rose and Julie walked towards the steps leading down to the beach, leaving Bryn to pull money out of his pocket for the drinks. She was wearing one of her favourite summer dresses, a bright blue 50s-style strappy top with a full skirt which flared out, especially when she walked on high heels with her arse swaying from side to

138

side as she did now. Her sandals weren't beachwear but she didn't care. She looked like a figure from one of her favourite Jack Vettriano paintings and felt as sexy.

Bryn caught up and put his arm round her shoulders as they strolled around the cliff face until they were out of sight of the harbour crowd. The rocky beach was deserted and quiet, the tide coming in in a desultory fashion with little lapping waves.

'A bit further on, in the cleft in the rocks,' breathed Julie. There was a tiny strip of sand along the edge of the cliff and she walked along that, wondering if the man at the next table had persuaded his girlfriend to take a walk.

The crack in the cliff wouldn't have hidden a grasshopper but it gave Julie a perch and she leant back against it and looked at Bryn. She felt her eyes narrow and lips part in anticipation. She wanted a quickie, like the first time they'd had sex. Although she hadn't forgotten about the other couple she realised that she didn't care if they were there or not. All she wanted was Bryn inside her fast with no domination role-playing.

He either sensed or knew what she wanted. The minute she backed on to the cliff and looked at him his hands were all over her breasts. She moaned as he pushed his hands inside the top of her dress and squeezed her nipples. They faced each other with calculated intent, both breathing fast, mouths slightly open and nostrils dilated.

She didn't want to tear her face away from his deep, glowing, brown eyes. Her hands reached out to undo his fly and she pulled his cock out and felt its size and solidity, as hard as the rock she was leaning against. Without wasting time on caresses, she pulled her skirt up and her knickers aside and pulled one of his hands out of her dress and rubbed it roughly against her sex.

'That's how ready I am for you. Fuck me hard, Bryn.'

Looking quickly over his shoulder, he pulled a condom from his pocket and fitted it on. Then grabbing her shoulders he turned her so he was the one braced against the rock wall. He reached again under her skirt and ripped her knickers off, then his strong hands lifted her and pushed her down on to his cock.

Julie whimpered with pleasure as she settled her arms around his neck and her legs around his waist. His muscled arms were moving her up and down on his thick cock and she dug her high heels into the rock to give her some leverage and moved with him. The sea-gulls cried overhead and the gentle waves sighed as they barely broke on the rocks.

They stared at each other in absorption as he pushed her down on to his prick then pulled her up again. Julie wondered if the couple was watching. They wouldn't be able to see much, as her skirt hung down over her arse and Bryn's cock. But they would know what they were doing.

His eyes burned into her as he gripped her harder to push her faster on and off his cock. His hands were on her hips with his thumbs spread wide to press down on her mons. She knew he was going to come quickly and she needed something more.

'Talk to me, Bryn,' she murmured. 'Tell me where you are inside your head.'

He spoke with an effort.

'I'm thinking of you and Monika and me and Branford on that white leather. I've got my tongue up one of you and I swear to God I don't know who it is and I couldn't tell you whose mouth is round my cock. All I know is that I lose everything except the use of my mouth and hands and cock and senses and I think we're all the same. Christ, it's all the same to me. I'm fucking coming, Julie, and at this moment I could be coming anywhere up anybody in anybody's fucking mouth or cunt or arse ... oh my God.'

Oh, yeah, that's what I wanted, Bryn. I'm coming now and that's what did it. I really wanted you to say that. I really want to be nobody just now except a hole for some

140

fucking fat cock. Jesus. Let me down, you shit, you bloody *man*, you're all the same. I love it. I fucking love it.

She collapsed on the sand and sat with her head bowed, recovering. Bryn dropped down beside her, alarmed.

'Shit, now I've upset you. I knew I shouldn't have said that. I thought it'd turn you on. Oh, Julie, don't be upset.'

He put his arms around her. She looked up and smiled.

'Don't be silly. It was great. That was the best thing you could have said.'

She turned her head slightly. No sign of the other couple. Oh, well.

'You sure?'

'That sort of honesty is such a turn-on. For God's sake, when I'm coming I'm not thinking, Oh, good, Bryn's doing this to me. I'm thinking, Oh good, I'm coming, and at that split second it could be a bloody chimpanzee for all I care.'

He smiled wryly. 'If you're getting involved in that sort of thing you can count me out.'

She laughed. 'No worries there. Mind you, talking of chimpanzees, I could do with a tea party right now. I'm starving. How about dinner?'

He groaned. 'Great. Don't worry if I'm ready. I'll just adjust my dress and follow you to the restaurant and I suppose if I'm lucky you'll let me foot the bill.'

'No way, we're going halves. Come on, put your prick away and let's go eat.'

They picked their way back along the sandy strip, Julie leading. Near the edge of the cliff she saw what she wanted to see. An extra set of footprints. The man had followed them.

She pointed them out to Bryn. 'Told you we were performing.'

He looked at her, puzzled.

'What sort of set-up was that?'

She shook her head. 'No set-up. Just the bloke at the

141

next table who was listening to us talking. I guessed he'd follow us.'

'You're kidding. You mean you were doing a live sex show?'

She winked. 'Yeah, I suppose. Though with your little story and confession I sort of forgot about him. Still, bit of added excitement.'

'So when you were talking about going round to Mark's and joining him and Monika –'

'Yup, I just said it to get that guy going.' She looked at him archly. 'Oh, sorry, are you disappointed?'

He gave his throaty laugh. 'No, relieved. It's one thing thinking about it, like just now, but I'm really not into orgies.'

The lights were on outside Tiny's as they rounded the pavement in the gathering dusk and she saw the man at the next table, still there as though he hadn't moved. But he was talking to the girl, their heads close together, and he was stroking her arm. There was sand on his shoes.

Rather than go home before the parish council meeting the next day, Julie took her car to work and spent a couple of hours doing the shops after leaving the office.

The town centre shops had started opening late on Thursday nights, mimicking London's West End, she supposed, to try to boost trade.

She asked Wendy to go with her, but she was going to a fringe play again.

'I suppose I could have guessed you wouldn't ask me,' said Julie, jokingly but feeling a bit put out.

'Oh, don't!' Wendy looked hurt. 'Honestly, I don't blame you for *Women in Love*. I'm going with someone else and, anyway, I knew you were working. Otherwise I would have asked you, really.'

'Who are you going with?' asked Julie, intrigued.

Wendy actually blushed. It didn't really go with her hennaed hair and red lips.

'With Doug Sandale. You know, the guy who runs the Phoenix?'

Julie vaguely remembered Wendy introducing them. He was cute.

'So how and when did this happen?'

Wendy giggled. 'Well, I went round on Monday night after Bob's sabotage to apologise. I suppose I didn't really need to because of course he didn't know it was thanks to us the council got wind of the play. Anyway, he was really touched and we went for a drink and – well, one thing led to another.'

'Ta-ra! Instead of wrecking your reputation with the local thespians I've led to you pulling dishy Doug. So you don't hate me!'

'Course not. And I really would have asked you and your cop to come tonight if it wasn't for the council meeting.'

'Theatre's not his thing. Perhaps if I get it together with Jonny Drew over the weekend I'll bring him to the next play. He looks like a bit of rough but he's been to university.'

Wendy did her Bette Davis impersonation. 'You've ditched the cop?'

'Don't be daft. He's a terrific shag.'

'So you're going to have them both at once.'

'Not literally.'

Julie laughed at Wendy's expression. She really was quite an innocent.

'Don't be shocked. There's seven nights in a week, after all.'

Good thing she doesn't know about Stevenson.

The leather jacket was waiting for her. The minute she walked through the door there it was on a model. She had to have it.

Collarless, zip fronted and royal blue. She put it on over her navy skirt and green cotton knit top. It looked good, but it could look much better.

Jeans? No, it'd look like she was taking the piss.

She rifled through the rails and came up with a short indigo denim skirt and an underwired black jersey strapless top. Heavy black and silver belt, long and loose to go diagonally from waist to hip.

Sexy as hell. All she needed was a pair of shades and some red lipstick. And in an ideal world, a cigarette dangling from the corner of her mouth. But she had enough bad habits already.

Friday night. The atmosphere was good, just like the last time Julie had been out with her new workmates. But now she was more aware of the relationships between the others and the possibilities relating to herself.

This time Monika came too. She wondered if she was normally included, or whether Mark had asked her to come as a result of their date on Wednesday, or whether Derek had. Did Mark know about Derek? Not that he'd care.

She looked affectionately at her various lovers, past, present and future.

Mark, talking animatedly to John about Wintersea Wanderers' chances the next day. She felt closer to him than ever, especially after his inspired housewarming ceremony, and his equanimity at her abandonment for Bryn and Jonny.

Stevenson, listening to Wendy telling him about the previous night's play. Without Julie's flexibility with regard to lovers, she had obviously stopped squirming over him now she had a man of her own. Julie felt turned on looking at him and wondered if there was any chance of some verbal sex before the night was over.

Monika. She remembered her fingers on her clitoris and her eyelashes fluttered involuntarily. She was still ambivalent as to whether she really wanted to have a scene with her.

Even Derek, now she knew about Monika's game, presented a possibility. He might be in his 50s, she

144

thought, but if you forget the lines and age spots and look at his eyes you could almost be looking at Jonny Drew. He dragged nonchalantly on his cigarette as he listened to Monika. What was she telling him? Maybe about Mark? Did she give verbal as well as Stevenson? Was that all there was to their game or was there something physical as well?

Derek looked up and caught her eye.

'Oh, Julie, I had a drink with young Underwood the other day.'

Don't worry, I remember.

'The man's an idiot and I told him so in no uncertain terms. I warned him there'd be a wall of silence from the reporters and it would bloody well serve him right.'

'I don't think he's even noticed,' said John. 'He's been quiet enough this week anyway getting ready for the new car registration ad supplement.'

'Well, like all little boys he gets off on cars,' said Derek contemptuously. 'Anyway, I told Bob he's lucky to have you on the staff and if he didn't sort himself out you'd be off and I would take great pleasure in telling David why.'

Julie raised an eyebrow. 'Almost seems worth leaving to get him a bollocking.'

'How about a mass resignation?' said Alan. 'All of us or him.'

Claire gave a brittle laugh. 'Nice thought but I'm not risking my pension. What if David said, "OK, off you all go"?'

Julie looked at the older man warmly. 'Thanks, Derek. You're a sweetie.'

Although she was having a good time, she decided to go to step after all. While exercising on top of alcohol wasn't very sensible, she'd only had two glasses of wine and reasoned that the exercise would be a whole lot better for her than another few drinks and a curry. As she rose and made her excuses, the photographer smiled archly.

'Maybe we should all come with you, Julie.'

'Now that would be a sight for sore eyes.'

'It can't be that hard. How long does the class last?'

'Hour and a half. Think you could stand the pace?'

'Anything you can do. But not tonight.'

She wasn't surprised to find Stevenson in the gym's juice bar when she left.

'I had a funny feeling you'd be here.'

He raised his eyebrows. 'I come here a lot, Julie Gibson.'

'Yeah. Especially after the pub.'

'You're right. I just wanted to find out what was going on.'

'Aha! Too much, this week. I'm absolutely shattered.'

'Did you go to step rather than come back with me?'

Julie shook her head. 'No. I just had a feeling that everyone'd be going off for a meal and it'd be too hard for us to escape without it being obvious. I really didn't want to have a lot to eat. What's more, I'm on at seven tomorrow, and I really have had a week of it.'

'Tell all.'

First she got an apple and carrot juice and a peanut butter and beansprout salad roll.

'Sunday I had lunch with Bryn followed by a car fuck. Monday afternoon you know about. After work I had dinner with a guy on Hornbeam who wanted to fuck but I was already meeting Mark, who in fact came back to mine and christened it, as he said, by screwing in every room.'

'He's got an impressive amount of energy. Monika's really pleased with him.'

'Wow, you can tell me about them. I'm sure he's avoiding me. Anyway, Tuesday, thank God, I had the day off but Wednesday I had Bryn on the beach with an audience.'

Laughter bubbled out of his mouth. 'How large an audience?'

She explained about the man at the next table.

'Then I was working last night but tomorrow afternoon I'm going back to the man at Hornbeam.'

'This is the biker you've just done the piece on?'

She nodded and sat back with a sigh. 'God knows why I thought I needed a power shower. Still, me and Mark are cooling it.'

Stevenson nodded with interest. 'You hardly need me to raise your sexual consciousness at the moment.'

'I think it's a bit too raised. I accidentally propositioned Tony Greene the other day.'

Stevenson's thin-lipped smile stretched from ear to ear.

'Great! Accidentally? So if he'd taken you up on it, what would you have done?'

She looked at him sideways and dimpled. 'Actually I find him very attractive – don't you think he is?'

He nodded. 'Sure. If you like older men.'

'Talking of which, I was looking at Derek in the pub tonight, thinking about him and Monika. He's got lovely eyes, and his clothes are so cool. But then I'm like, what am I doing looking at Derek sexually when there's too much on my plate already?'

Stevenson's pale blue eyes danced with amusement. 'You're greedy, Julie. That's what you are.'

'Yeah, you're right. It's like chocolates. Eating two or three should be enough. But I can't stop myself: I always want another one. And another one.'

'At least compulsive sex doesn't make you fat.'

'Exactly.' She looked at her watch. 'I'm on early shift tomorrow. I'm going to shoot.'

She looked up at him from half-closed eyelids. 'If you wanted to come back with me –'

'Oh, no. This is one chocolate you're not having. The rules still apply.'

Really, I don't think I dried myself properly after that shower. My knickers feel definitely damp.

Feeling very smug. Resisted going for a meal after work, did step instead after two glasses of wine, had healthy brown roll and juice after, plus a bit of conversation with Stevenson who – surprise surprise – turned up at gym. Resisted him too. No that's a lie I did ask him back here but I knew he'd say no. Would have liked to show him my new jacket though, specially with nothing else but the denim skirt on – see if it turned him on same way Jonny Drew did me. Well I know it would have done. He seems to think I don't need him at present but I got turned on just telling him about my busy week. Actually the thought of having him round for a meal dressed as above, me doing a lot of walking round in high heels with tits falling out, is getting me going now. Tempted to get vibrator out but might be better to save myself. So looking forward to tomorrow, apart from the work bit.

Chapter Seven

Evening Light, Saturday 29 June

SPATE OF CAR ATTACKS IN TOWN

A SECOND NIGHT of windscreen smashing in the town centre has led police to step up overnight policing.

Last night a total of 12 cars were hit in two locations, Harcourt Street car park and Torridon Square, following on from attacks on six cars on Thursday night in Dovercourt Road.

In each case the windscreens were smashed on the passenger side. Nothing was taken from any of the cars and Superintendent Tony Greene said the incidents can only be put down to 'senseless vandalism'.

It was Julie's first early shift on Saturday and she wasn't impressed. The police and fire voice banks had little to report first thing apart from a chip-pan fire with no casualties and a minor road accident. But 7 a.m. was too early to go round knocking on doors, especially when people had been up all night waving wet teatowels round their kitchen, and she found that the main job was opening the post and chatting to Claire.

She phoned the recorded messages again a couple of hours later and got the bare bones of a vandalism story so she was prepared when she went up to the police station.

Good. Tony Greene was on duty.

Julie hadn't seen him since she'd accidentally tried to bribe him with sex but had already decided how to play it.

Flirting with him was very enjoyable and she wasn't going to stop. The fact that he thought he could have had her added extra spice to the relationship. Nice to think that part of him would always regret turning her down.

He seemed worried about the windshield damage.

'There's no motive for this. Six on Thursday night and twelve last night – what's in it for them? They're not even taking the radios.'

Julie shrugged. 'Well, when they do all we say is, "What's the point of nicking the radio when there are so many stolen they can only get a couple of quid for them?"'

He shook his head. 'Yes, but a couple of these cars had good CD players in as well, and one even had a briefcase in it, for heaven's sake. These vandals were only interested in causing havoc – which they did. Glass everywhere, the motorists couldn't drive home, Wintersea Windscreens going hell for leather –'

'They must be the prime suspects.'

He laughed. 'Nothing would surprise me, but I think that's a bit obvious. I don't like motiveless crime, Julie. Robbery, burglary, even assault, you know what those yobs are after. This is bugging me.'

'It's bugging me, too. Harcourt Road is a bit close to work as far as I'm concerned. I wouldn't want to come out after writing up a night job to find my windscreen done in.'

'Yes. You take care, Julie. Your company car park is a bit dark and lonely at night.'

Oh, how sweet. He's worrying about me.

Another off licence had been done the previous night as well, and the police were studying the shop's CCTV.

'Mind you, the robbers were wearing balaclavas and Jack Clinton said there were no distinguishing marks, so we're not hoping for much there.'

At least the windscreen story would be simple to write up with no victims or witnesses. Julie should have hot-footed it round to Clinton's Wines to get the story from the horse's mouth but she lingered for a chat.

Tony was going to be visiting his mother in one of the town's many retirement homes that afternoon.

'She hardly recognises me, but I like to go at least once a week. My wife's given up coming – though I can't say I blame her. Anyway, she's always off playing golf on Saturdays.'

'Golf! Do you play?'

'No, doesn't interest me at all. Marion's addicted to it, though. That and bridge.' He smiled briefly. 'It means we don't see much of each other – but they say that's what keeps a marriage alive. So what are you up to this afternoon?'

The question hung in the air for a moment while Julie considered what might happen if she said she was free.

She really fancied him. And she'd never had a superintendent.

His marriage might be alive, but not exactly kicking. He'd just made sure she understood that.

In that split second she almost said she was doing nothing. After all, Jonny Drew could wait.

But this was a man who'd never given in to temptation in 30-odd years. He didn't want a one-off, however glorious. If he was going to be unfaithful to his wife, he was going to have a full-blown affair. With all the emotional disaster it would involve.

And in fourteen years of having sex, I've never made that kind of mistake. As much as, right now, I want to.

'Big excitement for me this afternoon. My second trip on a motorbike. On the pillion, I hasten to add. I've even got a new leather jacket.'

Was his smile a shade wistful?

'Great. I don't suppose you've seen the film *The Girl on a Motorcycle*? Marianne Faithfull in black leather having lots of fun on her bike. Of course, you'll be far too young to have seen it.'

He sighed. Maybe thinking she was far too young for him as well?

'No. Funny, someone mentioned Marianne Faithfull the other day – oh, yeah, I remember.'

The Mars Bar.

'So who's the boyfriend with the bike, then? Anyone I know? Not one of my men, I hope.'

Whoops.

'No, it's Jonny Drew. You know, the bike club man? I did a story on it yesterday, with Adam's help. He seems to think it's a great thing for the little yobs.'

'Oh, Jesus, Julie!'

She looked at him, surprised. Not the sort of reaction she would have expected.

He added quickly, 'Is it a treat for you, then, to thank you for doing the article?'

'Not really. I mean, it is a bit of a treat, I suppose – sorry, Tony, I don't really know where you're coming from.'

He had recovered his composure. 'To be honest – Jonny Drew's a nice guy in some ways, but he's rough, Julie. When I first started on the force he was what, about eleven years old, and he was always up to something. He wasn't just a yob, either. He's a darn sight cleverer than I am, to be honest with you, and that came out even then. He was a cool customer, always getting the other kids to do what he wanted.

'When he got to university I thought we'd never see him back in Wintersea. You know what they say about bright kids – if you channel their energy into learning they come good. The trouble with Jonny is he's got a self-destructive streak. He didn't really have to get married. OK, she was pregnant, but it wouldn't be the first time a woman had to bring up a kid on her own. It was as though he just did it for the hell of it, as though he didn't want to have a good job and a decent life. Instead he got into motorbikes, Sandra got into the booze, and they ended up divorced.

'He's not been on the wrong side of the law since he came back from university, or at least nothing official. But some of his friends are nasty pieces of work – well, I expect you know that, seeing as you were asking me about the Anderson killing. He's a wild card, Julie. If you're going to hang out with him, be careful.'

I don't want to be careful, Tony, I want life on the edge. But it's sweet that you care, and you have just made Mr Danger Man sound even more attractive.

The day plodded on. After the police and fire calls were written up Julie had a job out in one of the villages interviewing a ten-year-old girl who'd written to the Prime Minister asking him to save the village school which was due to close. She was a precocious little brat but Julie knew as well as anyone that kids sell papers.

On the upside was the fact that Claire was covering the Wintersea carnival. Julie gave thanks for her police station role as otherwise she could have been landed with that job, which would probably take Claire all day by the time she'd trotted round getting human interest stories and the results of the float competitions.

Two o'clock came at last and Julie was leaving the newsroom when she bumped into Mark on his way in.

'Hey, what are you doing here today?' she asked, surprised.

Of course. Ian Pewsey, one of the sports reporters, was on holiday and Mark was covering the Wanderers match. As he would be going anyway, it meant a free game.

'I'd love to get on to sport, Jules. What do you think the chances are that Ian'll leave?'

'Doubtful. You can always hang on for Bernie to retire. It must only be, what, ten years. Anyway, why are you here?'

'I said I'd meet Mike for a pint first.'

'Are you sure? I think he's gone with Claire to the Wintersea carnival.'

'Oh, sod it. Kit was talking about a sore throat last night. Bet Mike's having to do both jobs.'

Julie hung around in the corridor while Mark went to his desk. Sure enough, Mike had left him a note – Kit had gone down with a cold and he'd have to get to the match as soon as he could after the carnival.

'You'd better have your pre-match drink with me, then. I need a bit of Dutch courage for my Hell's Angels mama impersonation.'

'Oh, it's tonight, is it?'

'Afternoon. He's working till three so I'm going round about four. You ought to see the new leather jacket, Marko. I was just imagining it with my new short denim skirt, high heels and nothing else but red lipstick and shades.'

'Don't make that sound like an invitation unless you mean it.'

She nodded. 'Sorry, that was out of order. But I bet you don't need me in a leather jacket now you're hooked up with Monika.'

They reached the bar and Mark ordered. They sat down in a quiet corner before he answered her.

'I don't know exactly what's going on there, but you obviously do. And I am really a bit pissed off that you didn't feed me that little snippet about you and Monika getting together.'

Julie cleared her throat. 'Sorry. Believe me, I don't know the whole story either. Let's trade leads. You show me yours and I'll show you mine.'

'Right. One. Monika's bisexual. Two, she's having some sort of relationship with Stevenson and he's having one with you but he doesn't screw either of you, but you and Monika have had a scene together. Three, she's screwed the DJ from Hell and Back with another girl. Four, she does the dominatrix for Derek.'

'Dominatrix! Well, I'm not surprised. That was the missing part of the equation as far as I was concerned. God, does he look like a man who wants to be submissive?'

Mark grinned. 'If I was his age I'd have Monika any way I could, I can tell you. But apparently with the drink and all, he needs a bit of extra stimulation.'

'Wow. OK, I'll come clean about me and Stevenson.'

She explained about the game.

'I don't know about this, Jules. It's a bit like *Dangerous Liaisons*. We're all fucking each other in some way. I wouldn't mind if it wasn't for the fact that everyone's telling everyone else what they're up to.'

'Excuse me? I seem to remember a couple of weeks ago you were asking me for a speech on Yorkshire Cops I Have Fucked and when I wouldn't give you complained you wouldn't mind if anyone talked about you. That's why I told Monika about your ice-cream trick.'

He held up his hands. 'OK! And I'm glad you did. She's a real *überfrau*, or whatever they say in Denmark. But right now I feel that whatever I do with Monika, she'll tell Derek and Stevenson, then he'll tell you. It's pervy.'

'If it's any consolation, all I know is that she told Stevenson she was impressed by your stamina. I have to say that after last Monday I can only agree.'

Mark looked only modestly conceited.

She finished her drink and put her glass down firmly. 'So, you might as well tell me yourself. What did superwoman do for you? Come on, Mark. Get me warmed up for Jonny Drew. If the match is boring you can think of me with that bike vibrating underneath my pussy which you've revved up already.'

He sighed and moved closer to her as he lowered his voice.

'We went to the Breaker Bar and had a couple of cocktails. We left to go for something to eat and decided to walk along the beach up to Paolo's Pizzas. It was about nine, still light. As usual she's in high heels, practically no skirt and her legs look like stilts. Her arm goes round my back then she's got her hand on my arse, which is very nice, so I do the same to her except my hand actually disappears up inside the skirt and fuck me she's not wearing any knickers. Straight away I'm rock solid and wondering how I'm going to get through a pizza before we even talk about whose place we're going to when she turns towards me with that wicked smile and says we better fuck before we eat. I'm like, well, where? Under the pier, she says, with the druggies – they won't give a shit. Or in the shelter, but it's a bit busy. No, even better, let's get a cab to Paolo's. So she's whistling down this black cab and telling him to drive round and shut the partition and she'll tell him when we're ready and we're in the cab and she's on the floor pulling her skirt up and I'm thinking if we get near a bus the top deck will see everything but bollocks I haven't got my name written on my back and, Jules, she's shaved her pubes off. Straight away I want to get in there, no messing around, and I don't think she wanted me to hang about either. I give her a bit of a fingering as well and I come in about ninety seconds and so does she.

'So she just pulls her skirt down and knocks on the partition and directs him to Paolo's and there's me with this half-full johnny in my hand thinking I should have left it on and buttoned up. She just laughs and takes it and knots it and puts it in her handbag.

'I don't think I ever enjoyed a pizza so much. I mean, it's not like the usual first date when you're thinking, will we or won't we? So, we're having a normal conversation and eating and drinking then she says, "OK, that's the first hole satisfied, which one do you fancy next?"

'We finish and go back to her place and she opens this drawer and there's a load of leather gear in there and a mask and whips, for God's sake, and I'm thinking, Oh no, but all she's doing is getting out some KY and a vibrator. "Do you like anal sex?" she's asking me. Jesus, I've never done it before, so I tell the truth but like all men I've always fantasised about it. This time we both strip off and she puts some loud music on which is really throbbing through me and she's dancing in a really sexy way and it's making me so bloody horny. She sounds like she really enjoys me lubricating her and I try a finger and then another and she's no anal virgin, I can tell you. Mind you, I have to say I did think of you, Jules – your arse is nicer than hers. And she's telling me about being Derek's dominatrix and that sometimes she likes a bit of pain herself, so while she's attacking her front with the vibrator I push my cock slowly up her arse and she screams a bit but I think that's part of it. I get my confidence and go in long and steady and she's pushing herself back on me and writhing around and I'm grabbing her buttocks and digging my nails in and she's crying out for more. I know you can't understand, Jules, but that tight little hole is magic. Anyway, I dig harder and she's turning up the vibrator and what with the loud music and her shouting and the buzzing I don't know whether I'm in heaven or hell and back and I come like it's been weeks instead of a couple of hours.

'Then she changes the music for something quieter and we just chill for a bit and I'm thinking maybe I better get home and then she's stroking me again and saying, "Oh, well, only one hole left." I can't believe I can get hard again but I do and she gives me that bad girl look and goes over to her drawer and puts on this black mask, over her eyes like giant shades, a wide black leather choker and long black leather gloves. She goes down on me and all I can really see of her is the black mask and choker and black leather hands which incidentally are squeezing my balls gently and those dark lips round my cock and I've shot my load again. Only she hasn't come this time so fair's fair I do my turn with the tongue and knackered as I am that shaven slit is just beautiful. Anyway, we called it a score draw and I went home.'

He looked at his watch. 'And talking of score draws, it's time I got off to the ground. So now you know, and if that hasn't got you in the mood for sitting on black leather I don't know what will.'

She chuckled. 'Too right. Good thing I'm not the jealous type or I'd be, like, but you only came once with me on Monday! Anyway, very impressive. Looks like she's training you up for three in a bed.'

'Yeah, or a golf course. I'll tell you what, though, Gibbo, if I'm still hanging in there when you've finished with the biker and the cop, three in a bed would be a pretty good idea, wouldn't it?'

Oh, brilliant idea. Us three in the bed, Derek manacled to the wall and Stevenson taking the photos. Something for the staff magazine.

With the red lips and shades as well as the leather jacket, Julie felt she needed the appropriate soundtrack as she drove to Jonny's house. And loud. With the windows wound down she felt like a baseball-capped teenager thumping her bass around town. She realised why they did it. It was fun.

He was outside already, doing something to the bike, wearing what appeared to be his uniform: white T-shirt and jeans. The music announced her arrival before she'd even turned the corner of Elm View Road. She took the corner too fast; hell, she had an image to live up to.

'Hiya, Julie.' His devastating eyes lit up and his large mouth smiled as she got out the car. Not easy in a tight short skirt. It would be even more fun getting adjusted on the bike. 'You look delicious.'

He must have chosen the word deliberately to send a shudder through her.

If you want a taste you can have one now, especially as Mark's little story whet my appetite and wet my knickers. But I bet I'll be sweeter and juicier after I've been on the bike.

'Convenient you having a leather jacket,' he teased.

'If you're a betting man you'd have money on me having bought it specially,' she answered.

He gave her an unfathomable look. 'I am a betting man, Julie – did you know or did you just guess?'

'How on earth could I know?'

He shrugged and laughed. 'Well, you were talking about interviewing my ex. She might have told you about that particular naughty habit of mine.'

Julie pushed the shades on to the top of her head. 'She didn't. I haven't managed to get hold of her. What other naughty habits do you have?'

Dimples formed on his cheeks. 'I suppose wining, dining and propositioning journalists who come round asking questions about my old mates could be one of them.'

'I suppose journalists who come round and tell you they fancy you have only themselves to blame.'

'For sure.' He picked two helmets off the ground next to the bike. 'It's not often women say they want me to take them for a ride. Where do you want to go?'

Julie reached out for the helmet and her hand closed around one of his.

'How about showing me the coastline? I only seem to see it in little sections, like snapshots.'

'If you like. Though it's hardly the Corniche.'

She shrugged. 'We're on your patch. You take me where you like.'

Take me to the top of the hill and let me float down while I'm looking into your warm blue eyes.

He went inside and got his leather jacket, closing the door behind him. Julie folded her arms and pouted at him.

'What? What's wrong?'

'Well, it's just that you looked so sexy without your T-shirt on. With your jacket, I mean.'

Jonny laughed. 'You kill me, Julie. It's a long time since a woman's been as up front with me as you are.'

'So does that mean you take the T-shirt off?'

He put his jacket over his T-shirt and then for the first time he put his arms round her, pulling her towards him. Their faces were inches apart.

'I'm keeping it on for now, while I take you down town. But I'll take it off later. As long as you take your top off too.'

'You can put money on it. I'll take off whatever you like.'

Slowly their lips lifted towards each other and met, tentatively at first. They kissed experimentally, dry mouthed. Julie's sex was acting as though it already had a motorbike vibrating underneath it. His mouth explored along her lips and then his tongue parted them and she let herself go in the kiss, pulling his tongue inside her and then taking her turn to lick along his soft lips and around his eager mouth.

'If we're going to be doing any more of this we've got to get in the house,' he murmured.

'You're worried about your reputation?'

He laughed. 'Shit, that can only get better. This is upping my image one hundred per cent. What I'm worried about is messing my trousers.'

'You know how to talk nicely to a girl, Mr Drew.'

'I've always been a sweet talker. Get that helmet on and let's get out of here before I embarrass myself.'

He got on the bike and kicked the starter. Julie climbed

on behind him, her skirt up round her thighs as she spread her legs, and put her arms around him.

So, I know I can hold on to the bar behind me. I reckon I'd look pretty cool doing that. But just now I think I'll have the warmth of flesh and muscle under T-shirt, thanks all the same.

They roared round the corner, back in the direction Julie had come from, past the crescent with its boarded-up houses. A gang of youths drinking out of cans in the front garden of one of those looked up and called as they passed, and Jonny raised an arm in greeting.

For heaven's sake, don't tell me those yobs communicate with normal people.

They went through the town centre, past the office and the Vaults. Julie was co-starring in a remake of *The Wild One*, and she had no complaints about Jonny as a Marlon Brando substitute.

He turned down by the sea front and they cruised along the promenade slowly, past the pier, then he pulled into a parking space just in front of the funfair.

Taking off his helmet, he turned and smiled lazily at Julie. 'Bet you haven't had the real seaside experience yet. Let me get you a candy floss.'

He jumped off the bike and took Julie's helmet from her. She was amused to see that he did actually go up to the candy-floss stall, but only to shake hands with the guy in charge. He spoke to him then handed over the helmets and slapped him on the shoulder.

'Come on, babe, let's get our adrenalin going,' he said as he took Julie's hand.

Oh, how sweet. He just called me babe. What am I, a piglet? And here we are, hand-holding in public. Serves you right for going after a bit of rough. God knows what we look like. The wild one and the bimbo in the short skirt and leather jacket.

It was a role she quite enjoyed playing.

How long was it since she'd been to a funfair? Ten years? Each stall or ride was playing its own music and it was cacophonous but hugely enjoyable. Jonny won an ugly stuffed penguin on the rifle range and presented it to Julie. She spectacularly failed at everything she tried from shooting to bowling to quoit throwing, but happily accepted a consolation ice cream.

'Have your fortune told,' he said laughing as they came across Madame Zora's tent. 'See if we were meant for each other.'

She leant back provocatively against the railing nearby and licked her ice cream, then her red lips.

'There's a better way to find out if we were meant for each other, Jonny.'

He put his free hand on her waist where her top didn't quite meet her skirt and rubbed her skin lightly. It gave her goosepimples.

'Don't worry, we'll get round to that. Go on, see what Madame Zora says.'

I must be totally nuts coming in here. This woman's a complete charlatan, that's obvious. Still, maybe I could write a little piece about it?

Prediction: she was going to live for a long time. She was going to get married and have three children. She was going to go overseas, maybe to work. Although she would never be rich, she would be happy.

OK, Madame, that's the standard patter for youngish women without wedding rings.

Present: she was in trouble. There were many men in her life. One of them wore a uniform. One of them meant trouble. Danger loomed. She must be careful.

'I see fire. Breaking glass. Big trouble. Be careful, miss.'

Trouble from a man in uniform? That had to be Tony Greene. Obviously she'd be screwing him on his office floor, fire would break out in the station and they'd have to jump out the window.

As if.

Jonny was amused by the many men in her life. 'She's got you to a T, Julie. After all, you told me that I'd be number four in your life.'

'Not in so many words. Anyway, how do I know you're not the one who's going to cause the trouble?'

'You never know. Nice to think you're living danger-ously though, isn't it? And on that note, I think we ought to hit the Big Wheel.'

'I'm scared of heights.'

'Heights, bikes, what else are you afraid of?'

'What have you got?'

He laughed delightedly. 'Come on. It might not be the Millennium Wheel but it's brilliant.'

The ride was just about to start and they climbed in quickly. The attendant pulled the bar down over their legs. It didn't reach to the top of Julie's skirt.

'How very convenient,' observed Jonny, as the wheel slowly creaked into life.

What?

He put his arm round her and snuggled into her as far as he could. 'I'm glad you wore that short skirt.'

His other hand reached over and caressed her thigh.

'Don't you think someone might see?'

He laughed. 'How much can you see of the other people on here?'

True.

His hand eased itself between her legs and they fell apart automatically at his touch. Stroking her soft flesh, he moved upwards surely and swiftly to rub gently at the almost non-existent crotch of her G-string, drawing his breath in sharply when his fingers encountered the tiny scrap of silk.

Julie whimpered, her eyes closed, as his tantalising touch stroked her harder. She could feel the slick wetness oozing out of her and guessed it must be evident to his fingers. He lost no time in moving the silk string aside and probing blindly with his fingers to find the source of the moisture.

'Jonny. You'll rock the car. We'll fall out.'

He laughed softly. 'Don't worry, babe. I'm just going to rock that little button of yours.' His fingers moved to

163

her clitoris and circled gently, then harder. 'Is that OK? Have you ever come up in the air before?'

'Only on Concorde. No, I'm joking. You might call yourself an innocent but you've done this before.'

'Not on the Big Wheel. I wonder if you can come before it ends. How quickly can you come?'

Two and a half minutes, apparently. Not that I'm telling you. Anyway I'm not in the mood for speech. The carriage is rocking backwards and forwards, the whole bloody wheel's going round and my clit's on fire. Oh, shit, shouldn't have opened my eyes. No, it's OK, I'm not feeling vertigo. Just like I really am going to come, but not just yet. Anyway, we're getting dangerously near the bottom again.

Jonny moved his hand slightly as the wheel came down to ground level and put it back as they rose out of easy sight of anyone who might be watching. His assured fingers dipped in her wetness and stroked back up to her clitoris enough times to bring her almost to the brink. She moaned and he took the hint and started rubbing her clit harder.

'Open your eyes and look down while you come, babe. Take those sunglasses off. I want to see your eyes.'

She obeyed, near enough to orgasm that her eyes had opened involuntarily, although she was only half aware that Wintersea was spread out before her as they climbed halfway up to the summit.

'Come for me, babe. Look at me, look down. You feel fucking lovely down there, babe. I can't wait to get up inside you. You're wet and hard down there. Come on, we're at the top. Come on, Julie, come at the top. Brilliant, you've done it right on cue. You are one beautiful babe.'

He laughed with admiration as she pulsed against his hand, then he moved it and raised it to his mouth.

'Tastes great. Knew it would. I really want to get my tongue down inside you, Julie.'

'Is that all?' she asked lazily.

'No. Come on, let's get down. I want to get the fuck

out of here and get to somewhere a bit more secluded. And give you your trip down the Riviera.'

The wheel stopped and they got out and headed for the candy-floss stall. Julie resumed her shades and they picked up the helmets.

'Here you are, darling, on the house.'

'Oh, no, thanks, I mean I can't do the bike with one hand. I don't even know what to do with this.'

She held up the penguin.

Jonny exchanged amused glances with his friend. 'She doesn't do brave, Fred.'

'Go on. What's she doing with you, then?'

'You know, my other charms. See you, mate.' He took the penguin from her and put it inside his jacket. 'Come on, Julie. All you've got to do is hang on behind, and you can hold that in one hand as well and eat it when we get there.'

'Look, I really am not some girlie scaredy-cat. I just don't normally do this sort of thing.'

'Don't worry about it. Just enjoy the Riviera experience.'

He revved up and Julie held on for dear life, the candy floss waving in the breeze like a pennant behind her back.

First he carried on slowly eastward along what was left of the promenade. It wasn't long before the beach ended and the road ahead climbed steeply parallel to the top of the cliffs, passing the danger barriers where the landslip had been. He pulled into a parking area when they reached the summit.

'That's it for this end. The road goes inland now and you can't see anything. The sea looks pretty from here, though, doesn't it?'

It was Mediterranean blue, reflecting the sky. Looking down and to the west the whole town spread out before them: fronting the sea the caravan site, the funfair, the pier, the pleasure gardens, the harbour, the rocky beach and finally the sand dunes at Wintersea Point. Behind, the town sprawled out, windows and white buildings glittering in the early-evening sun. It looked clean and prosperous, its decay disguised by distance.

Jonny kicked the starter pedal again. 'Wintersea Point, here we come.'

Back along the promenade, past the gardens, looping round the narrow streets of the harbour and again near the beach, the gap widening as they approached the grassy scrub that backed on to the sand dunes at Wintersea Point. Jonny slowed right down and rode the bike over the bumpy grassland on a track through the gorse and briar and willowherb, stopping as he reached the dunes.

Pulling off his helmet, he propped the bike on its stand and took Julie's helmet off. She brought the candy floss up to her mouth and licked at it provocatively.

'You're not the only one getting your mouth round some sweetness, babe,' he murmured, his hands on her zip.

'Here? Is this what you call secluded?'

She looked round. True, they were now quite a way from the road and shielded by the bushes from the footpath through the scrub. The beach too was hidden by the dunes.

'Don't worry. There'll be no-one around at this time of day.'

She turned back and smiled at him, taking another wisp of spun sugar and holding it out to him. Her zip was now all the way down and he was sliding her skirt down under her belt and over her hips.

'No thanks. I want to taste you. Jesus, that is something else.'

The red silk G-string and the black and silver bullet belt obviously hit the spot.

He sat her backwards on the bike and stood looking at her. Slowly she undid the bows either side of the G-string one by one and pulled it out from under her and let it fall on to the grass.

166

'With that candy floss you look like some naughty kid. Lie back for me, Julie. I want my tongue inside you.'

She put her head down on the front seat and opened her legs, still eating as though unconcerned at what was about to happen. The leather seat was warm and her pussy was still vibrating from the bike's thrumming beneath it. But not so much that she didn't feel the warmth of his face as he knelt on the grass in front of her, holding her lips apart with his hands, and the heat of his breath as he moved his tongue towards her sex.

Julie closed her eyes and let her arms fall down either side of the bike, dropping the candy floss. The smell of leather and engine oil was heightened by the sun, now low in the sky behind her, and mingled with the coconut-oil scent of the gorse bushes. A skylark warbled overhead and Jonny's tongue connected with her clitoris and Julie clicked on line, on message and on heat.

He pushed his hands underneath her buttocks and lifted her so his mouth could reach her. Rimming her vulva lazily with his tongue, he seemed to hesitate before entering her for the first time with it, exploring her from inside. The delicate skin of her pussy was a mass of sensitised nerve endings and all Julie could do was thrash her head from side to side.

I wonder if he wants me to talk to him. I don't want to. I just want to feel his hot tongue pushing in and out of me. Lapping at my clit. I am just so sensitive to him. I could almost come now; his tongue's on my clit so gently it's unbearable. Down to my cunt. I hope he likes the taste of my juice because there's so much of it, it's running down on to the seat. Fuck me, Jonny.

'OK.'

So I do talk out loud when I'm excited.

He pulled her up off the bike and they kissed. His mouth was luscious and sticky with her nectar.

'You look delicious, you feel delicious, and you taste delicious. What are you like to fuck?'

167

'You'll have to tell me, but even if I'm a disappointment three out of four's not bad.'

He laughed and pulled her jacket off her shoulders. 'I want to see your tits first.'

The black top fastened with hooks and eyes at the back. She let him undo it.

'Christ, it's like a never-ending bra strap.' The last hook unclasped itself and he pulled the top away from her breasts. 'Oh, beautiful.'

'Don't forget you were going to take your T-shirt off as well.'

He pulled his jacket off impatiently and pulled his T-shirt over his head. His muscles rippled under smooth golden skin.

'Jacket back on,' she ordered. He smiled and obeyed. Julie put her jacket back on too, leaving it open to frame her breasts.

'I wanted you the first time I saw you like that,' she told him as she moved her hands down to his zip.

'You're not kidding?'

'The hell I am. Truth is I wanted you the first time I saw you standing on your doorstep, when I looked at your eyes, before I even had time to look at your body.'

'My eyes? Because they're blue?'

She reached inside his zip. No underwear. Just a warm, hard cock.

'Yeah. Baby-blue eyes. I don't suppose I'm the first woman to fall for those.'

She slid his jeans down to his thighs. Never mind his eyes, his cock was blushing baby pink, crowned with carmine. Slender but long, rising out of a wheatfield of blond curls.

'Or for this.'

She sat back on the bike again and opened her legs. 'So are you coming in or what?'

His lovely big mouth parted in a smile. 'If you've never fucked on a motorbike before, there's only one way to travel.'

168

Moving her gently off the seat he kicked the starter and the engine growled quietly.

'Get on and grab the handlebars,' he told her. She stood over the back of the seat and leant forwards. Her arse rose and the bike throbbed gently against her thigh. Nothing happened behind her and she imagined him contemplating the view of her two orifices. She was impatient for him to be inside her. The bike pulsing beneath her underlined the fast beating of her heart. She wanted him to ride her hard, as hard as she could take it.

Then his hands were on her hips and he was driving inside her. He pushed her further forwards until the warm pulsating tank was against her clitoris.

'How's that? Have you got your clit on it?' he asked breathlessly as he pushed in and out of her.

'I have. And how it is, is fantastic.'

'Best fuck you ever had?'

Her breath was coming so quickly it was hard to speak, like trying to sing when you were doing step.

'Best since the one up against the washing machine on spin cycle.'

He laughed. And laughed. Thank God it didn't stop him from ramming into her.

'Bet I can beat your washing machine.'

He leant over her shoulders and suddenly her clitoris felt like it was taking off, Apollo 2000, as he revved the engine harder.

'Coming yet, Julie? Yes, you are, I can feel it. Wait for me, babe.'

I'm time and tide, Jonny Drew, and I can wait for no man. And I want to come first because I want you to keep ramming hard inside me while I explode around you, and I want you to feel how powerfully your cock has made my muscles convulse and spasm so that you come as hard as I am.

Journalist or not I can't describe the orgasm Jonny gave me yesterday. It was like being fucked from behind with a cock that instinctively catches your G-spot, while at the same time rubbing a sandblaster over your clit. And I thought that shower was powerful, God knows I probably won't even feel it after having that bike shuddering on me. He wanted me to wait for him but I'm glad I didn't because it took for ever, I mean it wasn't only the biggest but it was the longest orgasm I've ever had. Then, I still can't believe this, we swam – nude – in the sea. The beach by the dunes is a nudist beach, he goes there a lot. First time I've swum completely naked, not even a bikini bottom, it was good. He's a brilliant swimmer. Went back to his place after for dinner, he'd bought it already, steak and salad and French bread and wine. He cooked it rare and bloody and we talked for ages. I just don't know what to think about him. In one way he is a bit of rough, but in another way he's smart and even worldly. He talked about France, he loves it, and goes over on the bike a lot. Course, he likes the food and wine. We talked about films and books, for God's sake, and growing up. He teased me about being middle class. It was funny him talking about being a tearaway as a kid after Tony had already told me. The great thing is he's so relaxed and spontaneous. Have to say I felt a bit disloyal to Bryn, specially as can't help comparing his intensity and strong smouldering silence with Jonny's carelessness. Stayed the night, God knows if the neighbours noticed my car, don't want them nudging and winking when I have to find more material for next week's Julie Gibson Weekend Feature. Perhaps I ought to do love in the time of squalor: reporter uncovers sex-crazed biker on run-down council estate.

Came home after breakfast (two bits of toast, butter and jam – after all that French bread and steak last night! What about the mighty arse?), read papers and chilled, napped on balcony – after all, it must have been two by the time we got to bed. And for the record did an encore this morning. Not on the bike, in bed.

I could seriously go for him, but then I really like Bryn too. He is different, though. Didn't wait for him to ask me out again, washed up breakfast things then just gave him a kiss, said had to go and I'd call him. He smiled – God, those eyes – as though he knew what I was up to and said, good, drive carefully. And that was that.

Wonder how long I can last before I phone him? I'll try to hang on till Tuesday.

Chapter Eight

Evening Light, Monday 1 July

RIOT!!! ESTATE ERUPTS IN CHAOS

by reporting team Julie Gibson, Claire Johnson, Derek West and Mark Williams

AN ORGY of crime and violence shattered the peace of the Hornbeam Estate last night.

While residents slept a gang of youths prowled around the estate attacking property, cars and local shops:

- The Hornbeam Minimart was broken into and looted
- Cars were set on fire
- Windows were smashed
- Youths wielding baseball bats roamed the streets

Residents who were woken by the noise of the rioting youths were afraid to leave their homes.

The mob dispersed after police turned up in full riot gear, and no arrests were made. Chief Inspector Adam

Arnside said this morning that police were devoting 100 per cent of their energies to investigating the incidents. However, he was keen to stress that he believed it was just youthful high spirits running out of control due to the continued hot weather, fuelled by drink.

'Don't you just love this,' breathed Mark, as he and Julie met in the middle of Ash Crescent, having started knocking on doors either end of the street. 'Bet you're glad I dragged you from the gloom of the frozen north down to this seething mass of unrest and violence.'

'You're not joking,' responded Julie.

They were both high on adrenalin generated by the palpable tension on the estate. The first news of it was when Wendy came in from her early trip to the fire station with news of burnt-out cars. Julie had been despatched to the police station early while the rest of the reporters phoned round to find out what was going on.

Adam confirmed there had been what he called an incident the previous night. Julie got as many details as she could then hotfooted it back to the newsroom and wrote them up. Derek and Claire had already gone round to the estate and were phoning in scene-of-the-action descriptions and quotes from the shopkeeper, owners of burnt-out cars and any residents who would comment. Together Julie and Mark pulled the strands of the story together for the 11 a.m. deadline and then went out to the estate to take over the house-to-house calls from the other two.

Leaving the buzz and nervous energy of the newsroom only to soak in the edgy atmosphere of the estate was almost intoxicating.

'You can understand why people want to be war correspondents,' enthused Mark. 'It's that feeling that danger could strike at any minute.'

'Yeah. Life on the edge.'

'That's right! Perhaps that's what I should try to get into.'

She looked at him sardonically. 'The other day you said you really wanted to get into sport. Give it another week and I expect you'll decide you want to be a train driver, but don't worry, Mark, by the time you grow up you'll have picked something else. Come on, let's do Sycamore.'

It wasn't coincidence that Julie took the odd side of the street – it was the one Sandra Drew lived on. And for once she was at home.

'Hello, I'm Julie Gibson from the *Evening Light*. I wonder if you heard or saw anything of the disturbances last night, Mrs Drew.'

Sandra Drew looked at her suspiciously. 'How do you know my name?'

Sod it. I was going to slip in the other bit later.

Julie explained she'd been trying to talk to her about the death of her partner.

'Well, you're wasting your time. On both counts. I didn't see anything last night and I didn't see anything on the night Greg died either.'

Sandra Drew was a washed-out blonde, her natural fairness spoilt by brassy peroxide. Her pale face was reddened by broken veins and her eyes were slightly bloodshot. There was a pinched look to her nose and her tight-lipped mouth was surrounded by premature lines. Tony Greene had said she was a drunk; that would explain her wasted features. After all, she must only have been in her early 40s.

Julie could see in her face the remnants of a delicately pretty woman, one who Jonny would have been attracted to. She felt oddly guilty looking at her, as though she was a mistress sizing up her lover's wife.

'I understand you'd only been living with Mr Anderson for a year or so? You must have been devastated when he was murdered.'

The other woman narrowed her eyes. 'I just told you you're wasting your time.'

Persistence, persistence. The most worthwhile quality in a journalist.

'Sure. The only thing is, I wondered if you had a photo of Greg? We don't seem to have one on file. I'd bring it straight back.'

'I hope you're joking. Someone else was down here just after it all happened and I told them the same thing. Read my lips. You – are – wasting – your – time. And I'll tell you something else,' she added venomously. 'You're wasting your bloody time with my husband as well. He's no good, never was and never will be. He ruined my life and he'll do the same to yours if you let him.'

She slammed the door. Shaken, Julie walked slowly down the garden path.

Mark came towards her. 'Did you get something from her? This is a bloody dead loss, I reckon.'

'No, she says she didn't see anything.'

'That's what they all say. Either that or they daren't say anything for fear of a brick through their window. Hey, are you all right?'

Julie smiled briefly. 'Sure. Look, it's half twelve. I think I'll call it lunchtime and pop round and see if Jonny's in.'

Mark shook his head. 'A woman obsessed. But if you're packing in so am I, which means I get to take the car, so how're you getting back? And what if bully Bob says we should have stayed longer? We've only been here for an hour.'

Think, think.

'Idea. You phone Monika and see if she'll meet you in Bubbles. Then you can park in the precinct car park – I'll pay, for God's sake – and meet me back here in an hour. Bob doesn't even have to know we've had a lunch break.'

He was already banging out numbers. 'You're a genius, Gibson. Monika Neilsen, please!'

* * *

'Had a feeling I might hear from you today,' teased Jonny. 'Did I see anything of what was going on last night? Do I have any idea who was involved? Is there something that might have sparked off the riot?'

She sat at the table opposite him. He was eating bread and cheese.

'You're asking all the right questions. Maybe you should have been a journalist.'

He snorted. 'When you live in trouble alley you're used to reporters sniffing around, always asking the same old thing. Hang on, let me get you a plate and knife.'

Julie took a chunk of bread and a piece of cheese from the board on the table and ate hungrily.

'Did you hear anything?'

He smiled. Surely his eyes could have set the estate on fire.

'Slept like a baby. Sleeping the sleep of the just.'

'I just spoke to your wife. Ex-wife. Whatever.'

He looked enquiringly at her. 'And? Bet you got a lot from her.'

'Nothing about the riot. Or the murder. Hey, you wouldn't have a photo of Greg, would you?'

'Bound to. We went on holiday together once. St Austell. I'll find it for you.'

'You star.' Julie cut another piece of cheese. 'By the way, your wife gave me a bit of a mouthful about you. She knows I'm seeing you and told me to watch out because you ruined her life.'

He finished chewing his bread and laughed shortly. 'Well, it's hardly surprising she knows about us. For one thing we had our tongues down each other's throats right outside the front door on Saturday afternoon. And your car was here all night. Even someone as intellectually challenged as Sandra can put two and two together.'

'Fair enough. So did you ruin her life?'

He blew out his cheeks. 'Interesting question. Perhaps she ruined mine. More likely neither of us were going to amount to anything anyway.'

The kettle boiled and he got up and made coffee in silence, bringing it to the table with milk and sugar. Julie waited.

'I'll tell you a story. I told you already about the kid. Well, when she first told me she was pregnant I told her to get rid of it; I didn't want to know.

'That was in the summer. I went back to university in October – it was my last year. My life was sorted: I was all set to get a good degree, and then I was going on to teacher training college.

'So I came back at Christmas and there's Sandra nearly five months gone. She said she tried to get rid of it, stupid things like drinking gin and sitting in hot baths, but it hadn't worked. Why the bloody hell she hadn't gone to the doctor to get an abortion I'll never know. Unless she really wanted the baby.

'My mum told me to wash my hands of her. She wanted me to go back to London, finish my degree, do the teaching course and just stay away. But I'd been going out with Sandra since I was sixteen. I was fond of her, in my way. Part of me felt guilty, and part of me agreed with Mum.

'Guilt – or whatever – won. We got married and got this house – but I did go back and finish my degree.' He laughed bitterly. 'I'm not even sure how I managed to pass the exams. I felt that once I came back here afterwards my life would be over. I went out nearly every night, usually drinking myself into a stupor.

'Charlie was born while I was in London. I wasn't really interested, to be honest. By the time I got my finals out the way and came back he was six weeks old.'

His voice softened. 'He was adorable. I knew everything was going to be all right. I decided that we'd just have to be on the breadline a bit longer, and applied to do the teaching course in Brighton. Then I realised that Sandra was hitting the bottle.

'She blamed it on me, of course. Because I wasn't there when she'd had the baby, because I made her feel that she trapped me, you name it, I got it. We had an almighty row one night and I thought, Fuck it, I can't go off to college five days a week and leave Charlie with this drunk. So I signed on.

'Then Charlie died. She blamed me, saying it was because I told her to get rid of him. I blamed her for drinking while she breastfed him. God knows, no-one was to blame. It was a cot death, just bad luck.

'We still rubbed along all right for a few years, till the night of Sonny Boy Burton's party. He was a boxer, could have been a contender. I used to hang round the gym and was in with that crowd. So anyway we're at this party, Sandra's pissed before we get there, of course, and she starts coming on to Sonny. They disappear and I think, Oh, fuck it, I don't care if he has her, and I get another few drinks down me. But time's going on and I head for one of the bedrooms.

'Sandra's on the bed and someone I don't know is fucking her. Her skirt's up round her waist and her blouse is open with her tits hanging out. There are four or five other men in the room. She sees me and smiles and says, "Join the queue." One of the other men who I don't know says, "Yeah, wait your turn, man."

'I wonder how many have had her already. I just say, "No, thanks, mate, I'm not interested; she's a real slag."

'Sonny comes in the room and does a double take when he sees me. Now we're talking big bruising heavy-weight here, and clever Jonny takes a swing at him. Very smart. Next thing I'm on the deck out cold.'

He looked evenly at Julie. 'I don't know how long I'm out for. All I do know is that when I come round she's still on the bed, there's a different man fucking her and another one's got his dick in her mouth and she looks like she's loving it.

'And that's how I ruined her life.'

Julie was silent.

'And that's how she ruined mine.' He sighed. 'Nasty class of people round here, don't you think?'

'What I don't understand –' Julie looked up, puzzled '– is why you stayed with her after that.'

He drunk his coffee and gave her a candid look.

'Neither do I.'

He moved to the kitchen and started to wash up. Julie trailed after him. 'You were still young. You could have gone to college after all. You could have moved away, started a new life.'

'Yeah. But I'd started working at Tommy McNally's bike shop by then, and, believe it or not, I was doing a couple of evening classes, keeping my brain ticking over.'

'Really?' she said, intrigued. 'Like what?'

'Politics and philosophy. I was sort of brought up with it – my mum was a real hardline socialist. When I was a kid she used to cart me up to London on demonstrations with her – the Vietnam War and so on – which was a real blast. I didn't really go along with everything she believed in, but as I grew up I had some ideas of my own I wanted to put a shape to. There was one brilliant teacher and some of the other students were really interesting people. It kept me going.'

He wiped his hands on a teatowel. 'Or perhaps it was just easier to stay than to go and start a new life. It was easy leaving home at eighteen. At twenty-five, I thought I was too old to start again. Or perhaps I was just lazy.'

'Or self-destructive.' She blurted out Tony Greene's verdict before even thinking.

But Jonny smiled, his eyes lighting up for the first time since he started his story.

'Nice one, babe. That's me all over. I'll piss on my chips instead of getting up for the vinegar.'

He put his arms round her neck. 'Don't feel sorry for me, Julie. I've done all right in a lot of ways. And some of us aren't destined to be teachers with nice houses and a cosy family. I don't think I was.'

They kissed and Julie realised to her horror that she'd been turned on by his description of his wife's orgy. He pressed his rigid cock against her and she wondered if that was what had aroused him as well.

'We'd better stop this. I've got a shop to open in –' he looked at his watch '– ten minutes.'

'How quickly can you come?'

He laughed, remembering, but shook his head. 'I really don't want to rush it with you. Me and Sandra both screwed around but apart from that one occasion we kept our little indiscretions from each other. Which usually meant quickies in cars or hand jobs in toilets. So I think I sort of deserve to spend a little time when we make love. If that's all right by you.'

Just don't say make love because I'm not being very sensible at the moment. And don't look at me with those blue eyes because I'm not so much self-destructing as melting before them.

Three Post-its on the monitor.

Pls phone Bryn.

Bryn. Already left msg.

Phone Bryn asap.

'You called?'

'Don't you spend any time in your office?'

'Maybe if your force didn't spend so much time in theirs I might not have to go out reporting on riots.'

'Come on, it was hardly a riot.'

Julie laughed disbelievingly. 'Yeah, I know the official line. And I know you don't want to talk about it, so let's change the subject. Are you missing me?'

'Like a hole in the head. No, seriously, I am. Say you're free tonight.'

'Let's check the diary. But aren't you on standby waiting for the Hornbeam Estate to erupt into a second night of violence?'

'Don't you mean an orgy of crime and violence? Bet you were responsible for that phrase.'

She giggled. 'Of course. Slowly but surely I'm trying

to eroticise the language of the newsroom. Anyway, glad you read my work.'

'So what about tonight? I've been working so hard I deserve a good night out, though Monday's a crap night in this town.'

'There's always bingo.'

'Or dancing on the pier to Terry Trilby's organ.'

Julie swivelled her chair round to face the wall and lowered her voice. 'Or my place.'

'Best idea yet. What time?'

'Well, if you deserve a good night, we'd better include dinner. I could cook it. But if you deserve a *really* good night, we could get a takeaway.'

'That sounds perfect. So, what time? About half-seven?'

'OK. I'll get some wine in and we'll think about the takeaway when you arrive.'

She put the phone down and it rang again immediately.

'Newsroom!'

'I suppose you're busy tonight.'

Stevenson.

'Only since the last two minutes. You should have phoned before.'

'You haven't been in.'

'What did you have in mind, anyway?'

She swivelled her chair round again. Better be careful – Bob would have a go about too many personal phone calls.

'I wanted to massage you. I've been thinking about your luminescent skin and I would like to get my hands on it. And I think you might enjoy it.'

'A foregone conclusion. I have to be at home by seven-thirty. As long as no more riots break out I'll be leaving here about four-thirty. But I need to buy some wine.'

'Go straight to my place after work. I'm finishing early so I'll get your wine for you and be home when you get there. How many bottles? Red or white? How much?'

'Listen, I want this to be supermarket stuff. Like I bought it myself.'

'Of course. One white, one red, maybe New World, under a fiver?'

'Brill. Not too cheap.'

'I'll put the white in the fridge for you.'

I would hate Bryn to know about this. But it's not like I'm going to fuck Stevenson. It's more like I'm going for an aromatherapy massage after work.

Phone.

'Newsdesk!'

'Don't think this is because I can't live without you –'

'Jonny! What's happening?'

'Calm down, it's not a riot. I just had Ben Dangerfield in the shop, lives down the road from me. He and his wife have got a few people together – they're setting up a tenants' association to try to get something done about the problems. They asked me to let you know. They're after a bit of publicity.'

'Oh, fantastic. You're a star.'

His laughter sounded just as warm and genuine over the phone. 'Why they couldn't phone you I don't know. Anyway. Their number's 555777 and they live at number nine. Got to run, babe. Catch you later.'

David Hammett sat back in his chair and ticked the points off on his fingers while Julie and Bob Underwood sat opposite him.

'OK. We can go with this in the morning and pour oil on troubled waters. Residents getting something done about problems, council behind them, it was all a flash in the pan. We're pleasing everyone.'

He looked up. 'Oh, what you don't know, Julie, is that Tony Greene was on earlier, very annoyed. Thinks we've blown the whole thing up out of proportion, just summer high jinks out of hand.'

'Yes, that's what Adam said. And that's what I put in.'

'I know, but he's seen that big headline saying riot and

your name's the first one underneath it. I think I calmed him down, but don't expect the red carpet at the station tomorrow.'

Shit.

'So. If we run this tomorrow he'll be pleased. So will Linda Edwards. She's been on about trying to get European funding for improvements, doesn't want bad publicity to prejudice it. And presumably Mr and Mrs Dangerfield will be happy too.

'On the other hand, we could save the tenants' association for your weekend feature.'

He got up and walked around the room. 'After a riot's broken out on the estate we'd look a bit silly if we ran a story on nursery schools or something.'

'But the continuing riot's not front-page stuff and we've got bugger all at the moment to splash on,' Bob objected. 'This would be better than nothing.'

'Do you want me to get round there again and get the story so we're ready if we need to use it in the morning?'

Which will spoil my plans for a massage. Unless of course Stevenson comes with me to get pics of Mr and Mrs D.

David thought in silence for a minute. Then he sighed deeply.

'If you do that, we've got to run it tomorrow, splash or not, or they might get pissed off and give it to the *Courier*. No, you need to spend some time on it and get the council involved. And it's perfect for the feature.'

He smiled with a touch of mischief. 'And who wants to keep everyone happy? We're a newspaper, not a community freesheet. As long as what we print is true, they can whistle.'

'You didn't get the impression that Adam Arnside was trying to fob you off this morning, Julie?'

Bob. Ever suspicious.

'No. No, I didn't. But when you think about it, it's

taking youthful high spirits a bit far. And it's not like the first problem we've had recently.'

'You're right, Bob. I think there's more to this than meets the eye and for some reason the police are playing it close to their chest. You get on well with Tony Greene, don't you, Julie?' David's eyes were twinkling through his glasses.

Maybe too well. I'll just nod.

'How about playing it this way. Tell him we know there's some agenda behind it, after all that's been happening lately. But get his confidence; tell him we're happy to go along with the official line – as long as he lets us know what's really going down.'

'I can try. But I don't know if he'll play ball.'

'I've got faith in you, Julie. Right. Go for it with Greene tomorrow, then get down to Hornbeam and tell the Dangerfields they're going to be your feature – that'll keep them happy. And let's all pray for a bit more action tonight.'

'Did you say amen to that?' enquired Stevenson, rubbing his thumbs in a circular motion along Julie's calves with blissfully scented oil as she finished telling him about the meeting.

She was lying face down on a linen sheet covering the chaise longue, breathing in the fragrance of the oil and the ylang ylang perfumed candles.

'I managed not to. I think he's asking a bit much of me with Tony Greene, though.'

'Yes, especially as he's already turned you down.'

'Hold your horses. There have been developments on that front.' She described their conversation on Saturday.

'Ah, so now you're in the driving seat. How satisfying.'

'Yes. But you know what I realised – oh, God, are you going all the way up my thighs?'

'Wait and see.'

'This is heaven. I realised that what's so great about flirting is the continuation of possibilities, as opposed to

184

screwing someone, where in no time you've exhausted them.'

'Congratulations! That's exactly what I was trying to explain to you.'

'Although I do think it's quite important to screw as well.'

His hands started to circle round her buttocks.

'I thought this was supposed to relax me, not excite me.'

'I didn't say that. Is it exciting you?'

Julie sighed as his thumbs probed perilously close to her anus. 'Everything's exciting me at the moment. I'm a walking mass of nerve ends. Bryn, Jonny, you, Mark telling me about his night with Monika, flirting with Tony, the riot – you know, I think the riot has really got me going. As Mark said when we were down there today, it's the tension in the air and the possibility that anything can happen.'

He laughed. 'Like flirting.'

'I suppose,' she said, surprised. 'That's it, isn't it? Not knowing. Whereas as much as I'm looking forward to seeing Bryn tonight, I could more or less script it in advance.'

'So don't. Tell him you don't want to fuck. Tell him you need to get away from the oppression of the orgasm.'

'Hey, great phrase.'

'Shame I didn't invent it. Your neck's stiff, Julie. Try to relax.'

'I can't. Too much anticipation.'

'Bryn?'

'No – what might happen on the estate tonight. Is that bad?'

He laughed and swept his hands down her back. 'No, just professional. Turn over.'

Julie felt suddenly shy as she turned on to her back.

'Our relationship is primarily verbal, Julie.'

'Yes? So?'

'So, don't lie there with your eyes closed not telling me

185

why you've got that slightly embarrassed look on your face.'

She opened her eyes guiltily. 'It's just that I've never been naked in front of you. A verbal relationship seems to me to be easier to handle with your clothes on, even if it's only a bra.'

'Practice makes perfect. You have a beautiful body. Your skin is so fine.'

'Hmm. I've got a big bum.'

'Womanly,' he corrected. 'Don't worry about it.'

His hands moved up her legs to her thighs. She sighed and parted her legs.

'This is how I feel with Bryn sometimes, vulnerable, as though I've surrendered to him. You could touch me anywhere you like. Or not. And I don't know what you are going to do.'

'I'm only going to massage you, Julie. But although you know that, you half expect I'm going to touch you, and even though you're seeing Bryn later you still have a faint hope that I'm going to let you climax.'

'God, I'm transparent.'

He moved his hands to her belly and started to describe deep circles on her flesh.

His thumbs were pressing on her mons. She murmured appreciation to try to stay his hands. An orgasm couldn't be far away. But they moved up her body, past her waist, then his fingers were probing around her ribcage.

'Julie, your exclamations of delight are all related to a touch that is on or near an erogenous zone. Concentrate harder on the rest of your body. Wouldn't you like all of it to be one big fantastically sensitive erogenous zone?'

She sucked in her breath. 'You're cheating. How can you be saying that while you're playing with my breasts? Sorry, massaging them?'

He laughed. 'I'm the one who makes the rules. Though you're right, I am cheating slightly. I want you to be ready for your policeman tonight. But really, you should try to conquer the tyranny of the erogenous zones. Then you can move on to escape the oppression of the orgasm. Now close your eyes.'

She lay in anticipation. He was going to touch her – but where?

Suddenly she felt his fingertips high on the inside of her thighs. The skin he had just massaged with firm, practised strokes was now tingling with a touch as light as a feather, describing minute circles on the satiny texture of her soft skin. Mindful of his instruction she tried to enjoy the sensation for itself, rather than hoping he would move up to touch her sex.

He stopped, but was still bent over her. She was molten with anticipation. Nothing happened for a full minute. Then, just as she thought he had finished caressing her, she felt the faintest touch on her clitoris. It was as though he was stroking her with thistledown rather than a finger. The bud of flesh felt as though it was on fire. Three times he stroked her, and then stopped. She waited, but no more.

'Stevenson. I am so on the edge of coming.'

She opened her eyes as he laughed softly.

'With barely a touch! Well, it should gratify Bryn if he brings you to orgasm so quickly.'

Julie's body didn't know what to make of the conflicting sensations of relaxation and excitement. But there wasn't time to think about it.

'I have to go. I need to shower before Bryn comes round.'

Stevenson cocked a surprised eyebrow. 'Why? You smell wonderful; your skin's as soft as silk and your cunt is weeping with desire. He'll fall on you as soon as you open the door.'

'Yeah – maybe I won't let him tonight. Perhaps I'll tease him and make him hold off for a bit. After all –' she had a glint in her eye '– I do want some information from the police. What's the point in relying on Tony Greene playing ball in the morning, specially if he's pissed off with me, when I can have a DI in the palm of my hand tonight?'

He looked at her sternly. 'If you value this relationship at all, Julie Gibson, you should think twice about gambling with it for a story that in the great scheme of things is of minuscule importance.'

She stood and started dressing. 'I know that. But sometimes there's a little devil in you that wants to try your hand.'

He sighed. 'It's rather sweet to see you taking on Jonny Drew's mantle of self-destructive behaviour, Julie, but don't you think it's a bit immature?'

Check.

'Or are you using him as well? Have you got him primed to stand in a darkened room with binoculars, calling you at the first sign of civil unrest?'

'No. Why didn't I think of that?'

Stevenson brought her wine in from the kitchen.

'Enjoy your evening, Julie. And don't upset your policeman. I like hearing about your exploits with him.'

Julie's diary, 1 July

I'm feeling guilty about Bryn. Jonny and Stevenson and Mark know about him and each other, well at least that the others exist, but he doesn't. Thought of telling him, like talking to S, to get him going, but we don't have that sort of relationship. Anyway we did say early on it wasn't going to be exclusive, and what with work we don't exactly see each other loads, so I'm sure he knows I'm up to something else. Maybe I'll come clean next time but not tonight – hopefully can get the lowdown on the riot from him. S told me off, thinks I'm using him.

!!Later: Shouldn't write the diary before the day's ended. So much for going on about poor Bryn being kept in the dark when he knew about Jonny anyway!!

* * *

'I'm definitely not complaining about your outfit, but I was expecting you'd be wearing your leather jacket for me. Preferably with nothing else. Or did you buy that exclusively for going out with Jonny Drew?'

Julie froze, a slice of pizza halfway to her mouth.

'How do you know?'

Bryn laughed. It was an amused laugh, she was glad to hear.

'This might be a big town compared to what you're used to, but I can assure you a pretty woman in a bright blue leather jacket and no skirt roaring through the centre on the back of a motorbike can't possibly escape attention.'

'Oh.'

'Even if you hadn't told Tony you'd got the new jacket.'

She chewed on her *Quattro Formaggi.* 'And Tony tells you what we talk about?'

That would be interesting.

'Not usually. He just mentioned your new incarnation as a biker's lady.'

'Oh.'

Bryn picked up his glass and swirled the red wine round. 'This is nice. Did you get it at Tesco's?'

'Yeah.'

I presume.

'I'll get some. Stop looking so shocked, Julie. You're not wearing my ring or anything. You said from the start you wanted your freedom.'

'So you don't care?'

He put his glass down with a sigh. 'That's neither here nor there. Let's say, I have no right to mind what you do when I don't see you. We're both adults.'

'You might be. I'm not so sure about me.'

He looked at her with his piercing dark eyes from under lowered eyelids. 'You did a great impersonation of one when I arrived.'

Julie rewound her mental video and relived the preceding two hours.

She had got home at seven, with plenty of time to shower and change. But Stevenson's words stuck in her mind and she sat on the floor and repeated them like a mantra.

I smell wonderful. My skin is soft as silk. My cunt is weeping with desire.

Repeating the last phrase aroused her even more. It wasn't as though Stevenson had really touched her sexually, after all. He'd just primed her for Bryn.

And as it was the first time they'd met at her flat, she thought he would appreciate a welcome.

So. Quick. Strip. Cleanse face. Wash hair. Moisturise. Dry hair. Make-up, not too much. Dress – in what?

He's a cop. Have you ever met one who didn't appreciate stockings and suspenders?

Black lace set on, thong, black skirt and little cardigan, undone to show cleavage, sleeves pulled up to the elbows. Lace-top stockings? God, no. The seamed ones. Wish I'd bought those fishnets. High heels.

Mirror. Do I look like a Parisian whore? Touch more lipstick.

Music – where's that old girl voice sex tape I pinched from somebody? There. Sit on sofa and think of Bryn to Chrissie Hynde.

Think of his dark eyes. His almost dirty laugh. That arrogant nose. His strength. The hair on his belly. How thick his cock is.

Segue into Madonna. Remember his eyes when he's pushing inside you – they're burning your face. Then they get that lost look and then close a split second before he comes.

Feel his hands on your arse. Imagine him taking your skirt off and finding your stockings. His mouth will be slightly open in its straight line.

Shame you can't leave the door open so he can come

in and find you stretched out on the sofa, one leg raised, just an inkling of stocking top.

Shit, I hate this one. Fast forward.

Entryphone. Come in, Bryn.

I stand against the door in my black and high heels, arms crossed under my cleavage. Motels – 'Total Control'. Yes, perhaps it's my turn for control over you tonight.

'I've been thinking about you. I stretched out on the sofa listening to some of my favourite songs thinking about you fucking me.'

'Julie.' He's brought me flowers. Blue, cottage-garden types, they're nice. 'You look like sex on legs.'

'I better tell you I haven't showered since this morning. I had this aromatherapy massage after work and I smelt so nice I didn't want to wash it off.'

'Napoleon told Josephine not to wash for three days before he came back.'

'That's gross. Anyway, apart from my skin being soft and scented, the massage turned me on. I thought you'd like me to be wet for you.'

'Let me smell you.'

His face in my cleavage.

'I want to strip for you.'

He sits down. I sway to the music and undo my cardigan, only three buttons. I leave it on but he can see my bra. I wriggle out of my skirt. I can hear him breathing. I take the cardigan off and turn round so he can see the thong. I take it off. He's unzipping and talking softly to me.

'Julie. Come here. Let me feel your wetness.'

'My cunt is weeping with desire.'

His big hand. It feels so good. I abandon myself to it.

He stands and strips. I love his dark body, brown skin, furred black. His solidity. His deep russet cock. With my heels on I'm taller than he is. I think of moving to the bedroom but decide not. First I want to taste him. I fall to my knees and lap up his cock to the eye, wiping away

191

its salty tear, then push my mouth down hard. The first time I've had my mouth around him, around such a thick stalk. Up, my tongue lapping, I feel his pulse as I reach the glans, then down. I feel his thighs tremble.

He lifts me off his cock and lays me on the floor, on my red poppy rug, then he's rubbered and poised at my slit. I feel that he will only have to enter me by a millimetre and my sex will suck him inside me, I want him in there so much. My muscles flex as I have the thought and he feels it too and he's in me and I close my eyes and concentrate on what I'm feeling until right at the end they open by reflex as I come, spasm upon spasm around him, and his groaning means he's coming too. I wish I could feel his cock jerking but no way can I feel anything but my own shudders.

'Dressing up as a whore, stripping and fucking is adult?'

Oh, that dirty laugh.

'If you weren't I'd be in my own nick. But. As I say, we're both free to do what we like.'

'Sure.'

They ate in silence for a minute. Julie had put her skirt and cardigan back on but left the buttons undone. Her bra and thong still lay on the sitting-room floor. She wanted to maintain the tension level. Especially when she went to put the flowers in water and found a pair of handcuffs round the stems.

'David told me this afternoon that my name's mud down at your nick, anyway.'

Bryn looked at her non-committally.

'Apparently Tony Greene's been on complaining about the riot story.'

He shrugged.

'Your front page was a bit over the top. Do you know how hot it was last night? Record temperatures for the third night running. Kids hanging round the street, drinking, too hot to sleep or even go indoors. It started off as a bit of fun, that's all, and got out of hand.'

'Yeah, I know the official line.'

He leant over her with a teasing smile and touched her nose.

'And that can stop twitching. Or I'll tie you up and rub your vibrator over you without letting you come.'

'Wow. That might be just what I need to help me escape the oppression of the orgasm.'

'Do what?'

Julie explained it away as a feminist theory.

Finishing her pizza, she sucked on her fingers, looking at him from under her lashes.

'So do you want me to dress up in my leather jacket while you handcuff me and tease me?'

He looked at her consideringly. 'No. Maybe next time. I can't stop thinking about your stockings and suspenders now. The sooner you get your skirt off again the better.'

Julie hit record temperature for the second time that night.

'Make a deal? You can handcuff me and do what you want. As long as I can do it to you after.'

Bryn breathed in sharply. 'I wasn't exactly seeing myself as the one chained to the bed when I brought those round. I thought you were the one who likes being dominated.'

'Sometimes. I just want to see what it's like.'

'Deal.'

She'd imagined that were she ever to be tied up it would be by a mock show of force, but Bryn wasn't into that. His only command was that she take off everything except her stockings and suspenders, then she lay on the bed while he attached her wrists to the brass bedhead. He tied her ankles together with the florists' ribbon, her legs bent so her sex gaped open for him.

But the lack of force was irrelevant. What was feeding Julie's desire and making pearly drops seep from her sex was the act of surrender. Her meekness as she took her clothes off and docilely opened her legs and permitted herself to be bound was sweeter to her than her earlier streetwise sexiness.

'What did you say before? Your cunt is weeping?'

'With desire. My cunt is weeping with desire.'

'I like that. Where's your vibrator?'

He turned it on, gently buzzing, as low as it would go.

'Say it again.'

She obeyed. Twice more. Each time her breath was shorter.

He touched her nipples with the vibrator and circled around them. Then he moved it down and pushed it against her pussy.

'Do you want it inside you?'

'I want whatever you want.'

'Jesus.'

He moved it to her clit and stroked gently. 'Do you do this to yourself?'

'Sometimes.'

'What you do think about when you do it?' He turned the power up.

'Fantasies. Or I read.'

She heard his breath suck in quickly, surprised.

'Porn? You read porno stuff while you're wanking?'

'Actually, I normally think of it as reading erotica while masturbating. Oh my God.'

'Are you nearly there? So what sort of stuff? Straight sex? Kinky stuff? Wait, Julie, don't come yet.'

He moved the vibrator and pushed it up inside her and replaced it with his fingers, soft on her clitoris.

'Take it a bit slower. I want you to tell me one of your fantasies.'

'You – making me do things, degrading things – bringing your friends round to fuck me, to make me suck them and take it up the arse from them, and they're all making comments about what a little slut I am and how much I'm dying for it. And you take bets on who can make me come the quickest and you all throw your stake money on me. When it's your turn you touch me and order me to tell you exactly what a filthy little whore I am and I'm so humiliated at having to say that in front of all the other cops I come in no time and you win.

'You win,' she repeated almost unconsciously as her orgasm tore through her, her sex muscles, strained to bursting point, finally unleashing control and spasming around the vibrator.

'Oh, sweet Julie,' sighed Bryn, his hand pressing down on her mons gently. 'Is that what you want me to do to you?'

She smiled indolently.

'No way. Fantasy, that's what we're talking about here.'

'Good. There's no way I could get into that sort of thing.'

'That's not quite true. You called me a slut the other day. And it was your idea to get Branford to hold me down.'

'Both times because I thought it would turn you on. You know that, don't you?'

He reached out and stroked her breasts. She smiled at him.

'Of course I know. Don't you want to fuck me? After all, I'm at your mercy.'

Bryn looked at her quizzically. 'I don't want to fuck you because you're at my mercy. I brought those because I knew you'd like them. This is not some fantasy rape scenario.'

'Oh, Bryn. You are so nice.'

'Tell me about it.' He undid the cuffs and the florists' ribbon. 'Sorry, Julie. I don't really see you abasing your-self for me.'

She rubbed her wrists. 'OK, you can abase yourself for me.'

'Hardly.'

'We had a deal, remember? You cuff me then I cuff you – you agreed.'

He sighed. 'If it makes you happy.'

As she shackled him to the bed, Julie noticed without comment that his erection had subsided since he had made her come. She ran her fingers over his face, feeling the softness of his dark skin and the sensual line of his hooked nose. His square jaw was clenched and his eyes closed, as though against impending assault.

'Relax, Bryn. I'm not going to hurt you.'

He opened his eyes and laughed. 'I'm a cop, Julie. As much as I do trust you – really, deep down – I still feel uneasy at being tied up.'

Bending her head to hide her smile, she stroked down his warm, black-velvet chest, past his belly to his pubic hairs, gently pushing her fingers through the deep pile of his dark curls. His penis stiffened in response, and she concentrated on lazily running her hands around it without a direct hit, then when it was looking as hard as it gets she moved her hands down to his balls and cupped them gently.

'Not uneasy now?' she asked him, intimately, like a lover.

He shook his head and with her eyes still on him she once again pouted her lips and sucked lightly on his cock, while one of her hands moved down to stroke lightly along to his arse. A sound escaped him but it was obviously appreciative so she continued stroking back and forth between his anus and the sac of his balls, increasing the pressure of her mouth around his cock and bringing her tongue into play.

She knew he liked her back view so she turned herself round, straddling him carefully, her seamed legs and suspender-framed arse facing him while she resumed her sucking and stroking with what she judged a perfect combination of efficiency and luxurious languor.

While she was using her mouth on him she wished he would use his to talk to her. She was turned on by the thought of the view he had of her round, womanly arse with the black suspenders either side, maybe with the

196

pink lips of her sex just visible. It would have been even more arousing if he had told her himself.

Needing more than her imagination to keep her tension up, she abandoned his cock with her mouth and with a fluid movement raised herself above him and with a sigh sank on to his massive penis. She heard a low moan come from him and once more thought about her back view. Raising her arms she crossed them behind her head as she rode him slowly, then brought them down to stroke from the back of her waist down to her arse.

'Julie, I can't last long like this.'

'No. I'm not doing it for long. Don't come. How does it feel?'

'Magic. You don't know what you look like from this angle.'

You're no mind reader, Bryn.

Twice more Julie raised herself slowly and lowered herself happily back on to his cock, then with a sigh lifted herself off him and turned to face him. His dark skin was flushed as though feverish with wanting.

'I've got to come soon.'

'Yes. I think I can again. Let's just have a bit of a breather.'

She lay next to him on her side, facing him, and as far as the handcuffs allowed he turned towards her. His cock pushed against her and instinctively Julie opened her legs and imprisoned it between her thighs.

'You know what's really exciting tonight?' she asked. 'We're up here in a scorching atmosphere of passion and erotic tension, and just a few miles away Hornbeam might be erupting again.'

'Why does that excite you so much?' he asked curiously.

'It's such a charge, like living on the front line. The thought of lying here, fucking you while someone starts throwing stones through car windscreens outside, and somewhere, something bursts into flames – doesn't that turn you on?'

Bryn laughed. 'The problem is if someone started throwing stones and lighting fires outside I'd have to try to do something about it. But I guess I can see what you mean in principle.'

Her hand moved round to his back, stroking the soft nap of his hair.

'What's going to happen tonight? Is it going to be an action replay? Or will they find something else to get up to? I know you have to stick to the official line but this is off the record.'

Impatiently he pulled away from her, his cock springing free from her thighs, but with his hands bound unable to move far.

'On record, off record, it's all the same. Nothing is going to happen. And even if I thought it was, I wouldn't tell you. And if this is why you wanted to cuff me, you can just fucking well get these off and I'm out of here.'

A slow-burning anger sparked in his eyes.

'Bryn, no, honestly, I'm not just trying to get stuff out of you. Really, I'm sorry.'

She held his face in her hands and they locked eyes, his now wary and ungiving, hers appeasing and sincere – she hoped.

She felt deceitful, ashamed – and almost aggressively excited.

Again her hands moved over his body. His quick flare of anger had had no effect on the immensity of his erection. She held him two-handed, one thumb and forefinger holding him at the root and the other hand sweeping up and down his cock. Their eyes were still on each other's.

'Come on, Bryn. It's time now. How do you want to come? I don't mind. If you want to download inside me, on my arse, my tits, or in my mouth, I don't mind. You can come all over my face if you like, rub it into my hair. Whatever you want.'

'God almighty, Julie, give me a minute. If you keep talking to me like that I'll come in ten seconds flat.'

'OK.' She relaxed her grip. 'It turns me on, talking.'

'You don't say. I'll tell you what I want. Loads of saliva on my cock. Spit all over it.'

And then wank me off, added Julie mentally. She worked her mouth to force out as much saliva as she could all around his cock.

'Undo the cuffs.'

He rubbed his wrists. 'I'm not here. Pretend I'm not here, and you're wanking, like you said earlier. Go get one of your books.'

Julie smiled slowly and went to her bottom drawer and pulled out her favourite erotic novel. She turned to look questioningly at Bryn.

'I'm not here,' he repeated, moving off the bed and sitting in the wicker chair. 'Do what you do on your own. Don't look at me.'

OK. Let's pretend: God, I feel horny now I've tried these seamed stockings on. Book in left hand, find my favourite bit. Legs wide apart, dip finger in wetness – wow, my clit feels silky. Rub it slowly then back down, up inside me. Concentrate on the book. I love this bit – the heroine's at some way-out strip joint where this beautiful blonde's being whipped by a woman in black who licks her out afterwards, then she goes upstairs with the blonde and loses her bisexual virginity. Oh, brilliant, this always works: I can feel it starting to build up, a bit more on my clit and then back and forth, right on it now, the little bud of it, my eyes are on the book but right now what's turning me on is knowing that Bryn's eyes are burning into me. Shit, dropped the book – oh my God oh my God, Bryn's kneeling over me, he's wanking really quickly with his cock pointed at my face, I'm closing my eyes now, come on, baby, I'm murmuring, then it hits me, hot on my eyelids and my cheek and my mouth, and as I open my mouth to whisper some gets inside but I don't mind, and he's holding my head now and pushing my spunky face into his chest.

Who gives a toss about a riot anyway?

Cleansed and moisturised, Julie snuggled up to Bryn again. He stroked her hair.

'You didn't mind?'

She tutted. 'It was me who told you to come where you liked.'

'And you didn't mind doing it yourself?'

'Nah. Makes a change, anyway.'

Oh-oh. It's not as though we see each other every night.

But he was smiling. 'A change from all your men?'

'Hey, that's not fair. I haven't got a string of them.'

'Well, I know you've got at least one more.'

Julie kept quiet for a bit. She didn't really know how to play it.

'Bet you got turned on being on the bike, didn't you?'

'Oh, wow. I was terrified at first, but it's really full-on. Have you ever tried it?'

'Yes, a while ago.' They cuddled in silence. 'What does he make to the riot, then?'

Julie lifted her head and look at Bryn quizzically. 'Haven't you asked him?'

'Nothing to do with me. Haven't you?'

'Not in so many words. I did call in today but he was talking about his ex-wife.'

'Right. So does he think it's going to blow again tonight?'

'Don't know.'

'So why did you ask me and not him?'

She sat up properly. 'Obvious, isn't it? You're a cop. He only lives there. I expect he's waiting to see what'll happen as well as everyone else.'

'Right.' Bryn sighed. 'Anyway, time I was tucked up in my own bed.'

Julie pouted. 'How long do we have to go out for you to spend the night?'

Zipping up, he shook his head. 'Years, kid. A good policeman likes to be on the end of his phone, woken up by his own alarm clock and two yards away from his car.' He kissed her. 'Don't get up. I'll call you.'

The door closed.

Oh, well, always sleep better alone anyway. Just hope if there is any trouble tonight it confines itself to Hornbeam. I don't want flashing blue lights and sirens interrupting my beauty sleep.

Chapter Nine

Evening Light, Tuesday 2 July

VIOLENCE SPREADS TO CUTLER ESTATE

An Evening Light exclusive

THE VIOLENCE that hit Hornbeam Estate on Sunday night was replicated on the Cutler Estate in the early hours of this morning.

Again yobs smashed cars and windows with baseball bats. The sub post office was attacked but security grilles prevented theft.

Wintersea Police Divisional Commander Superintendent Tony Greene said that there was obviously a link between the two incidents.

'After Sunday night's disturbances a heavy police presence was maintained on the Hornbeam Estate last night. Whether this made the vandals move to the Cutler Estate, or whether that was targeted for attack in any case, we do not yet know.'

He added that police were taking both incidents

extremely seriously. 'We are determined that no estate, no street in Wintersea, will become a no-go area. To that end we are pursuing several lines of enquiry and are in contact with Scotland Yard.'

'You're causing me sleepless nights, Julie.'

Tony Greene wasn't smiling. His mouth was set straight and without the lines which usually enlivened his face he looked as stern as a judge. But not unattractive; his severely angled features and the iron-grey hair gave him a distinguished look Julie hadn't noticed during the teasing, laughing hours they'd spent together before.

'Tony, I know you're annoyed. David told me you'd been on. But honestly, I had nothing to do with the headline. The sub-editors do that side of things. I reported the story as it happened, and quoted Adam saying it was a bit of summer fun.'

She wrinkled her nose at him apologetically. If she had wanted to be completely honest she could have told him that although the sub-editors might make up the headlines, the reporters suggested their own for each story. And of course hers had been 'RIOT!!!'

He shook his head. 'I know. David told me all that. But really – what was it – "an orgy of violence" was going too far.'

'Actually, it was "an orgy of crime and violence",' she corrected.

Leaning back in her seat Julie looked him steadily in the eye. 'Tony, you know that I respect you, and Adam, and I am only too pleased to co-operate with you as far as possible in what I report and what I don't – within reason. But my first loyalty is to my job.

'I don't believe you think for a minute this was summer high jinks. It's up to you if you want to share your information with me, on or off the record, but I can't go into the office and pretend that I believe you. For one thing, David Hammett is damn sure there's some hidden agenda here. Not only Sunday night, but everything that's happened in the last couple of weeks – the smashed cars, the increase in robberies, the race attacks. So if you think I'm prepared to compromise my reputation at work by pretending to be your gullible pawn, I'm afraid you're wrong.'

Silence. Have I been too blunt?

Tony sighed and relaxed back in his seat. 'OK, Julie. You said on or off the record?'

'Yes. As long as we know what's happening, or what you think might be happening, and we're the first to get the story when it breaks, off the record will be fine.'

'Right. Well, first of all I have to say that even off the record there's not a lot to tell you. But I can say that yes, we do think there's something behind it. Or someone.'

'You mean like organised crime moving into the town?'

He shrugged. 'We don't think it's anything too sophisticated. I'm not talking Yardies or Yakuza or Triads here, just – possibly – a local operation. But we're not sure of the motive yet.'

'What about the personnel? Do you have anyone fingered?'

He looked up from his desk and tapped his pen on the pad in front of him. 'No names yet. One of our officers is going to London today to meet with a couple of guys from the Met. That might give us a better handle on it.'

Julie drew in her breath. 'You mean someone from London has come down to Wintersea to stir the town up? Why?'

For the first time that morning, he smiled. 'Why? Who? If I had all the answers, Julie, we'd have an arrest by now and you'd have your story. Now get out of here.'

'Hey! You haven't even given me today's report yet! What are you covering up?'

'Well, if you hadn't come steaming in with conspiracy theories you'd know by now that we did actually have another incident last night.'

'Oh, for fuck's sake – oh, God, sorry, Tony.'

He was laughing now. 'What am I lumbered with here? A crime reporter who's foul-mouthed as well as over-colourful in her reporting, not to mention over-insistent in her questioning!'

'Go on, I said sorry. What happened?'

The Cutler estate, a smaller and more respectable neighbourhood than Hornbeam, had been hit, but on a smaller scale.

This time she got an official statement.

Julie snapped her notebook shut. 'Amazing, isn't it. I phoned the Dangerfields on Elm View Road first thing and they said it had been a quiet night. It didn't occur to me they might strike anywhere else.'

A sudden thought struck her. 'Has anyone else got this? I mean, South Seas FM?'

Tony smiled. 'Actually, no. Unless they've heard on the grapevine and gone down to the estate, but I can't believe they wouldn't have been on if they'd heard.'

'Terrific. And if they do come on? Could you stall them till this afternoon?'

He pursed his lips and then nodded. 'OK. This once. But I've no control over what the press office at HQ do. They'll probably put it on the voice bank.'

'Sure. I must rush, Tony.' She was already getting her phone out of her bag.

He picked up his phone and passed it to her. 'Allow me. The least I can do.'

'You're a star.'

Yes, he was. And as she spoke to Bob, trying to take in what he was saying about sending John and Stevenson out to the estate and for her to get back to the office, she was aware of his hazel eyes on her all the time. What a pity. He seemed so fond of her. But the circumstances were what they were, and nothing was going to change them.

The editor's eyes were twinkling so brightly through his glasses he was in danger of starting a fire himself as he walked into the newsroom and high-fived Bob and, to her surprise, Julie.

'Bloody good job we hung on. Fantastic hunch work on all sides. Good job, Julie.'

She shook her head. 'You know I thought afterwards maybe I could have walked out of the police station without even getting the story, having gone in there and had Tony sulking and then talking him through the off the record bit. He'd more or less said, "OK, now piss off" before I remembered to get last night's list and there it was.'

'No, he wouldn't have not told you,' said David confidently. 'He likes you. Good move of mine, putting you on police calls.'

Bob almost laughed. 'I get it, David, this has only turned out all right because of your decision?'

More twinkling. 'That's what being an editor's all about, Bob. Making the right decisions. As you might find out for yourself one day.'

'Hopefully not on this paper,' muttered Wendy as David left the room. If Bob heard anything, he didn't react.

Instead he looked at Julie. 'So, if you're finished, weren't you supposed to be getting on down to interview Mr and Mrs Tenants' Association?'

She groaned. 'God, no rest. Can't I at least stop for a coffee and cake on the way?'

'You don't want to get fat. Might spoil your relationship with Tony Greene.'

She poked her tongue out at him.

'Don't be daft, of course you can.'

It was a day of surprises. No sooner had she sat in the corner with a muffin and what the canteen laughingly called a cappuccino than Bob appeared and sat down next to her.

'Hope you don't mind – didn't want to say this in the newsroom.' She looked suspiciously at his closed face.

He gave nothing away. 'How deep are you in with Jonny Drew?'

'Is this actually any of your business, Bob?'

He put his ugly face closer to her. 'No, but I know you're going out with Bryn Edwards. Now you're going out with Jonny Drew. I really think you're putting yourself in a very stupid position.'

Stung, Julie crashed her cup on to the saucer.

'Stupid? Bryn knows I'm seeing Jonny. So what's the big deal?'

He sniffed. 'And does Jonny know about Bryn?'

She nodded. 'Yes, he does. Well, he knows I've got a boyfriend.'

'But he doesn't know he's a cop. Think about it, Julie. How did you first meet Jonny Drew? Because one of his old mates is a murderer. And incidentally, the bloke who got murdered was living with his alcoholic slag wife.'

'Oh, come on, Bob!' she said exasperatedly. 'Alleged murderer. Ex-wife. Don't you think you're being a bit dramatic?'

He sat, stubborn and unmoving, in his chair. 'No. I think you ought to be careful. Jonny Drew's got a reputation for being against the law. I think you must be absolutely barmy if you think you can go out with him as well as a policeman. Still, it's your funeral. Just a word of fatherly advice.'

'Cheers.'

'As you say, it's none of my business.' He got up. 'See you later.'

Bloody woman hater. Bet he can't stand the thought of young, single people screwing each other when he's stuck with his wife.

She picked up her muffin then put it down again. Suddenly, she wasn't hungry.

Ben and Carole Dangerfield were delighted to hear their new association would feature in the paper on Friday, and Julie was equally delighted that they had practically organised everything for her.

Other tenants, the postmaster, even pupils and teachers at the junior school had been lined up for Julie to talk to. They all seemed genuinely optimistic that any problems with the estate could be sorted.

'You've got such a great atmosphere here, it's hard to believe how the riot happened in the first place,' Julie commented as she sipped tea and nibbled on Hobnobs in the Dangerfields' cosy kitchen.

Carole tutted and shook her head. 'I know. Most of the problem's the council's fault. They dump all these young-sters here who've left home just because they don't get on with their parents. And they're not bad lads, Julie, but you can imagine if you're eighteen or whatever and on the dole life has got to be frustrating. They want beer and clothes –'

'And bloody drugs,' Ben put in. 'I bet you that had a hand in it. What did the police say, fuelled by drink? Not just bloody drink if you ask me.'

His wife sighed. 'Well, you might be right. The other thing is boredom, of course. You can't do much without money, so they're just sitting around all day watching telly and listening to music, or they go down the precinct and make a nuisance of themselves. The younger ones hang out with them if they let them and before you know it they're on the same path.'

Ben sniffed. 'They're lazy bastards, that's what they are. When I was a kid –'

Let's get back to the point here.

'So do you think if the council found somewhere else for these kids you'd have no problems on the estate?'

'Definitely. But then some other poor buggers will have the problems, won't they?'

Check.

Julie looked at her watch. Nearly one. Might just catch Jonny.

'I think we're more or less done, Carole. I'll get on to

the council this afternoon and get their input, and I'll give you a ring if I need to check anything.' She put her cup down and said as casually as she could, 'I might as well go and see if Jonny's in while I'm nearly next door.'

Carole put her hand to her head. 'Oh, no, you won't! I completely forgot, he asked me to tell you he won't be back at dinnertime today, but he'll give you a ring tonight, or was it this afternoon?'

Have to be this afternoon. He hasn't got my home number, or even my mobile. Why didn't I give him one of my personal cards?

'Oh, thanks.'

'It's a shame Jonny's not more like his old mum. She would have put a stop to all this rioting business.'

Julie's ears pricked up. 'Really?'

'Oh, yes. Old Sal was a real battle-axe, in a nice way, I mean. She was a councillor, you know! The first one off the estate, in the days when most of the councillors were a bit posh, if you know what I mean.'

'Really? Jonny said she was a socialist and took him on protest marches and stuff.'

Carole started clearing the tea cups. 'That's right, dear. She was a real fighter, always putting the world to rights. Shame she died so young – she was only in her sixties. It'll be, what, three years ago.'

Julie hesitated. 'Well – what I don't understand – Jonny was a real tearaway, right, when he was a kid? How did she let that go, if she was such a battle-axe?'

Ben chipped in. 'That's right, Julie. She was too bloody soft on him, I can tell you that. But I'll tell you what she did do for him: she made sure he got on at school and went off to university.'

Carole sighed. 'Yes. She was never the same after he married Sandra Braithwaite, though, was she?'

Her husband shook his head. 'Broke her bloody heart. That and the Thatcher government.'

Julie remembered she still had a paucity of information concerning Sandra's murdered lover.

I can kill two birds with one stone here. Turn to the back of the notebook.

'That reminds me, Carole, how well did you know Greg Anderson?'

As the afternoon wore on Julie was increasingly disappointed not to hear from Jonny. As she called the mayor and the social services department at the council she subconsciously expected one of the others to bring a message over. They didn't. When she came back from interviewing a woman whose child had fallen in the park pond she looked eagerly at the notes stuck to the screen. None from Jonny. She shrugged and banged out the pond story and then finished the feature on the tenants' association.

Stevenson strolled over to her desk near to home time with a pretext of checking the spelling of a name.

'Good time last night?'

She smiled. 'I think you would have found it oppressive.'

He laughed. 'One day you'll have had enough of all this instant gratification, Julie Gibson, and you'll understand my point.'

'I can't wait. I'm a bit pissed off, though. I was sort of hoping to hear from Jonny about tonight, but he hasn't called.'

He raised his eyebrows. 'Don't you ever feel like a day off?'

She laughed. 'It's not that. God knows I do need a day off –' she lowered her voice '– sex, after last night. I just want to talk to him. If he'd been around at lunchtime, that would have been fine, but he wasn't.'

Stevenson shook his head. 'So what's your problem? You know his number, don't you? Phone him and say you want to pop round for a quick chat.' He looked at her meaningfully. 'If that's what you really want.'

'Yes, it is. Trust me.'

A ghost of a smile flitted across his lips. 'I don't think it's me who needs to be told to trust you, Julie.'

Got it in one.

'Newsdesk!'

'Hiya, babe. Get my message?'

Oh, sweet relief. She made a thumbs-up at Stevenson.

'Yeah, cheers. Everything OK?'

'For sure. I was a bit busy today so I worked through the dinner hour. Go all right with Ben and Carole?'

'Terrific. Thanks for putting me in touch with them.'

Was she imagining Bob's eyes boring into her?

'Don't thank me, I was just the messenger. Anyway, I was wondering if you fancied coming round tomorrow? I'll cook. Or we could go out, if you want.'

She turned away from Bob's direction. 'Well, that'd be great, but I'm going out with the girls from work. You can't do tonight?'

'Sorry, no can do. Then Thursday's bike club, unless you come round after nine?'

'Yeah, cool. The only thing is, I sort of wanted to see you today, just for a bit of a chat.'

'What, you mean to do with work?' His voice had become guarded.

'No. Just a quick word, really.' Oh, please, I sound so wimpish. 'Can I pop round in half an hour or so?'

There was silence on the other end of the line.

'Well – look – I'm just off for a swim. How about meeting me down at the Point?'

'Great. See you in the water.'

His laugh bubbled through the phone line. 'I'll be the one with the silver St Christopher.'

Ah, that was what the charm was.

'I'll be the one in blushes.'

Julie guessed right in parking near the track Jonny had driven up on the bike, and passed it as she walked through the dunes. It wasn't hard to recognise his jeans and leather jacket, carefully folded under, bless him, two towels, in a deserted part of the beach. There were a few others, all correctly unclothed, scattered around but none nearby.

There were only two people swimming as opposed to splashing around in the shallows and Julie immediately identified Jonny's blond head and strong crawl. She stripped off as quickly and casually as possible, folded her clothes and tried to walk unselfconsciously down to the water.

Jonny had obviously seen her for as soon as she launched into her ladylike breast stroke he swam vigorously in her direction.

'Hey, babe.' He stopped and trod water to kiss her. 'How's it going?'

'Fine.'

He looked up and down the beach. 'Shame there's a few people here. I'd like to lift you on to my cock and see if I could fuck you while I was treading water.'

She giggled. 'Great, we both drown but die happy. Perhaps they'll all go.'

'They'd be mad. It's beautiful at this time of day. And great after a hot day at work.'

'Do you come here every evening, then?'

'When I can.' Julie was again swept away by the warmth in his eyes. Like the water, light danced in their blue brilliance. Impulsively she put one arm round him and kissed him deeply. She frogged her legs to keep upright and felt his cock stiffen as she brushed against it.

'Leave it out, Julie. I don't think I could swim with a hard-on.'

She laughed teasingly. 'Sorry, I didn't really intend to touch you. I just wanted to taste your tongue.'

'Yeah, nice. But I want to do a bit more swimming, then we can dry off and talk. You coming out?' He indicated the horizon.

Julie started off with him but knew her limitations and turned back after a while, leaving Jonny to swim out to where he had been before she arrived. She turned on to her back and floated lazily, kicking her legs indolently. The sun was still hot, though nowhere near as fierce as it had been at its height. It felt good and she thought maybe she too should come every day after work. Except, of course, that Jonny might think she was stalking him.

And really, she'd probably enjoy it just as much with a cossie on. Much less embarrassing if she met anyone she knew.

They met on the beach ten minutes later, and Jonny handed her one of the towels to lie on.

'Very considerate of you,' she told him.

He smiled. 'Well, it occurred to me you weren't prepared for this. I could hardly lie on my towel and leave you on the sand.'

They lay down and appreciated the sun on their wet bodies for a few minutes. Julie's hand crept out towards Jonny and he clasped it when it touched his.

'Managed to lose your hard-on, then.'

'Yeah, I don't think they're very welcome on the beach. But don't start talking sex or I won't be able to stop it.'

'As if!'

'So what did you want to talk to me about?'

Julie's resolve wavered. 'Well – I don't know if I should tell you or not. It's . . . it's about my other boyfriend.'

He laughed softly.

'What's so funny?'

'You said your other boyfriend. Like, I'm your boyfriend too. I was pleased.'

Were you really? Wow. I feel ridiculously pleased that you're pleased.

'Right. Well, whatever. I just thought you ought to know about him.'

Jonny turned towards her. 'What about him? Has he got some deep dark secret? Does he beat you? Is he impotent?'

She smiled at him. 'What would you do if he was?'

'Which? If he beats you up I'll sort him, no worries. If he's impotent, all I could say is poor sod.'

213

'Neither. He's a cop.'

'Right.'

His eyes hadn't betrayed the slightest flicker of concern or interest.

'And why is that my business?'

She took a deep breath. 'I just thought you ought to know.'

He traced a line down her face from her forehead, over her nose to her lips. She kissed his finger.

'Do you think I'm a villain, Julie?'

'No! Of course I don't! But, you know, what with your mates and the murder and stuff, I just didn't want you to think I was spying on you or anything.'

'No. I see what you mean.' He sounded reflective. 'At least – when you say spying, has he asked anything about me?'

She couldn't help looking amused. 'Actually, the police seem to know all about you anyway, even if your criminal career is all in the past. I don't think he looks on me as a grass.'

'Still, you've obviously talked about me.'

Julie laughed. 'I didn't have to. As he said to me, as soon as I dressed up in leather and rode around town on the back of your bike I was a marked woman.'

Jonny laughed his easy laugh. 'Yeah, this is a small town, that's for sure. Who is it, anyway? Seeing as he knows who I am.'

She hesitated – why? – and told him.

He nodded. 'Yeah, I know who you mean, though we don't move in the same circles. Well, thanks for telling me. When I plan the perfect bank robbery, I won't ask you to be the getaway driver.'

'Shame. I've always fancied a bit of lawbreaking.'

He sat up. 'Serious? How about a bit of public indecency back behind the dunes?'

'What, a replay of Saturday? Are you asking for trouble?'

'That's me. Come on, put your top clothes on. We don't have to fuck. I just want to cop a feel.'

'Your seduction patter gets worse,' grumbled Julie, while still feeling slightly thrilled at the thought of Jonny's fingers on her. Shame she felt sore from the night before.

He pulled his jeans on and Julie her top and skirt and holding the rest of their clothes they walked gingerly across the hot sand to the gap in the dunes. Soon they were sheltered from the beach, and the thick gorse and wild roses hid them from the roadside path. He arranged both towels on the sand again and sat down.

He looked so sexy, wearing nothing but jeans, with his little silver chain round his neck, laughing at her so carelessly and confidently.

'Get your skirt off again, Julie, and come over here.'

She unzipped her skirt again and moved to stand in front of him, shivering with expectation despite the heat, waiting for his touch. Suddenly his head darted forwards and with no preamble his tongue was on her clitoris, fretting it as if to prise the little bud from its sheath. It took her breath away; she had been expecting a finger, a hand, but not the warmth and moisture of a tongue. Then it relaxed and he swept down to her vagina with the flat of it, darting it inside her and then back again.

Just as quickly he stopped, his face smiling up at her.

'You taste like the sea, but with your own juice mixed in. It's great.'

She pouted her lips. 'That was nice.'

'You want more? I thought you were a bit unwilling when we were back there. Seems to me you were just doing it to please me.'

'Sod off. It's just that you've started something now.'

'And you want me to finish it?'

She made a face. 'I'm not begging you.'

'Oh, why not? I was just looking forward to you saying pretty please.'

Julie knelt down on the towel next to him. 'Perhaps I can persuade you another way.'

She unzipped his fly and his cock sprang out happily, a deep rosy pink after its sea and sun bath.

Usually she prefaced a blow job with a few licks up the shaft and around the head but in an echo of Jonny's direct assault on her clit she clamped her mouth firmly over his penis and sucked. Once she gauged the shock had worn off she used her tongue as well, lapping him while she sucked hard, and then lifting her mouth off him to give the glans a special hard-tongue job and then back on him, pulling him as deep in her throat as she could.

'Fucking hell, Julie, that's bloody wonderful. If you keep that up I'm going to come. Where the hell did you learn to do that? I'm going to – oh, fuck.'

Julie's turn to stop midstream.

She raised her head and looked at him innocently. 'Who's begging now?'

He laughed. 'I am. I haven't got anything with me so I can't fuck you, babe. Please go down on me again. I'm begging you.'

That feels rather nice.

'Would you mind saying that again?'

His eyes.

'I don't mind at all. I'm begging you, Julie. Please suck me off. I won't come in your mouth if you don't want; I just want your mouth round me for a bit longer and I do most definitely need to come but I'll tell you when and you can get out the way. Please, Julie, otherwise I'm going to have to wank myself off.'

She smiled triumphantly, excited. 'Since you put it so nicely, how can I refuse?'

'Unless you want me up your arse. Do you do that, Julie?'

'No. Anyway, it's illegal.'

'Yeah, that's why I like it.'

'Hmm. It's all anyone seems to talk about these days, so maybe I'll try to get into it.'

He raised his eyebrows. 'You mean your cop wants to break the law?'

She laughed. 'No, I don't, I mean a friend was talking about it. Anyway, do you want this mouth or what?'

'How many times do I have to beg?'

That'll do. Though I must admit it's made me feel pretty good. I'll definitely get into domination one day.

Sometimes blow jobs could be so enjoyable. Jonny's enthusiastic approval of her technique made her apply herself even more. She wanted it to be the best he'd ever had.

And really, it was nice to suck on that warm pink shaft, so hard but covered in such tender flesh, to employ lips and tongue to heighten the pleasure, cheek and throat muscles to pull it firmly down inside her mouth. Letting it have a little moment of release and murmuring with her own excitement and desire before starting again with her little tongue flicks up the throbbing vein to the eye and then sucking gently and wetly with open mouth just down an inch or so, before plunging down, down with her mouth and pulling him in again.

It was so nice that when Jonny warned her he was going to come she kept right on going and let him come in her mouth. And because she didn't want to let him go until she'd felt him pulse for the last time, she did something she rarely did. She swallowed.

He lifted her up and kissed her. It was almost tender.

'Oh, babe. That was beautiful. There's no other word. You're the best.'

She smiled. 'Can I have that in writing? You never know when you might need a reference.'

Laughing, he stroked her hair. 'You can have anything you want after that. I don't want to sound presumptuous, but you enjoyed it too, didn't you?'

'Yes, sure. Was it obvious?'

He nodded. 'That's why it was so great. Being sucked

off is usually a bit like having a wank. I mean, it's being done to you by a mouth or a hand. It's good but it's not like making love with someone. But what you just did was more like making love. You didn't just try to bring me off as fast as you could, you did it with feeling.'

Julie was quiet. His language disconcerted her: making love, feeling. But when you translated it, all he meant was, having sex, care. Hell, it was probably just a generational thing.

Jonny squeezed her. 'I was so happy I'd forgotten what I was doing when you started that.' His hand moved down.

With a flash of insight Julie realised that she didn't want it. She honestly and truly did not want to come.

She sighed. 'No, not now.' Turning on to her stomach she rested her head sideways on her hands, looking at his questioning blue eyes.

'Have you ever heard the phrase "the oppression of the orgasm"?' she began.

The decibel level was incredible. Especially as it was all coming from their group.

Number of telesales girls: 8. Reporters: 2. Receptionists: 2.

'It just shows you what a sexist world we live in,' snorted Wendy. 'All the telesales staff are women, and only three of the reporters. It's totally wrong.'

'Oh, yeah, and what you mean is that reporters are somehow better than telesales,' said Monika fiercely. 'I really resent all that shit.'

'I'm not saying that at all!' protested Wendy. 'It's the stereotyping of roles that infuriates me.'

Monika drew on her cigarette. 'Let's face it – you did have four women reporters until recently. It's only thanks to bloody Bob that Gail and Penny moved on. It's not that David doesn't take on women, it's that they don't stay.'

She had lowered her voice slightly and Julie realised it

was because Hilary, Bob's former mistress, was on the next table.

'So what does Derek make to that?' asked Julie curiously. 'He seems to get on all right with Bob. Does he realise he's causing people to leave?'

Monika shook her head impatiently. 'I shouldn't speak for Derek. But, between us three – and I mean that – he can't stand him. Even David realises he's no good with the staff, but the newsroom was totally disorganised till Bob took over. Unfortunately organisation alone doesn't make for a happy office.'

'He had a word with me about Jonny,' confided Julie. 'Told me I was stupid going out with him as well as Bryn.'

Wendy pursed her red lips. 'Actually, I think he might be right this time, Julie. I don't want to slag off your Jonny but he doesn't exactly move in the best circles.'

Having spent half the day pulling together the various interviews about Greg Anderson and Peter Grimley ready to accompany the verdict on the next day's murder trial, Julie had to agree.

'Bollocks!' snorted Monika. 'What difference does that make? Bob's just trying to undermine your confidence. You've started off too well too fast as far as he's concerned. He knows you're not going to crawl under his thumb like Wendy.'

'Cheek!' said Wendy indignantly. 'I am not under anybody's thumb. I just do my job.'

'Yes, and when Bob says jump?'

Monika left the question hanging and stood, picking up what was left of the kitty and the list of drinks. 'Everyone ready for another round? We'll do last orders here and then head over to Capri.'

The club was having a Rolling Stones night. Stoked up with tapas and wine from the Barcelona Bar and now vodka and sundry other spirits from the Far Pavilion, the girls were ready to go for it.

Except Wendy, who bowed out. Monika caught Julie's

eye with a dismissive gesture when she heard her. She was joined by Fi and Lyn, two of the telesales girls, claiming waiting boyfriends, and Hilary.

Monika managed to get waiter service and tucked back in next to Julie. She was looking incredible as always in a fringed pale suede skirt and matching bustier. Julie had thought she was pretty cool in the tie-dyed vest dress she'd worn for the flat's christening but guessed she'd never outdo Monika.

'Are you sure you haven't got someone waiting for you at home?' she asked as she sipped her vodka and cranberry.

Monika smiled mischievously. 'I thought about it. It's nice to know there's someone to go home to. But if you do pull, you feel a bit mean that they've waited in your flat for you.'

'Hey. You mean if you pulled you'd go back with someone and leave the other person at home?'

'Sure. It can be a bit of a turn-on for them. Not knowing if or when I'm coming back. Maybe at two in the morning with someone else, and turn them out of the bedroom. Or let them join in. Or watch. Or maybe come back in the morning stinking of sex with someone else.'

'Jesus. That might be a turn-on for a masochist.'

Like Derek.

'How's Mark coping with you? I feel like I've led a lamb to the slaughter.'

They laughed. 'He's doing just fine. I saw him last night – it was wild; we watched some porno videos. How about your cop?'

'Good. Handcuffs on Monday.'

'Biker?'

'You won't believe this. I saw him briefly last night, sucked him off by the nudist beach, but as for me, I decided to escape the oppression of the orgasm.'

'Shit! Don't tell me Stevenson has made a convert?'

'Not really.'

'So you'll be desperate to pull tonight.'

Julie smiled faintly. 'I don't think I've got your energy, somehow. Bryn and Jonny are enough for me.'

Monika pouted. 'Boring! Anyway, let's go. I'm ready to boogie. OK, gang?'

The appeal of Capri was its tackiness. It was small and rundown but pulled in the crowds for its theme nights. The girls hit the place on a good run of 'Brown Sugar', 'Tumbling Dice' and 'Honky Tonk Women' before 'Angie' came on.

'Shit, that's too slow. Come to the bar with me, Julie.'

Fine. Just don't ask me to the loo.

Monika surveyed the swaying mass from the bar. 'Not much talent in here tonight. I think we'll just have to make do with each other.'

Julie shook her head. 'Mon, I really am not ready for that.'

'For what? You've already let me touch you. Don't you want to find out what it's like to touch me? And don't tell me you're not intrigued to know what it's like to kiss a woman.'

'Yes, but –'

'But shit. You want to get a close-up of my shaved pussy, don't you? Put your mouth over it? Squeeze my tits?' She moved her head closer to Julie's. They were standing side by side with their backs to the bar. Anyone who saw them would have thought they were discussing the dancers, or even the price of fish.

'Yes. I do. But life's too complicated at the moment.'

'Don't be pathetic. Come on, your place or mine?'

Julie hesitated – but what the hell. Monika's bare arm rubbing lightly against hers and the occasional jostle of her hips was as arousing as any man's touch. 'Mine. This is all too much as it is without any accessories from your box of tricks.'

Grasmere Avenue was quiet as the taxi pulled up outside Julie's flat. As usual she briefly eyed the Clio, making sure it was still there with all glass intact. It was fine. But parked three cars behind it was Bryn's Volkswagen, with him curled up in it.

She tapped on the window and spoke tersely when he opened it. 'Special surveillance? Or just can't get through the night without me?'

He held up both hands in a placatory gesture. 'Don't get mad. I was just making sure you were all right. You weren't supposed to see me.'

Monika had paid the taxi and joined them. 'Shame on you, Julie. You pretend to be shocked at me for having a little supper waiting at home, and you've got your cop here all the time. Hi, Bryn, nice to meet you properly.' She put her hand through the window for him to shake.

'So are we going in or what?'

'Not me. I was just seeing that Julie got home. I'm off now.'

Monika hadn't relinquished his hand. 'You're joking. We want you to come in, don't we, Julie? I've got a very big appetite, Bryn. I usually eat little girls like Julie for breakfast.'

'Literally,' Julie sniffed.

'So for supper I might need something I can really get my teeth into. Come on. We both want you to.'

Bryn turned to Julie questioningly.

This is out of my control. 'Whatever.'

She opened the door and went up first to unlock her flat door, leading the way into the sitting room in silence.

'You've gone into passive mode, Julie. Have you experienced that, Bryn?'

'Oh yes. But I thought it was only with me.'

He raised an eyebrow at Julie.

'You started it off,' she said defensively. 'Then with Monika, I guess I just didn't know what else to do. Why am I explaining myself, anyway?'

'Indeed.' Monika was taking charge. 'Let's just sit and chill for a moment.'

She sat on the sofa and patted the cushions for the

others to sit down. 'Julie, you can get in the middle after you've put some music on.'

Shame I haven't got anything experimental and avant-garde to mirror the action. But I can put the two lamps on and kill the overhead and light those two ylang ylang candles, and if Monika says anything about it looking like Stevenson's flat I'll kick her out.

Monika was giving Bryn the lowdown on her and Julie's relationship so far, diplomatically omitting Stevenson's role as facilitator, and explaining that she had planned on a proper seduction that night.

'It's like that book you like,' said Bryn slyly. 'The one you read the other day when we both –'

'Yes, I know,' Julie broke in exasperatedly. 'But I would be happier if we didn't all have to discuss every step of our respective relationships so far.'

'Sure,' said Bryn soothingly. 'I think the important thing now is, what do *you* want?'

They both looked at her expectantly.

'Hang on. I'm thinking.'

I'm thinking: a: I fancy Monika. b: I love fucking Bryn. c: It's about time I had some bi experience. d: Ditto three-way. e: I think I'm fed up with passive mode.

'Mon, you agree with Bryn, that what I want is the important thing?'

Monika nodded agreement.

'OK, I'm in charge. Which means going back to the original plan for tonight, i.e. Bryn, you are temporarily redundant.'

'But I can watch?'

'Yeah. I reckon we'll want you on hand a bit further down the line.'

She was back in control of herself and turned to Monika as Bryn moved off the sofa to sit on an upright chair at the table. There was no point in trying to chore-ograph a scene with Monika, when Amazon woman would do it so much more imaginatively.

'So, how were you planning to seduce me?'

The Great Dane smiled wickedly and tutted as she rose from the sofa and walked around Julie.

'You've provided the soft lights and the sweet music. I know what that means. You want a nice little chocolate-box seduction, with me tenderly touching you, giving you girlie head for the first time, exclaiming on how much better women understand cunnilingus than men, murmuring sweetly, fingers lingering over each other while we go on about how soft our skins are compared to coarse blokes. Right so far?'

Julie had to laugh. 'Sure! I've read the books! What else should I expect?'

Monika smiled back at her. 'Something a bit more . . . raunchy?'

Swiftly she moved over to the stereo and revved up the volume and turning back to face Julie unzipped her skirt and pulled it down quickly. She was wearing suede knickers that matched her outfit, with fringed ties at the side. But where the crotch would usually be there was nothing, just two more suede strings either side of the shaved slit. She twirled round imperiously to no great purpose except to show her bare arse. Looking at Julie almost mockingly, she put her hand down to her naked labia and pushed two fingers inside herself. They came out glistening.

'Looks like you've got me quite horny,' she said as she put them to her mouth and sucked on them. 'How about you, Julie?'

She didn't want an answer. Before Julie had the chance to reply, Monika moved towards her and pulled her into her arms and brought her mouth down to meet Julie's.

When they had embraced in the studio at work, Julie had resisted a kiss. What an idiot, she thought now, losing herself in responding to Monika's tongue, the tongue that had flicked so knowingly over Stevenson's cock. Now it was hard and questing and Julie met it with her own, sucking it in, revelling in the feel and taste of the soft lipsticked mouth against hers. Monika smelt of

224

cigarettes and gin and the steamy animal scent of suede on hot flesh.

How horny am I? My nipples are pressing hard against my dress. My sex muscles are dancing out of control.

Monika's hand was suddenly in Julie's knickers, rubbing her clitoris and then a slight graze of long nail against skin and a finger was burying itself inside her. Just as quickly she brought it out and, pulling her mouth away, inspected the creamy moisture. Smiling triumphantly, she then pushed it inside her own sex, mingling the juices of their excitement.

'Dress off,' she ordered, watching as Julie pulled the dress over her head; not the best choice for a seduction but she'd hardly expected it. She stood there in nothing but her briefs and shoes.

'Nice to see your tits properly at last,' observed Monika as she grabbed one in each hand, then pressing her sex to Julie's started dancing, her hips gyrating to the music. Julie's pubic mound pushed towards her, feeling the taller girl's bone above her, and she too joined in dancing.

Monika's total lack of inhibition was infectious. Suddenly it wasn't a seduction at all. Just two sexy women doing what came naturally.

Thumbs scuffing over nipples while hands mashed breasts. Julie's hands squeezing handfuls of Monika's arse, rotating it, pulling her apart, remembering Mark's second hole. Her hands moving from the buttocks around the suede ties to the front to run a finger down Monika's blatant bareness, scooping up sap from her wet slit to come back to her clit and start a steady stroking. Monika shouting approval and pushing forwards to meet Julie's finger, her own hands moving from Julie's breasts to push her knickers aside and delve inside her to rub the cream on to Julie's clitoris in turn.

Facing each other, mirroring each other, both still swaying hips to the music while concentrating on the other woman's finger. Both narrow-eyed, wide-nostrilled, plump-lipped with excitement.

Monika's hands on Julie's shoulders, pushing her to her knees, then flat on her back on the poppy rug. Pulling her knickers off.

'Open wide, Julie. It's my supper time.'

Yesterday Jonny's tongue was on my clit. Today it's Monika's. Hers is smaller – but the effect is instantly more exciting.

There's no point in holding on. Orgasms are not going to be rationed tonight. It's building up now.

Julie bucked her hips forwards to meet Monika's tongue as it licked and stabbed and sucked and yes! – she was there, contractions ripping through her, rolling over and over down the hill, until she slowly, finally, stopped at the bottom.

'Hey,' she said, lazily. Monika raised her head and regarded her through her bent legs.

'Hey yourself. I won't even ask if you liked that.'

'Yeah. I'm just wondering about your turn.' She turned her head. 'Bryn, get your clothes off, will you?'

Monika winked at her. 'Surely you're not really going to let me at lover boy?'

I might regret this some day. But right now, I really feel like being a voyeur.

Julie's diary, 3 July

I'm writing this at 7 a.m. on Thursday. I am so tired. And hungover. And sore.

From the top: last night girls' night out, Monika came back with me, Bryn was here. He said to see I got home safely. Why? Probably find there was another riot last night. There was definitely one in here.

Had incredible scene with Monika while Bryn watched, not what I expected at all, more wham bam hard rock sex than tender seduction. She brought me off with her mouth and though I wanted to do the same for her I wanted something different first. Anyway Bryn must've been split-ting his jeans open by the size of his hard-on when I let him get undressed. His face was amazing, like it was cast in bronze. God, he's so intense.

I liked watching Monika suck Stevenson last week so I thought it'd be pretty good watching her with Bryn. Thought I might feel jealous but I didn't, just really hot even though I'd just come. Part of it was thinking, so maybe he'll like it better with her. Self-destructive!! I think I'm starting to see why Jonny gets off on that. It was cool seeing Monika so impressed with the size of him.

I changed the music over to that trance sampler that I don't like much but it was pretty good background music. I got Bryn lying on the floor then gave Monika carte blanche. No messing, she just sat right on him, back straight and frigging herself saying, can't wait to come, you just lie there and don't move, and she's bouncing up and down with fringes flying. God she is so verbal, it was amazing. Tony Greene thinks I'm foul-mouthed, he should hear Monika in the throes of orgasm. It was something else watching her tits falling out of the suede and her shaved cunt shifting up and down on Bryn while she rubbed herself, just like she was using him like a vibrator – or a gearstick, even! I knew he was having trouble restraining himself but she didn't take long.

Then she was off and on all fours, looking over her shoulder at him, inviting him in, not that he was hesitating. He's not even looking at me, I was saying to myself, trying to make myself feel good through feeling bad. All he cares about is his cock up inside her and shooting his load there. God knows I was getting hornier and had to join in. I slid on my back under Monika so Bryn's balls were almost banging my head and licked around both of them. I knew she wasn't going to come again yet but thought she'd appreciate my input. She was shouting that she did loud enough. Then Bryn came and it was just us girls and she was pushing fingers in and out of me really fast and rubbing my clit hard and I came again and I was shouting as well. So we'd all come at least once and sat around stroking a bit till Bryn got hard again and fucked

227

me standing up while I was bending over the sofa and Monika was rubbing herself all over his back. She was giving a running commentary so I knew what was going on, then I asked Monika if he could give it to her up the bum for a special treat cos he won't be getting it with me and he did and loved it.

Was I jealous? Like hell. Just turned on again. Of course Mon's arse was too much for Bryn so he came again. Men really are useless except we sent him off to get some drinks while we got the vibrator out. Mon wanted to see my books but we were both a bit too pissed for reading, so she's taken a couple home for those lonely nights – as if. She's got a good memory because after she started on me with the vibrator she got Bryn to come and hold me down like Branford did at the club only more so and he was really quite rough, like kneeling on me, and Mon started real mean with the vibrator and she was talking to me about pushing it up my arse whether I wanted it or not and what with Bryn's hands holding my legs apart and his legs over my arms I came so hard even though it was the third time it was like the first time you come after a long layoff, megavolts that won't stop going through you. Think I'll thank Stevenson for that – bet if I had given in to the oppression of the orgasm with Jonny on Tuesday I wouldn't have been so horny last night. Anyway after a bit of a rest me and Bryn got hold of Mon then and tied her to the table with a couple of scarves and shoelaces, not v aesthetic, and then just teased her and didn't let her come and fucked in front of her and she's calling us everything under the sun. We finally both stormed in big time and she came in major fashion.

Bryn went after that, must have been about five. Me and Mon fell asleep then the alarm went off five minutes ago and she went home to get ready for work. This is top secret at work I said. She smiled cynically and said apart from Derek and Mark. Oh yeah, I said, and Stevenson. Might as well put it on the front page.

Chapter Ten

Evening Light, Thursday 4 July

DEAD MAN 'STOLE MY GIRL'

A WINTERSEA MAN accused of murder brought chaos to the Crown Court today as he shouted that his alleged victim had 'stolen his girl'.

Sandra Drew, who lived with the dead man, Greg Anderson, 42, screamed abuse at the accused, Peter Grimley, of Elm View Road. He is charged with murdering Mr Anderson last year at the home he shared with Mrs Drew in Sycamore Avenue, Hornbeam Estate.

Grimley, 45, denied murder but admitted stabbing Anderson with a kitchen knife. He claimed he had gone to see him on the night of the attack to 'get Sandra back'.

Mrs Drew, 40, a divorcee, gave evidence that Grimley came to the house with a bottle of whisky on the night of the attack, saying that he wanted to have a drink with Anderson. She denied any involvement with Grimley, and said he was 'talking rubbish'.

The trial continues.

'What the hell was all that about?' Julie asked, puzzled, as the reporters scanned the front page of the late edition.

'You might be able to find out more than the court,' said Claire dryly. 'All I know is that when I went to cover John so he could phone this story in he said something about there being more to it than anyone's letting on. Anyway, nothing much happened while I was there.'

Shit. I don't want to be called a snob but it's a bit of a downer when your lover's ex-wife is screaming in court about whose woman she's supposed to be.

'And I must say, Julie, your boyfriend looks even better in the flesh than he does on film.'

Julie looked over, astonished. 'What, he was there?'

'Oh, yes. Looking very sexy in a leather jacket and jeans.'

Glad he made an effort.

'I suppose they were all friends. Though why on earth anyone would want to be friends with someone like Peter Grimley – is he as awful as his police mugshot makes him appear?'

Claire shook her head, shuddering. 'Worse. He's an absolute brute. I can't believe he ever had a chance with Sandra Drew. He's just lost it, I think.'

Julie sighed and stood up, throwing her notebook and phone in her bag.

'Stuff it, it's not my business. I've got to get down to the Hotel Bristol. Some of the refugees are organising a self-help group because of the attacks.'

'Must be catching, what with the Hornbeam tenants' association,' said Wendy. 'What a shame that people need to band together like that against the rest of the world.'

'No, you've got it wrong, dear,' said Derek. 'What they're doing – in both instances – is creating community spirit. The most natural thing in the world. Or should I say, in the civilised world. Not the one we live in.'

He was right, thought Julie, as she unlocked one of the

pool cars. All they were doing was what should have come naturally.

She was dead tired. Two hours' sleep was not enough for someone approaching her 30th birthday. The euphoria of the night's events had kept her going at first but the court report had brought her down fast.

Forget Sandra Drew. Never mind murders. Think about last night. Remember Monika's tongue moving faster and harder and you coming. Watching Bryn fuck Monika.

She shivered. It had got cooler overnight, but she was dressed for 22 degrees. Maybe the hot spell was over.

Perhaps after last night the hot spell in my life is over, she thought wryly. At least for now. Calm, that's what I need. A sensible, measured approach to life for a bit. Think maturity. Think the big three-o.

Bullshit. Think raunchy, think horny.

Shame she was so sore for Jonny tonight. Maybe take some KY round. It was always so nice and slippery, anyway, sore or not. If he guessed he wouldn't say; probably wouldn't care. As long as he didn't take it as an invitation to move on to the second hole.

Before she went inside the Hotel Bristol she phoned the office.

'Photographic!'

Good, it was Stevenson.

'You want to hear a good story?'

He laughed softly. 'You mean the same one I just got from Monika?'

'It's not fair! She's got Mark and Derek to tell –'

'Sshh, Julie Gibson. All she said was, I wonder how long it'll be before Julie tells you about last night. I said, were you there? And she said, better believe it. She bet you'd meet me for lunch.'

'Great. Why am I so predictable? So are you on for lunch or not?'

'Of course. Sounds very exciting. Where are you, anyway?'

'Hotel Bristol. Reckon I'll be about half an hour, maybe a bit longer. Let's get right away from the office. The Breaker Bar's handy for me – what do you think?'

'Superb. See you there in forty-five.'

It was always nice to have something to look forward to.

Julie was pleased to see the bar was almost empty – just a few holidaymakers clustered near the windows complaining about the drop in temperature. Stevenson was already there, relaxing on one of the beige sofas, with two glasses and a jug of what looked like sangria on the bleached wood table.

'Is this a joke?'

He smiled, obviously pleased with himself. 'Great, isn't it? I thought your sordid little story would be best accompanied by something really tacky.'

'Hey! It was not sordid! I cannot believe that someone as sybaritic as you could actually drink this stuff.'

He poured and lifted his glass to her. 'Sometimes I prefer to tickle my sense of humour rather than my tastebuds. Skol, or whatever Danes say. Spill the beans, Julie. My imagination's working overtime picturing Monika shackling you and your DI together with his handcuffs and marching round shouting and cracking her whip like an SS guard.'

'Wrong! Well, except for the shouting. No accessories at all, you might be surprised to hear. Just a suede bustier and matching crotchless knickers.'

'How beautifully vulgar. Tell all.'

At the end of her narrative he smiled cynically.

'So much for your desire for a night off. You had the chance on Tuesday but instead met Jonny Drew, and then exchanged the opportunity for a chaste night on Wednesday for an orgy. I think I should despair of you, Julie.'

'A three-way isn't an orgy. We decided that last night, because Bryn always says he doesn't do orgies. And you might be impressed to know that on Tuesday I did your thing.'

'Which?'

'The oppression of the orgasm. I sucked Jonny off then decided I'd go without.'

His thick eyebrows almost met his hairline. 'Congratulations. I am amazed. And impressed.'

'So what about last night? Wouldn't you have liked to have been there?'

His voice lowered. 'Oh, yes. I am a bit disappointed that you and Monika made it without me being there to watch. Although I wouldn't have wanted to play an active part.'

'God, you are so controlled! Not even slightly active? Not just to come once, perhaps, when you finally couldn't bear not to?'

'No – unless – your DI sucked me while I watched you and Mon.'

Julie had thought nothing could excite her after last night. But the thought of Bryn's mouth round Stevenson's cock brought an immediate tingle to her sex.

'The thought of that is such a turn-on.'

His thin lips stretched into a pleased smile. 'Good. I didn't want the turning on to be all one-sided.'

'But you did mean it?'

'Yes. Though of course I wouldn't want to climax, just get close and then go down on him and make him come.'

'Stevenson. You have never confessed these homoerotic fantasies before.'

'Not to you. We haven't had much time together. And if I get this job in London, we'll have even less –'

'What job? You're not leaving! I've only just got here!' Julie wailed, horrified.

He shrugged. 'I haven't had a final offer yet – we're negotiating. It's *Slice* magazine.'

'Wow.' Only the hippest magazine around, the barometer of the front line of urban culture.

'Yes. I'm rather pleased. And don't tell me you

expected me to stay in Wintersea for ever. I've been here too long as it is. I've decided to go for success, and don't tell me it won't bring happiness. I'm not a monk any more.'

'Fantastic. I'm so pleased for you, but I'll really miss you.'

He laughed richly. 'Well, you do also have a detective, a biker and a shrieking Valkyrie. If they're not enough for you, I'm sure Mark will be only too pleased to fill in from time to time. Not to mention Tony Greene. Oh, and Luca at *Adesso!* was asking after you, and –'

'Enough already! Will you give me phone sex?'

'Of course. Anyway, plenty of time before I go – if I go. David will insist on his month's notice.'

Julie fell silent. The thought of losing him was a definite downer.

'Maybe you could get me a job there.'

He looked at her incredulously. 'Julie, do you know yourself at all? Could you really give up the buzz of the daily deadline?'

'Wow. You're right. Never thought of that. I don't know actually how I managed to work on a weekly for so long.'

'Quite. Now you've had that daily fix you won't give it up. You haven't got the patience for a monthly. You're a once-a-day girl.'

'At least.'

They both laughed, Julie's quickly turning to a sigh.

'Talking of work, must be time to go. I can't say I'm looking forward to finding out what happened in court this afternoon. Still, I'm seeing Jonny tonight after his bike club, so I expect I'll get the lowdown from him.'

'Julie, I cannot let you go back to work so dispirited.'

'Yeah. Well. What with this Sandra thing, you leaving, I've only had two hours' sleep, and God knows it's heartbreaking talking to those poor refugees – give us a cuddle.'

That was better. Nothing like a warm male chest in your face to cheer a girl up.

A rich savoury aroma drifted from Jonny's kitchen out to the hallway as he opened the door to her.

'I'm glad you cooked. I took a chance and didn't eat.'

He grinned as he put his arms round her and kissed her hello. 'What if I'd eaten already? Would you have starved?'

'No way! All I had for lunch was sangria and a bun in the canteen afterwards. I reckoned I might be able to persuade you to take me down to the chip shop.'

'You mean you wanted to get on the bike again – wearing that jacket's a pretty good hint,' he teased.

Julie followed him into the kitchen where two pans were on the hob. He prodded the contents of one with a fork and drained it, then handed pan and fork to Julie.

'I expect you know how to mash potatoes?'

'Of course. Just show me where the milk and butter are.'

She started breaking down the potato.

'Actually, you're right. I was thinking another go on the bike'd be pretty exciting.'

He laughed. 'Yeah. Maybe after dinner. I'm starving.'

It was a beef stew.

'Sounds a bit mundane for you.'

'What if I'd said *boeuf en daube*? Or *boeuf bourgignon*? That would have got your tastebuds going, but it's all variations on a theme.'

Julie opened a bottle of wine while Jonny dished up and waited till they'd tasted both food and wine before she mentioned the trial.

'John said you were in court today. This stew is delicious.'

'Thanks. Yeah, Sandra needed a bit of moral support.'

'I thought she hated you. That's what it sounded like when she spoke to me.'

He shrugged. 'You can't live with someone for nearly

235

twenty years without still having a bit of friendship, despite everything. Anyway, she was hardly going to tell my new girl that she missed me and wanted me back, was she?'

'I suppose not. So, how was it? The news tonight said it'd been adjourned till tomorrow but there didn't seem much put forward in the way of evidence, just what everyone already knew.'

'Yup, that was it. Not much evidence to be had, is there? He says he only intended to frighten Greg and it got out of hand. Seeing as Greg can't tell his side of the story, who can prove anything?'

'True. What was all that this morning about Sandra being his girl?'

An odd look crossed Jonny's face for a moment. 'He had some crazy idea about her. That's all he said, then she started shouting at him, and when the prosecution started on him again he just clammed up.' He put his fork down with a clatter. 'Look, babe, if you don't mind, I don't really want to talk about it. Being in court, trying to cheer Sandra up, all the neighbours asking about it, it's all a bit of a pisser.' He took a large swallow of his wine. 'You know what? I feel like a break. What do you think?'

Julie stared at him uncomprehendingly. 'What do you mean? Go away somewhere for the weekend?'

'Weekend, it's hardly worth it. Let's go to France for a week or so, get away from everything. It'll be great. We could stay with my friend Guy near Paris to start with, then move around a bit. Come on – let's go for it!'

Shaking her head, she laughed incredulously. 'You're crazy! I've got work! I've only just arrived. I can't just take a holiday at the drop of a hat! And what about your shop?'

'Bloody work, it spoils everything. That's why I work for myself. As long as I've got no repairs booked in, I can close up and go off any time. Put a sign on the door, "Gone fishing".'

What a fantastic, crazy idea. Just take off and go. But you can't start a new job and ask for time off after three weeks. Maybe one day I'll work for myself – maybe even write my novel. Or get loads of freelancing work from *Slice* . . .

She speared another piece of meat. 'It's funny you should say that, though, because I felt really fed up today too. Stevenson, one of the photographers, might be leaving. He's one of my best friends at the paper. Things just won't be the same without him.'

Jonny had an amused look on his face. 'Is he another boyfriend?'

'No. No, not really. He's just a . . . just a friend who I talk about sex to – it sounds too bizarre.'

'It sounds great!' His face had lit up. 'I love the way you don't give a shit, Julie. I remember when you first met me you said you had a boyfriend, and someone you sometimes screwed, and someone else – I suppose that's the photographer guy?'

She nodded.

'Is he the one who did the bike club pictures? Long hair, all in black?'

'That's him.'

Since we're talking about my sex life I might as well open the throttle a bit more.

'You might be even more interested in what happened last night.'

He cocked his head on one side. 'Why?'

She licked the sauce from her lips. 'Well, it was a sort of a first for me. It started off as a girls' night out. Except after we left the club, me and Monika Neilsen had a bit of a girls' night in. If you know what I mean.'

Laughing delightedly, he pushed his chair back and walked round the table to her. As she turned her head towards him he bent and fixed his mouth on hers, kissing her hard, insistently, the weight of his head pushing her back so she was bent backwards from the waist as far as the chair would allow. The excitement wasn't just in the kiss itself, but in the fact that the only contact between them was their mouths and tongues. Julie kept expecting his hands on her breasts and her nipples tingled with anticipation. But he didn't touch her.

Just as suddenly as he started he lifted his lips from hers.

'You really are something else, you know that?'

She looked up into his warm eyes. He was so appreciative of her, and she wasn't sure why.

'You think I'm great because I fuck different people? I can tell you, it's more exhausting than anything else.'

He laughed. 'No, it's just that you just go for it, and you don't try to hide it.'

'I'll be honest – given the choice I wouldn't have met you all at the same time, but I wasn't, so I've just got to put up with it.'

He regarded her avidly. 'Exactly. You just do it, Julie. And I don't mean just sex. It's the way you look, the way you dress, the way you eat and drink – I bloody love it. I mean, how many women do you know who have sex with other women?'

'Only one – at the moment,' she said with a significant look. 'But what about you? If you think that's so great, does that mean you've had sex with a man?'

'Ah. Not exactly. I mean, not penetration.'

There was a secretive smile on his face.

'Jonny, don't tell me you're praising me for being so open and you're not going to give.'

His smile broadened. 'Come on, babe, I never said I wasn't full of shit.'

He settled back in his chair. 'OK. When I was at university a couple of the guys I hung out with tried it. They reckoned all experience was valuable, seize the day, that sort of crap. But to me it was a class thing. They were middle class, been to public school, and they'd probably already had it thrust upon them. I decided they were talking bollocks about experience and just fancied each other. As far as I was concerned if you weren't a proper gay you were just reliving your schooldays if you made it with another bloke.'

Interesting theory. I'll put it to ex-public schoolboy Stevenson. It might explain his cocksucking fantasies.

'Anyway. Gay sex is not the sort of thing that hits you in the face in Wintersea, as you may have noticed. I would probably never have given it a second thought, until about ten years later, when I was staying with Guy in France.'

Julie sat up straighter. 'Is this serious? Your French friend's your gay lover!'

He burst out laughing. 'Can I finish this story or what? Hang on, let me show you a photo of Guy.' He went to the back of the armchair and pulled out the same photo album he'd taken Greg Anderson's picture from. Turning the pages, he thrust the book in front of her. 'I love Guy like a brother, and even if I didn't there's no way I could fancy him.'

Point taken. Guy was small and dark, almost bald, but with a little pointed beard and moustache. The look on his face was stern, and he must have been in his mid-50s at least.

Julie nodded. 'Go on.'

'Guy had another friend staying with him. He was in a bit of a state. He'd been in a protest about something and the police had given him a good hiding. He was just hanging out at the house licking his wounds, so we spent quite a lot of time together. I liked him. He was about my age, which was, what, about thirty at the time, and spoke good English. He helped me with French. We had a bit of a laugh.'

'So how badly hurt was he? What had he been protesting about?'

'He'd been beaten around the head and arms, not life-endangering stuff, but quite a lot of bruises and a black eye. He'd fallen on broken glass and his hands were cut quite badly. As to what the protest was about, I don't even remember. You know what the French are like, they take to the streets at the drop of a hat – farmers, lorry drivers, students – that's what I like about them.

'So one day I came in from a walk. Guy was at work of course, and I called out to Christian. He said come in, from the spare room, so I did – well, I was staying in it too. He was on the bed, with no clothes on, and he was wanking.'

Julie held her breath.

'At least, he was trying to. His hands were heavily bandaged and I knew they were still very painful. "Jonny, *je t'implore*," he said, and I don't suppose you need a translation.'

'Wow.'

'Yeah. And I thought, Shit, why not? This poor guy can't even wank. God knows when his injuries would heal enough for him to actually go out and find someone to fuck. He was a nice-looking bloke, dark, slim, lots of body hair, and we got on. It was a world away from the prospect of bending over in front of one of my university chums.'

'So you gave him a hand job?'

'I started off with my hand. But as you know, dry is not the best way, so I spat a bit on it, then I thought, Fuck it, and went down on him. I quite enjoyed it.'

'And that was it?'

Jonny shook his head. 'God, no. He was so pleased he insisted on returning the compliment. And I'll tell you something, it was the best blow job I'd ever had.

'We were there together for another five, six days, and it was every day after that. It wasn't like being a gay couple. I went down to the town and got a couple of girlie mags and we'd look at them, just a couple of straight guys getting off on soft porn except we happened to be wanking or sucking each other off at the time. Then we found *L'Histoire d'O* in Guy's bookcase, not that I'd even heard of it but of course being French Christian had. It was good for my French as well.'

'So? Have you seen him since?'

Jonny shook his head. 'No. If I should bump into him again, I'd be pleased to see him. But that was it.'

Julie looked at him curiously. 'But haven't you ever felt like doing it with another man?'

'No, it was a one-off.' He leant over the table, his eyes blazing into hers. 'I'll tell you something, though, Julie. I've had a lot of women's mouths around my dick since then but nothing's ever been like Christian's – until yours the other day.'

A frisson of delight ran through Julie. What was he, this strange man? Ostensibly a working-class man coming up to middle age, living on a rundown housing estate in a decaying town. In reality: university educated, impetuous, living for the moment, up for anything that came his way.

'You're a mystery to me. But don't think I'm complaining.'

He beamed at her. 'You're my kind of girl, Julie. I wish you'd come away with me. I'd love to spend some time with you properly.'

'There you go! You're saying how great I am because I'm up for anything, but I'm not even spontaneous enough to take time off work. It only comes down to sex at the end of the day.' She wrinkled her nose in self-deprecation. 'As you said the other day, I don't do brave. I was even afraid of going on the bike at first.'

'At first, yes. But now you love it, and the faster the better.' He put his hand over hers. 'Julie, there are loads of things I'd like to do with you. Take you rock climbing, paragliding – so many things that are such a turn-on.'

Julie shook her head. 'I just couldn't. It's like swimming, I suppose. I know I can swim for ages without getting tired but I still don't have the nerve to go out as far as you do.'

'Oh, well. We can't all be the same. I need a bit of danger in my life.' He looked at her affectionately. 'I still think there's a wild child in there waiting to come out. I bet if we'd met when you were at your old job you'd have said, "Fuck it, I'll come with you." Wouldn't you?'

Would I? Am I this bold, free, impulsive woman he thinks I am?

She dimpled her cheeks. 'Anyway, how do you think I could cope without my policeman friend, or Stevenson, or Monika?'

'Don't forget the other one, the occasional one,' he reminded her slyly. 'Well, I don't know if you intended to, but you've put me in the mood to rip your clothes off and fuck you till you beg for mercy.'

'Never been known,' she said dryly. 'And you better believe your story has had the same effect on me. But I wondered if you might fancy something else first.'

He sighed exaggeratedly. 'What? Don't tell me, I'm a mind reader. You want a ride first.'

She nodded. 'What was it you wanted me to say? Pretty please?'

'Yeah, yeah. I knew that was coming. Anyway, that's why I only had one glass of wine.' He looked up mischievously. 'Deal? You wash up, I'll take you for a ride, then we'll come home and fuck like rabbits.'

'Deal.'

'How fast exactly were we going?'

'Just a touch over a ton. Were you scared?'

'Terrified. But it was brilliant.'

Jonny smiled delightedly as Julie took off her crash helmet and unzipped her leather jacket. She knew why. She could feel her face flushed with wind and exhilaration and her eyes sparkling with elation. And if he hadn't noticed before that she wasn't wearing a bra she thought he could hardly fail to see her erect nipples straining now against her charcoal sweater as her breasts rose and fell with her breathless excitement.

They were at a truckstop at the eastern end of the bypass, just before the motorway. Julie had noticed the green sign telling them that London was 60 miles away, and half expected Jonny to roar on to the motorway and go to the city just for the hell of it. Instead he stopped at the van and ordered two coffees.

Apart from a couple of lorries there were several bikes parked nearby. As Jonny gave his order, one of the bikers gathered in a knot at one side of the van came up and clapped him on the back.

'Hey, man, wondered when you were gonna get here.' He looked at Julie briefly. He was the stereotypical biker, with long, dark, greasy hair, moustache and shades, despite the fact that darkness had long since descended.

'I'm not stopping,' said Jonny. He handed Julie her coffee. 'Hang on, babe, I've got to have a quick word here.'

When they had pulled up at the van the all-male presence had pushed Julie's pulse up to a new high. Being the only woman in a group of men, especially truck drivers and bikers, sent her sex muscles pulsing. But without Jonny standing next to her she felt selfconscious and sipped her coffee quickly. The two men were immediately deep in conversation, standing apart from the other leather men, but not for long. Jonny was half smiling as he shook the man's hand and came back to Julie.

'What was all that about?' she asked curiously.

Jonny laughed. 'I'll assume your instincts as a journalist are taking over here, rather than you want to know my business.'

Stung, Julie shook her head. 'I'm not being nosy! I was just interested.' He had irritated her. 'I don't give a shit about your business. Perhaps for a minute I forgot we're nothing but semi-strangers who've screwed a couple of times.'

'Hey. Don't.' He took her cup and put it with his own back on the counter then led her round the side of the van. Holding her against it, his eyes fixed on hers. The look in them was patient and tender.

'I wasn't being out of order, Julie. That didn't come

out like I meant it to. And don't say you meant that, about us being strangers.'

She still felt hurt.

'Let's not make a big deal out of it, Jonny. We're not a couple and I don't have any right to know your business. It just came out.'

'I sort of wish we could be a couple.'

Julie shrugged. 'Well, so do I, sort of. But we're not and as we both only sort of want to, let's forget it. I didn't ask you.'

'Yeah.' His hands were on her breasts. 'I can't forget that you're not wearing a bra, though.'

'Thought you hadn't noticed.'

Her annoyance faded as she concentrated on his hands, his thumbs on her nipples through the fine rib, his eyes on her.

'To be honest I hadn't till we got here. When you unzipped that jacket your nipples were standing out like bullets. The thought that every bloke standing round this van noticed and got turned on but you're with me, has really got me going. Can you feel that?'

He was pressing against her, his erection hard under the fly of his jeans. His words had mirrored her own feelings and her anger evaporated in her excitement.

'Of course I can. Specially as I've got no knickers on either.'

'Julie, you want to go home and fuck? Because I do.'

She smiled slowly. 'Well, I don't know. Just before you pulled up here I was reading the signs and thought we might be going to London for a quick ride round, and I still think that'd be cool.'

His face fell.

'But on the other hand I do want to fuck. Now, or at least soon. But not here.'

'You mean you don't want to wait to go home.'

'No. I want to go somewhere . . . different.' She gave him a challenging look.

244

He obviously wasn't fazed by her request. 'Come on then.'

Accelerating quickly, they thundered back down the bypass and then he took the town centre turn-off, past the old industrial estate, then past a 40 mph sign which he ignored. Suddenly he slowed and turned into a back alley and stopped between the rear of a row of shops and a double garage. Obviously the backyard of Drew's Bikes.

'Will this do you?' He had taken off his helmet and was turning a key in a garage door. 'Fancy getting yourself down on a greasy floor?'

'Yeah. I reckon that'll do nicely.'

Oh, yes. As he switched the light on Julie looked round. It was greasy all right. There was a bike in the middle of the floor, stripped of paint. It looked weird. All around the walls various tools and bike parts were hanging.

Julie lifted her arms and experimentally grabbed hold of two large hooks high up on the wall. She had to stand on tiptoe.

'You going to take your clothes off, Julie?'

Jonny was smiling his usual easy smile but his voice was suddenly throaty. She realised what she must look like, almost hanging from the wall as though she were chained ready to submit to a whip or a crop. Her sweater had ridden up to expose her belly and her breasts, framed by the two sides of her jacket, were pointing skyward under the fine wool.

The break in his voice excited her as much as a caress. Letting go, she faced him and took off her jacket and sweater then undid her drawstring trousers. She stepped out of them and stood naked apart from her short black leather boots, knowing that he could see the desire on her face.

'Lots of possibilities in here,' she said huskily. 'Like this bike. Looks so bizarre without paint on it.'

She moved to stand at the side of the bike, running her

245

hands over the grey metal, her back to Jonny. She knew he was watching her and planted her legs apart and folded from the waist over the seat, pressing her mons against the leather.

'Feels pretty nice on here – what do you think?'

Silence, then she heard him unzip his jacket and then his jeans. She could hear his breathing, hard and fast, and imagined him taking in her spread legs, their muscles tensed from the high heels of her ankle boots, her round arse in the air thrust impudently towards him, and a tantalising glimpse of her pink sex.

Shall I just wait here for his cock to plunge inside me, almost anonymously? Actually, no. This is a bit too much like a Bryn domination scenario.

'I think I do like the idea of the greasy floor after all,' she decided, lifting herself from the bike and turning towards him. His jeans were off and she watched him remove his boots. 'Take your T-shirt off, Jonny, but you can put your jacket back on.'

'Thanks, miss,' he laughed, watching her wince as her back touched the cold floor. 'You sure you're comfortable down there?'

It was cold and gritty and smelt of oil and petrol and dirt. She wondered if it was worth trying to explain to him that sometimes there was nothing as luxurious as discomfort.

She rubbed her back from side to side on the cold, greasy floor like a dog rolling on grass. Pushing her fingers inside her wet, waiting opening she looked up at him, her eyelids heavy with sensuality and her lips full and open. 'I'm pretty comfortable down here. That's all I'm interested in and it's all I want you to be interested in.'

He sucked in his breath and lowered himself to his knees. 'Whatever you say, babe.'

'Never mind the talk. Just get your cock inside me,' she ordered, raising herself on to her elbows to watch him approach her. He knelt in front of her like he was

246

paying homage to her sex and then took his weight on his hands and pushed inside her. His silver medallion swung above her face as he thrust in hard and she wrapped her legs around his back, over his leather jacket, squeezing tight against it.

She lowered her back to the cold floor again and lifted her hands above her head. Jonny caught them in one of his and his mouth opened in his big smile as he pushed into her again. She was seized by a sudden rush of tenderness towards him as she noticed for the first time signs of age on his face.

She thrust her hips up to meet his cock. The lack of foreplay, apart from their clinch by the van, had excited her and she thought him as well. Their previous couplings had taken place after plenty of preparation; this time she wanted it immediate and hard.

Thinking again of the bikers and lorry drivers at the truckstop fired her up even more. Was Jonny right? Had they all seen her erect nipples, guessed she wasn't wearing a bra? Perhaps the man he'd talked to had said something about her. It would be something crude, lascivious. She pushed faster, correcting his rhythm, feeling the leather of his jacket against her thighs, rubbing her heels on his back.

'What are you thinking about?' he asked breathlessly, his voice warm and tender.

Good one, Jonny. Telling you will make me come, no problem.

'About the blokes at the van. You said they'd all noticed my tits. Just thinking about them all fancying me, and what they might have said about me after we'd gone. And thinking perhaps we should have just fucked round the side of the van; we were both up for it, and so what if someone came round and saw us, called the others round to watch, oh fuck, fuck me, Jonny, oh God . . .'

It worked. And for him, too. Just as she was wringing

the last contractions from her pussy, Jonny groaned and came with a final convulsive thrust.

After collapsing on top of her he rolled on to his back and swore.

'Christ, this floor's cold on my arse. How did you stand it, Julie?'

She looked at him and they both burst out laughing.

'What the hell are we doing here?' Jonny demanded. 'I remember telling you I wanted us to be special together, have sex in bed, that sort of thing, rather than just getting down to it anywhere we can. Now look at this.'

Julie raised herself up on one elbow. 'Now I suppose you're going to tell me that you had all your adulterous adventures here.'

His devastating blue eyes turned on her blazing with humour, satisfaction, enjoyment. 'No, I didn't. In the shop, Christ, I hate to think how many girls I've fucked over the counter. But not in here.'

She paused then smiled broadly. 'I was just about to say, "Oh, how sweet, you brought me somewhere else," then it occurred to me if you picked up a girl in a pub or club or whatever she'd probably be a bit pissed off if you brought her back to a greasy garage.'

'Got it in one, kiddo.' He was grinning too. 'But I guessed you'd like it. Though I didn't realise there were so many possibilities in here till you leaned over that bike and hung yourself from the wall.'

'You're not joking. If only I'd taken the gym more seriously and got into pull-ups, I'd have been able to hang on to those hooks and lift and lower myself on your cock.' Her mouth formed itself into a pout. 'I'm getting horny again thinking about it. Not to mention the possibilities on the bike –'

She walked over to the stripped-down bike and sat backwards on the pillion, then lay down and reached behind her head for the handlebars.

'Hey, Jonny, what about this? Bit like we just did, but you'd have to stand up.'

He stood.

'I didn't necessarily mean right now –'

'I should hope not. Lying on that floor's enough to shrink your manhood for a week.'

'To be honest with you, after Monika going at me hard with the vibrator last night I'm too sore to go again.'

He smiled and straddled the pillion, imprisoning her legs in his. 'Got to be time you lost your other virginity, I reckon. How about it, when we get back? I'll be gentle with you.'

'No, thanks. I'm saving it for marriage.' She looked at him impishly. 'And before you say anything, that is most definitely not supposed to be a hint.'

'Thank God for that. So, how about we get home and clean ourselves up and finish off that wine in comfort – like bed?'

'Yeah. What time is it?'

Shit. Gone eleven.

'I have to say, I'm dead tired. My eyes are prickly.'

He ruffled her hair. 'If you want, go home, babe, or you're welcome to stay and I'll wake you up early tomorrow for work.'

She yawned. 'I suppose I should just go home. But the thought of a nice warm bath and snuggling under the covers with you and a glass of wine sounds too good to refuse.'

'Yeah, make the most of me.'

In the middle of pulling on her trousers, Julie registered what he'd said. 'What do you mean?'

'I told you, I might go over to France for a while.'

'Oh.'

Silly me. I didn't realise you would go without me.

'Sure. OK, back to yours.'

'Julie. The alarm's gone off.'

'Uh.'

'Come on. It's seven.'

'Oh, God.'

She had slept so deeply she hadn't heard the clock.

'Reset it for half-past. I'll still just about make it.'

'No, get up. I've got to go to the court, and there's stuff I've got to do first.'

She sat up, rubbing the sleep from her eyes. 'Great. You mean you're kicking me out?'

'Not quite yet. Get in the shower and I'll get you breakfast.'

Grumpily Julie complied. Why on earth he couldn't do what he had to do while she was in bed, she couldn't imagine.

After a quick shower she felt better. Not that she'd had anything like enough sleep to make up for the previous night but hell, it was Friday. Get through the day, step could go on without her – she was staying in tonight. Hopefully she'd be firing on all cylinders by the time she met Bryn on Saturday night.

She sat down just as Jonny put the tea and toast on the table.

'Have you written this background story about Greg and Peter?'

'You could say that. There wasn't much background to find, as you know.'

'So that'll be in the paper today?'

She shrugged. 'If they reach a verdict it will. The idea is we splash on the verdict and today's evidence and then the background'll be on page two. Why?'

He sighed. 'I want to tell you something, babe. The real background.'

'For fuck's sake, Jonny, couldn't you have told me before?'

'No, it's not for publication. Not for my sake, but for Sandra's.'

He chewed on a piece of toast, avoiding her eyes. 'I wasn't going to tell you at all. Pete had obviously kept quiet about it, but after his outburst in the dock yesterday he might be having second thoughts. I don't know if it'd

250

make any difference to the trial, but in any event I'd rather you found out from me.'

Julie watched him exasperatedly. 'You're not making any sense, Jonny.'

He sat back in his chair, facing her with a strange look on his face. Defiance? She wasn't sure. Embarrassment?

He told her.

They had been playing their weekly poker game. Jonny, Greg Anderson and Peter Grimley. Sandra usually went out and left them to it but she said she had no money so they were banished to the spare room while she watched TV with a bottle of vodka in the sitting room.

Spare room? Must be the door next to the bedroom. Don't know why, I thought it was an airing cupboard. Maybe because the other doors are always open.

Peter Grimley was on a winning streak and the other two were starting to get low on funds. Sandra came in, drunk. Jonny asked her for a sub.

She'd laughed. No bloody way. Served him right for gambling, he could just bloody well lose. She'd sat on the edge of the table, turning her back on Jonny and smiling at the other two, letting her skirt ride up her thighs.

Piss off if you're not going to help me out then, said Jonny. You're a waste of bloody space, Sandra.

The others protested and Jonny got mad. Tell you what, he said, if you think she's so wonderful, what'll you give me for her? She's on the table already. How much do you think she's worth? A hundred? Two?

Leave it out, Greg had said. That's no way to treat a lady.

What lady, said Jonny.

You bastard, said Sandra, I'd be better off without you. What do you think, guys? See if you can win me.

And so Jonny had carried on playing, using Sandra as his stake. And lost.

'Peter won. He stood up and grabbed her, saying, "Come on, Sandra, we're going home." Of course, there was no way she was going with him. I told him not to be stupid, I'd pay him back the money, it was all a joke. But he was furious. We all had a flaming row. At the end of it, Sandra said whatever happened she wasn't staying with me after what I'd done, and she went home with Greg. Me and Peter had a bit of a bundle and he went off.

'Sandra didn't come back. But Peter always reckoned she should have been his woman, and though we all stayed mates, carried on with the poker games, he got a bit out of order a couple of times when he was drunk. None of us realised he was carrying a knife round with him.'

Oh my God.

'Jonny. Let me get this straight. You're saying it was just a joke?'

He shrugged. 'Christ, I don't know. It seemed perfectly reasonable at the time, but when you're pissed lots of things seem reasonable.'

Julie pushed her chair back, aghast. 'But you treated her like a . . . a chattel! It's like selling her to the highest bidder, like a slave!'

Jonny was looking at his teacup. 'I suppose it seems like that. At the time it was a bit of a laugh. Anyway, once we'd all sobered up, no-one really took it seriously. It's not like she went with Pete. He was the winner, after all.'

'No, but she went. Didn't you feel guilty? Or miss her? Try to get her back?'

He shook his head impatiently. 'Jesus, Julie, I told you about me and Sandra. It was a relief to be on my own, to be honest.'

'All right, but that's not the point. Someone died because of this.'

He looked at her. 'Yeah, right. Poor old Greg. I feel sorry, too, Julie. But that's life, you know. Sometimes you have to make decisions like that – the throw of a dice, the turn of a card.'

She was shaking her head in denial. 'I don't believe

this. I just don't believe that I could be going out with someone who would do something like this.'

'What did you say the other day, I was self-destructive? I suppose that's part of it. Sometimes something presents itself on a plate and you go for it, even though you know it's a bad idea.'

She sighed. 'I knew we didn't have much in common, Jonny, but we really are on totally different wavelengths. I could never understand you.'

'Julie, one day you're going to have to make a decision that could change your life. You might spend hours, days, deciding – but you've still only got a fifty-fifty chance of getting it right.'

'That is so cynical!'

'Really? Open your eyes. How many marriages break up these days? You might as well pick a husband on the toss of a coin as give it any intelligent consideration. You're as likely to get it right.'

'God's sake. Is that what you did when you found out Sandra was having the baby?'

He gave her a flat stare. 'No. I threw a dice.'

'Jesus.'

He sighed. 'I'm not arguing about it, Julie. Christ knows I spent enough time arguing with my mum. She never spoke to me after that.'

'Surprise surprise.'

'Yeah, well.'

He leant over the table and caught her hand in his. 'I know, you're shocked, horrified, all the rest of it. Just try not to make any judgements for a bit. You're not exactly a conventional person yourself. Don't fold your arms and tut like a seaside landlady.'

She almost smiled.

'And now, you better get going or you'll be late for work, unless you're going on duty in leather.'

At the front door she looked at him in dismay. 'I don't know, Jonny. I don't think I can still go out with you now I know this.'

She wondered if she'd ever see the sun rise in his eyes again as he smiled at her. '*Que sera, sera*. I'll tell you something, though, I've had a bloody wonderful time with you. The best.'

Tears sprang to Julie's eyes. 'Are you really going away?'

'Probably. I'll give you a ring when I get back. If you want, just tell me to fuck off.'

'Hey. Meant to give you this.' Her personal card. 'Best not to ring me at work. So. Have a nice time, then.'

'Yeah. Take care.'

She clung to him briefly, then looked into those blazing blue eyes.

Will it be for the last time?

I can't make any decisions now.

Julie's diary, 5 July

Second time writing early next day. I feel like shit, not to mention a bloody fool. I've been prancing round with Jonny on the bike feeling like I was Marianne Faithfull and it turns out that all along he's the fucking Mayor of Casterbridge. No wonder Sandra Drew hates him. No wonder she said he'd ruin my life. God knows who *I* might have ended up with. But I am: a. tired b. slightly hungover and c. possibly over-reacting so all I'm going to do now is go to work, keep my head down, get through the day and come home and go to bed till I see Bryn tomorrow night. As long as Peter Grimley doesn't tell all in court today, then at least it's only my problem. I couldn't stand it if everyone knew. I keep wanting to cry but for God's sake it's not like I'm in love with him or anything. Think I'd feel better if he'd not told me, just said goodbye and good luck, at least I could tell people like S and Mark. I'm not used to not being able to tell friends when things go wrong, I feel so bloody lonely.

Chapter Eleven

Evening Light, Friday 5 July

MANSLAUGHTER IN ANDERSON DEATH: EIGHT-YEAR SENTENCE

by our Court Reporter

WINTERSEA CROWN Court erupted with cries and jeers from the public gallery as the jury returned a verdict of not guilty of murder on Peter Grimley this morning.

However Grimley, 45, was convicted of the manslaughter of Greg Anderson, 42, last year. The jury took less than an hour to deliver their verdict.

In his summing up the judge told the jury that to return a verdict of murder they must be 100 per cent sure that Grimley had gone to see the victim with the express purpose of murdering him.

Sandra Drew, who lived with the dead man, screamed abuse at the jury. Grimley had said that he had gone to get her back from Anderson, but there was no evidence to prove that she had ever had any involvement with him except as a friend and neighbour.

John had phoned the story in and the copytaker told the newsroom the verdict. No surprises.

'Anything else happen today?' Julie asked almost casually.

Hazel the copytaker shook her head. 'All he said was cries and jeers et cetera at the verdict, and Sandra Drew screamed abuse. Seems like it was just summing up, jury out, back and sentence. Wasn't really much else that could happen.'

That's what you know.

John was back in the office only half an hour later.

'I don't know, murder trials, you look forward to them and then what? Hardly any evidence, no weeping and wailing apart from a bit from Mrs Drew, and then they get off. This job can be a pain in the arse sometimes.'

'Jonny dressed up again?' she asked, her voice slightly high-pitched.

John shook his head. 'Not there. Suppose he thought one day off work was enough.'

What do you mean? He said he was going.

Get the phone.

'Newsdesk!'

'Hihi. Didn't see you around yesterday. Still fancy me?'

'Yeah, I love you and want to have your babies.'

'Back to you! Listen, what about tonight? With Mark?'

'No way.'

Is he looking over at me? Shake head in his direction.

'And Bryn, I mean.'

'That's even worse. He won't want to know. Three's the biggest crowd he's doing, he told you that. Anyway, I'm seeing him tomorrow. Alone!'

'OK. You'll be in the Vaults tonight, though?'

Julie sighed. 'Maybe for one. That's all. I need an early night.'

She hung up. Well, at least if she stopped seeing Jonny, life would be more manageable, especially now Monika seemed to be staking a permanent place on the scene.

Not surprisingly the day dragged, but Julie was grateful that it was uneventful. The most heinous crime overnight had been a stolen mountain bike, the report of which she got in two minutes from one of the inspectors, both Tony Greene and Adam Arnside apparently in a meeting.

When the paper came round she was pleased with the Hornbeam tenants' association feature, though the background on Peter Grimley and Greg Anderson was pretty lacklustre. It amused her that one of the photos Jonny had given her of Greg with Sandra was captioned – on holiday together in 1996 – but failed to mention that at the time they had been just friends.

Lunchtime finally arrived and she went out just to get some time to herself, walking like a zombie round the shops. Wendy had gone out half an hour earlier, asking if she wanted to join her, but she'd pleaded tiredness. She could just imagine their conversation: Hey, Wen, so pleased you and Doug are going such great guns. Me? Well, I might be splitting up with Jonny since I found out he lost his wife by gambling with her, and as for Bryn, well, we had a terrific night on Wednesday taking turns to screw Monika.

After lunch she met the mayor to talk about the appeal for the new bandstand, which fortunately didn't demand too much concentration. She dragged the story out as long as possible, chatting to Wendy desultorily as she worked.

Phone. Tony Greene.

'Hey, missed you this morning.'

'Yes, lots to do. Julie, I have something to tell you. Can you come round some time this afternoon?'

She looked at her watch. Three o'clock.

'Sure. I can be there in ten minutes if you want. I've

nearly finished what I'm doing. But what is it? Something really hot?'

'Not really. Just something I want to tell you first.'

'You sweetie.'

He sounded embarrassed. 'No, it's not really a favour. Anyway, no rush, I'm here till late.'

Tired, pissed off, depressed – she forgot all about it as her journalistic instincts took over and she bashed out the end of the bandstand story, mentally rubbing her hands together in anticipation of an exclusive. Then just as she was about to pick up her bag and tell Bob where she was going, a thought occurred to her.

This isn't a story. He's going to make a pass.

He had seemed embarrassed. And said come any time, I'm here till late.

Shit, could have been a big mistake to say where she was going. Hold the front page – Julie's got an exclusive. Superintendent propositions reporter!

She told Bob a Hornbeam man had just been on about a sponsored bike ride, didn't know when she'd be back, if it was too long she'd go straight home. He nodded testily.

It was cheering her up even more than the prospect of an exclusive. Of course she'd let Tony down gently, because she genuinely did feel regretful that they just weren't meant to be. This was exactly what she needed right now. Not exactly a *Brief Encounter* scene, but wistful sighs and yearning looks, the fleeting touch of his hand on hers . . .

She popped into the ladies on the way out to re-lipstick and mascara. She looked a bit tired but nothing too drastic. Certainly the prospect of the scene ahead had brought the sparkle back to her eyes.

Thank God for serial shallowness.

'Julie. Come in.'

He rose and put his hand on her back and closed the door behind her – a first.

She sat down and faced him, smiling. 'Hi, Tony. Do I need my notebook?'

A guilty look crossed his face. 'No, actually – how did you know?'

Folding her arms on his desk, Julie looked at him encouragingly.

'I didn't. It was the way you sounded on the phone. I wasn't sure what to expect.'

He cleared his throat. 'I don't know how to tell you this. A few things have happened that have drawn us to certain conclusions. Nothing proved, nobody charged – yet. But we think we've got it sussed and as for what happens next, it's being discussed higher up.'

This is not a pass.

'It really sounds to me like I ought to be making notes.'

'No, Julie. As I said we're still deciding where to go from here. I'll talk you through it. Remember we had a video from the Clinton's Wines job last Saturday? Well, one of the home-beat bobbies recognised one of the lads. He's got a slight limp, not that you'd notice if you didn't know him, but McNichol got it in one. So we went round to see him and his best mate. Not only had they got booze and ciggies hidden under the bed but baseball bats and balaclavas. Both mums were furious and came in with them for a little chat. What with us and the mums they admitted they were involved in the riot and named a couple more names.

'We pulled in some more lads. They deny they're a gang, but coincidentally they just all happen to hang out at the motorbike club.'

I am not reacting. I will not react.

'Not that that means anything. Except some of the things the lads said didn't gel. They sounded like they were quoting someone else saying something they hadn't properly understood.'

'What sort of things? Like something political?'

He smiled uneasily. 'Yes, sort of. They were definitely under the influence of someone they admired.'

Sighing, he sat back in his chair. 'The thing is we'd already been alerted by the public order boys at the Met thanks to a video from the riots up in London. Bikers were involved, obviously part of some organised group or other – you can guess who one of them was.'

Oh, please.

'For God's sake. This is the second – sorry, go on.'

Concern was in his eyes. 'You sure you're all right?'

She nodded.

'Jonny Drew's always been politically inclined, taking part in any protests going, reclaim the streets, exporting calves, that sort of thing, but there's no law against it. Anyway after the disturbances one of our officers went up to London to see if we could get any further forward.

'Years ago Special Branch were keeping an eye on someone, a Frenchman who was over here teaching evening classes.'

'Guy somebody.'

'That's him. It wasn't just the syllabus he was teaching.' He cleared his throat. 'There have always been revolutionary groups around. You're too young to remember when they were at their height in the late sixties and early seventies, but they've never gone away. I know it sounds a bit melodramatic, but they reckon Jonny Drew's part of an international anarchy group.'

'Oh, please! Anarchy in the UK?' She shook her head impatiently. 'And you seriously think Jonny started the bike club just to teach kids to make trouble? What's the point? Working-class kids smashing up their own estate, their parents' cars – what's that achieving?'

'Maybe that's just a practice ground. And wherever the trouble occurs, it all contributes to a gradual breakdown of law and order. You have enough people stirring up enough kids all over the country, and God knows what sort of society you end up with.'

He sighed. 'Let's be honest, Julie, it's a divided country. It's not hard to stir lads who've got nothing and not much chance of improving matters up against our society.'

'You almost sound like you approve.'

Tony shook his head. 'No, I don't approve of lawbreaking. But neither do I approve of a society that creates the sort of envy that makes lawbreaking seem a logical option. So, that's where Jonny Drew's coming from. The Met have been trying to track down web sites various groups set up but haven't had much luck. They have learned from phone bill records, though, that Mr Drew spends a lot of time on line, as you may know.'

'No, I didn't know, Tony.' But let me guess what's behind that spare room door.

'The top and bottom of it is that the youth of Wintersea have been given a free crash course in civil disorder while supposedly learning about motorbikes. They worked their way through a programme from wind-screen smashing to burglary to riot.'

'So-called.'

Tony smiled tenderly at her. 'So-called.'

Julie was starting to get annoyed. 'Oh, you forgot the nastier side of it – stoning refugees and attacking students.'

'Interesting, that. We didn't think it was his style, and it turns out a few of the younger kids decided to show a bit of initiative and got a few of their mates involved. They were kicked out the bike club.'

'What a relief,' she said tartly. 'So what you're telling me, Tony, is that someone I'm, let's say, involved with, is suspected of being an anarchist of long standing who has been subverting law and order in this town by corrupting minors and orchestrating street violence. Not to mention taking part in large organised violent demonstrations in London.'

'In a nutshell, yes.'

Julie was silent. It was a shock, but hell, as far as she was concerned it was better than gambling with your wife.

She looked up at Tony Greene's concerned face. 'You know what? He told me he liked life on the edge. It was pretty dim of me not to think that there was more to his life than running a bike shop and a club for yobs. No wonder you tried to warn me off him. So did Bob Underwood – don't tell me he knows you were keeping an eye on Jonny.'

'No, that's coincidence. He probably fancies you himself. It's not nice to think of someone you like involved with anyone else, let alone a bad lot.' His look was wistful. 'I know that only too well.'

What a sweetie. He obviously doesn't know about Bryn.

'And then we found out that you and DI Edwards were involved.'

'Oh, shit.'

He laughed. 'Told you before about your language. Problem was he was the one co-ordinating our little anarchy problems. When I told him you were going out with Jonny Drew he had to tell all.'

A faint smile came to Julie's lips. 'Not all, I hope.'

'Julie, you're quite something. Do you feel all right?'

Slumping down in her chair, she yawned and looked Tony Greene in the eye.

'I feel awful, actually, but that's not all down to your news. I'm having to take too much on board today. The thing is, why are you telling me? You said the higher-ups are deciding what to do. What's to stop me driving straight round to Jonny and telling him to get away for a bit?'

'Too late, Julie. He's gone.'

'Oh, right. Gone fishing.'

'Sorry? He's left a friend in charge of his shop. He says he doesn't know when he'll be back.'

'Don't tell me. Another biker, greasy-looking, dark hair?'

Tony nodded.

So that's why we went to the truckstop last night.

That's why he wasn't in court. Those things he had to do after I left this morning: could packing have been among them?

She almost felt amused. 'He said he was thinking of going over to stay with his friend in France for a few days. I didn't realise he meant to lie low.'

'Well, he'll know we're on to him. For one thing there won't have been many faces at the bike club last night, and those who did show will have told him about the others being questioned.'

'So what happens next? Will you put out a warrant for his arrest?'

'As I said, that's out of my hands. We could get him on some conspiracy charge, incitement to riot, but unless the kids talk the evidence is circumstantial. Half of them are under age in any case, and the other half are not exactly Mensa material. And let's face it, we don't really want this sort of thing in the public domain. We spend a lot of time trying to reassure people that we don't live in a lawless society. It won't help public morale to think the next generation are being influenced by activists under our noses.'

'But surely you can't just let him come back and carry on!'

Tony laughed. 'Hardly! Oh, I expect he'll come back to England all right, but he'll go somewhere else, where he's not known, and start again.'

'Yeah. Well, thanks for telling me. I think.'

Tony leant over the desk and took her hand. 'Don't worry, Julie. I'd put money on the whole thing fizzling out, then nobody will have to know.'

'Suits me. But if there is going to be any action, I presume I can trust you to let me know first.'

He burst out laughing. 'An *Evening Light* exclusive! Of course!'

She smiled wearily. 'OK, I know. At a time like this I shouldn't be thinking of the paper.'

'No, I'm glad you are. It's a healthy sign.' He looked at

her slyly. 'Anyway, DI Edwards is more your mark. Much better looking. And younger.'

She looked across at him from under lowered lashes. 'True, but you know I do have a thing for older men.'

'Get out of here! Look, are you sure you're all right? Can I get some coffee or something before you go?'

Timecheck: 4.55.

'No, thanks, but I'll borrow your phone and give the office a quick call. Think I'll meet the gang in the Vaults. A large vodka is what I need at the moment, not coffee.'

He handed her the receiver. 'Look, I'll get Bryn to come down and see you –'

'No way! I'm seeing him tomorrow. He's got some explaining to do – Mark Williams, please.'

'Don't blame him. He was agonising about it, but it was too good to be true, you going out with him.'

'Yes, I bet. Hi, it's me. Are you just off to the Vaults? Yes. Yes. Nothing, just tell Bob this story was a complete waste of time, I've finished in the office and I'm going home. See you in the pub in ten.'

She handed the phone back. 'Cheers, Tony. And thanks for being so nice.'

'Thank you for not breaking down in tears. Mind you, I wouldn't have minded comforting you.'

He stood up and Julie followed suit as he walked round the desk and grasped the door handle. Before he could open it, she reached up and kissed him on the cheek.

'See you Monday.'

'Yes, Julie. You take care now.'

For God's sake. I've taken this so well and now I'm walking down the corridor and tears are coming into my eyes.

'Bloody hell, Jules, you're taking a bit of a risk going off to see lover boy on a Friday afternoon.'

Her hand paused mid-air, the glass suspended inches from her mouth.

'Wrong, Marko. Who said I did?'

'Bob thought so. He was looking at his watch and huffing and puffing and when I gave him that message about the story being a waste of time he just glowered, as he does.'

'For God's sake. He's such a prat. For your information, which you might pass on to him, Jonny's gone to France on holiday.'

'Oh, sorry. Seemed a bit obvious, though. You get a phone call and you're telling someone called sweetie you missed them this morning, then you rush off on some unlikely story, what's more to Hornbeam – well, you see my point.'

She almost laughed.

'See what you mean. Actually it was Tony Greene.'

'So why didn't you say so?'

'Didn't know what he wanted. Thought he was going to make a pass.'

'Gibbo! A super! Brilliant!'

'Shut it, Mark. Anyway, he didn't. Must have lost his nerve. Anyway, he knows about Bryn now.'

'Wow. Did you tell him before he made his pass or after?'

'Told you, he didn't do it. And just as well – I wouldn't want him making a fool of himself. He's too useful as a good mate. He'd only hate me if he tried it on and I said, "Oops, sorry, I'm shagging one of your DIs."'

'True. Oh, and you might be amused to know that the other thing Bob was pissed off about was that sod all's happened today and unless there's another riot overnight they're going to have to splash on your bandstand story.'

'Just when you thought nothing could make you laugh –'

'Why not? Missing lover boy number two already? You can always change your mind about tonight.'

'No way!' she said emphatically. 'I'm shattered. I'm going home to crawl into a hole. It must be your round.

Get me a large one. I'll pay you back. I just need a bit of anaesthetic.'

'What for?'

She sighed. 'Just do it. I'll tell you one day.'

Stevenson appeared while Mark was ordering and sat down next to Julie in the seat Mark had just vacated.

'Julie, on a scale of one to ten you're about nine at the moment.'

'The looking-like-shit scale? You don't have to tell me.'

'So why? Didn't bikeman come up to scratch last night?'

'Briefly, I had a lovely time last night. But just between us, today has been one of the worst days of my life.'

He looked impressed. 'Tell all.'

'No. This is something that's not for telling. Anyway, there's no sex in it.'

Laughing, he handed her the vodka and tonic Mark was waving in her direction. 'That's why it's been such a bad day. You need some tension raising.'

'Oh, no, I don't. I need to be alone.'

She downed the drink in two swallows and rose. 'See you all next week. I'm going home for twenty-four hours' sleep.'

The others must have chorused their goodbyes but she wasn't listening. She was out the door on automatic, in a cab and home in bed without letting a single thought into her conscious mind.

'Are you all right?'

I'm getting sick of people asking me that, thought Julie.

'Fine. What are you doing phoning me? I said I was coming home for twenty-four hours' sleep.'

'Yeah, I've heard that one before, Jules, and you always moan afterwards that you end up waking up at the usual time.'

'How wonderfully predictable I am. OK, I'm awake, I'm up, and I'm all right. Why shouldn't I be?'

'Why? When you so obviously weren't last night? After

the way you sunk that large vodka in ten seconds flat, Stevenson couldn't stop going on. It was all I could do to stop him coming round and trying to look after you. Mon says she's never seen him like this. He's really fond of you.'

So fond he's buggering off to London, but I don't suppose you know that.

'He said you said it was the worst day of your life.'

'I didn't want him to tell the world. And as I said, you'll find out, when I'm ready.'

'OK, OK! I'm not hassling you. We were just worried about you. Anyway, I'm off to meet Mike before the match, but Mon wants a word. If that's all right.'

'Oh, yes, you're still ace footie correspondent. Put Monika on if you want. I'm only reading.'

'Hihi. Are you still in bed?'

'No, why?'

'The lad here's going off to be a boring sportswriter and leaving me in bed, and I thought it'd be a nice idea if we had a little phone sex and wanked together – Fuck off to your stupid match – shit, now he wants to stay and watch. Piss off, Mark.'

Julie heard his voice but not what he was saying then the door banged.

'He's gone. Hey, what do you say? I thought what a brilliant idea, both of us lying in bed and turning each other on talking and playing with ourselves.'

In spite of herself Julie felt a tingling heat gather in her sex. 'It is a brilliant idea, Mon, but I'm not really in the mood at the moment.'

'Shit, this is just what you need to take your mind off it, whatever it is. I got dressed up for Mark this morning and now he's fucking off. It seems such a waste.'

'Dressed up? Go on, tell me.'

'You'd love it. It's a red PVC corset, quarter cups, tits hanging out, done up with black hooks, suspenders and black stockings and red patent stilettos.'

'And he's gone out leaving you in that? I can't believe it.'

Monika snorted. 'He was going straight out without even a good-morning fuck, but after I put this on he managed a quickie. He's a real tart as far as lingerie is concerned. As I expect you know.'

'I remember it well. He was always complaining about my white vest and pants.'

'That sounds sexy. Is that what you've got on now?'

Julie laughed. 'Embarrassed as I am to admit it, I'm still wearing yesterday's knickers. I haven't showered. I just got up and put them on and a pair of drawstrings and a sweatshirt.'

'Dirty cow. So no vest. Come on, strip off. Let's wank together.'

'Sod off, Mon. You can if you like.'

'You better believe it. Christ, I'm soaking wet. That is so good. Hey, how do you fancy one of these stiletto heels pushed up you?'

'No way! Sounds painful.'

'I'd do it gently. You can do it to me. No, I know. How about a stick of Wintersea rock? We can get on each end of it. Our clits will be banging together as we push in and out on it. Shit, that's fucking brilliant. What an idea! You'll do that with me, won't you, Julie? Shit, I'm getting close.'

'Sure, Mon. With Bryn watching?'

'Oh, yeah. Oh, fuck, Julie, oh, shit, I can't wait to get together with you again. I'm coming again. God, that's better than Mark did this morning. Wow, that is fucking unbelievable.'

Monika's voice came back to its normal volume after her shouted climax.

'Hey, that was a fantastic orgasm. You sure you don't want one? I've got your erotic books here. I'll read to you over the phone.'

'No, Mon. I'm saving myself for Bryn tonight.' She yawned. 'If I can keep awake.'

'Hey, that was some idea, that rock. Just think how sweet we'll taste afterwards. You won't let me down on that one, will you?'

'No chance.'

'So, if you're not going back to sleep, how about a little retail therapy?'

'I know I keep saying no, but I really don't want to do anything except sit here and read and listen to some music.'

'And wait for Bryn.'

'That's it.'

More like decide how to play it with Bryn.

'See you, Mon. Have a nice day.'

'Are you sure you're all right?'

Not again.

'*Yes*. Now, goodbye.'

After buzzing Bryn in she opened her flat door and walked to the bedroom. She propped herself up elegantly on the bed on one elbow, one knee raised and her pussy exposed. All she wore was the leather jacket, open.

'Julie?' She heard his puzzled voice as he didn't find her in the sitting room, then his footsteps in the kitchen. Then he was framed in the bedroom doorway.

'Julie. Are –'

'Don't!' Her voice rang out fiercely. 'I am sick and tired of people asking if I'm all right.'

'Sure. Hey, you look fantastic. I was worried about you, but Tony said you'd said you'd see me tonight –'

'Yep. So here you are. This is what you were looking forward to, isn't it?' Her hands swept down the jacket and over her bare hips and thighs. 'Wanted to give you what you want. After all, you'd only take it, anyway.'

'Oh, don't. I won't take anything you don't want me to have, you know that. Anything I've done that seems that way I've done for your pleasure, I told you. I thought you understood.'

269

She smiled cynically. 'I thought I did too. Until I found out you were using me to keep tabs on Jonny Drew.'

He sat on the bed, his face troubled with remorse. 'That's not true, Julie. Using you was just what I didn't want to do. I couldn't believe it when I found out you were seeing him, but what could I do?'

Her lips smiled at him but she couldn't make it reach her hurt eyes.

'Don't look at me like that. I couldn't warn you about him in case you told him we were on to him. And say I'd just asked you to stop seeing him – you'd have thought I was pushing you into a commitment you weren't ready for and got scared off. I was in a catch-22.'

'Sure. So now he's gone you can stop feeling guilty about using me. I'm so pleased for you.'

'I was *not* using you. Be fair, Julie, I didn't ask you about him. I was worried about you – why did you think I was waiting up for you on Wednesday?'

'Oh, come on, don't say you thought I was with him and might come to some harm?'

He shook his hands in frustration. 'Look, believe me! I care about you, Julie. Very much.'

'OK. So you were playing Sir Galahad, but it didn't stop you jumping in between me and Monika, did it?'

'Christ! Look, I know you're entitled to be a bit unreasonable at the moment, but I really don't think I can take the blame for that! It was her idea and I said we should do what you wanted, as you well know.'

She was trembling. 'Fuck off, if you think I'm being unreasonable! Hang on, I'll give you Mark's address! Monika's there – they'll be only too happy to invite you in!'

'Stop it! Just stop it! Stop shouting and stop blaming me for things I haven't done and don't plan to do!'

His hands were gripping her shoulders hard. She glared at him, her rage white hot. 'Go on, then, hurt me! Why don't you just fuck me and get out of here? That's what you want to do, isn't it?'

Breathing heavily, his face a mask of misery and despair, he let her go and put his hands on the duvet.

'No, sweet Julie. What I want to do is take you in my arms, tell you everything will be fine, that I'll look after you, and make all the pain go away. But if you want me to, I'll leave. Just don't expect me to stop caring about you.'

Her fury dissipated in the tenderness of his words. She felt tears pricking her eyes and realised that, despite what she had been saying to everybody, she hadn't been all right; but that she was going to be.

'Don't go, Bryn. I know I'm not being fair. Let's start again. Could you just go and get us a drink? There's some wine in the kitchen.'

While he was gone she wiped the wetness from her eyelashes.

I've never been a cry baby, and I'm not going to start now.

He was back in two minutes with full glasses and sat on the edge of the bed looking at her. She felt much better.

'OK?'

'I'm fine. After all, what am I so upset about? The fact that I feel a bit of a fool? It's not like he was the love of my life.' She took a sip of wine.

'Bryn?'

'Yes?'

'You caring about me so much. That's really nice.'

'Good.'

'But I don't think I'm ready for any commitment. Not quite yet.'

With Jonny gone, Stevenson going, we're practically exclusive anyway. But let's keep all the options open.

'That's fine. As long as you're happy that I care about you, I can work with that.'

'The only thing is, I really don't want to give up that intense, animal, wordless, smouldering sex. I'm a bit

271

worried that this caring stuff might interfere. Do you think you can still do it?'

She put her glass down and raised her hands behind her head to grasp the bedposts. The jacket fell to her sides, exposing her breasts. As Bryn's face took on its wonderful, familiar look of sensual concentration she slid her back down and opened her legs.

'Don't say anything!' she warned him. 'Just do what seems right.'

What seemed right to him was right to her too. He stripped and got on the bed, crawling towards her on all fours, his mouth hesitating for a brief second before settling on hers firmly as though it had found its home. She responded just as ardently and gasped when she felt his fingers on her sex, caressing her with almost quiveringly light strokes then dipping into her moistness, making sure she was ready for him. Then with a sigh that evoked a thousand words, his cock was inside her, driving hard, fully in and almost fully out, so that each time she opened up for him gratefully. The warmth and solidity of his body and the sensuousness of his face and deep glittering eyes felt so right. One of his hands was on the bedhead and the other was on her clitoris, stroking her surely, and she saw his lips part and his eyes start to slide into a dream world and she knew he was almost there, and so was she.

Julie's diary, 7 July

Perhaps I'm more girlie than I thought. Bryn cares about me, a lot, and I like it – a lot! It might make up for missing Jonny. Though much as I adore cops, I can see the attraction of being a gangster's moll. Having a relationship with a lawbreaker is a bit of a turn-on – though if I'd known at the time might have been different. Feel a bit glamorous. At first thought it would be so embarrassing and how could I tell people, but now I've calmed down think it gives me a nice dollop of street cred. Will I ever grow up?

Great sex with Bryn last night then went to One Nation – brilliant. Laitan said he missed me on Friday! Came back and did not do an encore, just got in bed and cuddled and he *stayed the night*, feel v significant! This morning had an early-morning quickie then he got papers and did scrambled eggs, sat and ate and read like old married couple. Then he said, I need a shower, how about you? I knew what that meant. Washed each other really slowly then I couldn't resist showing him how powerful shower was. He just loves thought of me wanking when he's not here, made me do it with shower, then he held the showerhead and fucked me standing up from behind, made me bend over and hold on to end of bath, kept moving shower to different bits of me. He was back to dominant mode and I am so not complaining. He left abt 3, working tonight, as he went I said, hey, ever thought of buying a motorbike? He laughed and said if it guaranteed seeing my tits framed by the leather jacket he'd think about it – wonder if he meant it?

Epilogue

e-mail from Jonny Drew to Julie Gibson, 14 July

Hello babe. I expect you know by now why I went away and why I'm not back. It's a bit of a pisser – I was hoping to be able to carry on in Wintersea. Apparently there's no warrant out for me but there would be for sure if I came back. I'm staying in France for the rest of the summer then I might come back to England – try the north, perhaps, it'll make a change. Probably something I should have done years ago. Hope you don't mind if I stay in touch, I'd like to know what you're up to.

It's a holiday here today and there's a funfair in the town. I'm going on the Big Wheel and I'll think of you. We had some great times, didn't we? Do you remember that fortune teller predicting one of the men in your life would cause big trouble? I'm sorry if I messed you up, I shouldn't have got involved with you but I'm getting soft in my old age. Shame it wasn't someone like you I was married to all those years, what a waste. You take care, babe. You can e-mail me here if you want, Guy will always pass a message on if I've gone, think I'll head off to the Alps and spend some time climbing now all the other excitement's gone out of my life. I really hope you don't hate me. There's no way I could make you understand, but maybe one day some idea or cause might speak to you, and you might get my drift. Have a wonderful life, Julie, and from time to time do something that scares you, just for me.

J.

BLACK
lace

BLACK LACE NEW BOOKS

Published in September

DEVIL'S FIRE
Melissa MacNeal
£5.99

Destitute but beautiful Mary visits handsome but lecherous mortician Hyde Fortune, in the hope he can help her out of her impoverished predicament. It isn't long before they're consummating their lust for each other and involving Fortune's exotic housekeeper and his young assistant Sebastian. When Mary gets a live-in position at the local abbey, she becomes an active participant in the curious erotic rites practised by the not-so-very pious monks. This marvellously entertaining story is set in 19th century America.

ISBN 0 352 33527 0

THE NAKED FLAME
Crystalle Valentino
£5.99

Venetia Halliday's a go-getting girl who is determined her Camden Town restaurant is going to win the prestigious Blue Ribbon award. Her new chef is the cheeky over-confident East End wide boy Mickey Quinn, who knows just what it takes to break down her cool exterior. He's hot, he's horny, and he's got his eyes on the prize – in her bed and her restaurant. Will Venetia pull herself together, or will her 'bit of rough' ride roughshod over everything?

ISBN 0 352 33528 9

CRASH COURSE
Juliet Hastings
£5.99

Kate is a successful management consultant. When she's asked to run a training course at an exclusive hotel at short notice, she thinks the stress will be too much. But three of the participants are young, attractive, powerful men, and Kate cannot resist the temptation to get to know them sexually as well as professionally. Her problem is that one of the women on the course is feeling left out. Jealousy and passion simmer beneath the surface as Kate tries to get the best performance out of all her clients. *Crash Course* is a Black Lace special reprint.

ISBN 0 352 33018 X

Published in October

LURED BY LUST
Tania Picarda
£5.99

Clara Fox works at an exclusive art gallery. One day she gets an email from someone calling himself Mr X, and very soon she's exploring the dark side of her sexuality with this enigmatic stranger. The attraction of bondage, fetish clothes and SM is becoming stronger with each communication, and Clara is encouraged to act out adventurous sex games. But can she juggle her secret involvement with Mr X along with her other, increasingly intense, relationships?

ISBN 0 352 33533 5

ON THE EDGE
Laura Hamilton
£5.99

Julie Gibson lands a job as a crime reporter for a newspaper. The English seaside town to which she's been assigned has seen better days, but she finds plenty of action hanging out with the macho cops at the local police station. She starts dating a detective inspector, but cannot resist the rough charms of biker Jonny Drew when she's asked to investigate the murder of his friend. Trying to juggle hot sex action with two very different but dominant men means things get wild and dangerous.

ISBN 0 352 33534 3

To be published in November

LEARNING TO LOVE IT
Alison Tyler
£5.99

Art historian Lissa and doctor Colin meet at the Frankfurt Book Fair, where they are both promoting their latest books. At the fair, and then through Europe, the two lovers embark on an exploration of their sexual fantasies, playing dirty games of bondage and dressing up. Lissa loves humiliation, and Colin is just the man to provide her with the pleasure she craves. Unbeknown to Lissa, their meeting was not accidental, but planned ahead by a mysterious patron of the erotic arts.

ISBN 0 352 33535 1

THE HOTTEST PLACE
Tabitha Flyte
£5.99

Abigail is having a great time relaxing on a hot and steamy tropical island in Thailand. She tries to stay faithful to her boyfriend back in England, but it isn't easy when a variety of attractive, fun-loving young people want to get into her pants. When Abby's boyfriend, Roger, finds out what's going on, he's on the first plane over there, determined to dish out some punishment.

And that's when the fun really starts hotting up.

ISBN 0 352 33536 X

If you would like a complete list of plot summaries of Black Lace titles, or would like to receive information on other publications available, please send a stamped addressed envelope to:

Black Lace, Thames Wharf Studios,
Rainville Road, London W6 9HA

BLACK LACE BOOKLIST

Information is correct at time of printing. To check availability go to www.blacklace-books.co.uk

All books are priced £5.99 unless another price is given.

Black Lace books with a contemporary setting

FEMININE WILES £7.99	Karina Moore ISBN 0 352 33235 2	☐
DARK OBSESSION £7.99	Fredrica Alleyn ISBN 0 352 33281 6	☐
THE TOP OF HER GAME	Emma Holly ISBN 0 352 33337 5	☐
LIKE MOTHER, LIKE DAUGHTER	Georgina Brown ISBN 0 352 33422 3	☐
THE TIES THAT BIND	Tesni Morgan ISBN 0 352 33438 X	☐
VELVET GLOVE	Emma Holly ISBN 0 352 33448 7	☐
DOCTOR'S ORDERS	Deanna Ashford ISBN 0 352 33453 3	☐
SHAMELESS	Stella Black ISBN 0 352 33485 1	☐
TONGUE IN CHEEK	Tabitha Flyte ISBN 0 352 33484 3	☐
FIRE AND ICE	Laura Hamilton ISBN 0 352 33486 X	☐
SAUCE FOR THE GOOSE	Mary Rose Maxwell ISBN 0 352 33492 4	☐
HARD CORPS	Claire Thompson ISBN 0 352 33491 6	☐
INTENSE BLUE	Lyn Wood ISBN 0 352 33496 7	☐
THE NAKED TRUTH	Natasha Rostova ISBN 0 352 33497 5	☐
A SPORTING CHANCE	Susie Raymond ISBN 0 352 33501 7	☐
A SCANDALOUS AFFAIR	Holly Graham ISBN 0 352 33523 8	☐

---------------------✂------------------------------

Please send me the books I have ticked above.

Name   ....

Address   ....

            ....

            ....

            .... Post Code ....

Send to: **Cash Sales, Black Lace Books, Thames Wharf Studios, Rainville Road, London W6 9HA.**

US customers: for prices and details of how to order books for delivery by mail, call 1-800-805-1083.

Please enclose a cheque or postal order, made payable to **Virgin Publishing Ltd**, to the value of the books you have ordered plus postage and packing costs as follows:

UK and BFPO – £1.00 for the first book, 50p for each subsequent book.

Overseas (including Republic of Ireland) – £2.00 for the first book, £1.00 for each subsequent book.

If you would prefer to pay by VISA, ACCESS/MASTER-CARD, DINERS CLUB, AMEX or SWITCH, please write your card number and expiry date here:

....

Please allow up to 28 days for delivery.

Signature ....

---------------------✂------------------------------